# *Almost Always*

## A NOVEL

## MICHAEL MANOSCA

EDITED BY
### REGENA SLATER

*For everyone who has loved across distance and time,*
*who has waited in the space between "almost" and "always,"*
*and who understands that some connections transcend*
*everything we can imagine, until they meet the things we cannot.*

Love is born into every human being: it calls back the halves of our original nature together; it tries to make one out of two and heal the wound of human nature.

From a speech given by Aristophanes in the *Symposium*.

PLATO

# Preface

There are certain places that hold memories like amber—preserving not just what happened, but how it felt to be young and uncertain, standing on the edge of becoming who you were meant to be. For me, one of those places was a dark stairwell in Chicago's Boystown, leading up to the pulsing lights and endless people of a now-defunct club called Medusa's.

It was the late eighties, and I was an art student navigating those brutal Chicago winters that seemed to last half the year. But on certain nights, when the cold became too much and the weight of my own shyness felt unbearable, I would find myself climbing those stairs to another world entirely. The dance floor at Medusa's was where masks fell away, where the carefully constructed personas we wore during the day dissolved in the heat of moving bodies across two floors, lost in the driving rhythms of New Order and Dead or Alive. I still have the mix tapes from those nights—now converted to streaming playlists that can transport me instantly back to that smoky, electric atmosphere where nothing would surprise me.

Layered over those memories was something else: a growing crush on a fellow student, someone I admired from afar but never had the courage to approach. I was too afraid of my own shadow then, too paralyzed by the possibility of rejection to take the risk that might have changed everything. He remained a beautiful mystery, a path not taken that I would wonder about for years.

Later, life surprised me. I was approached by a kind, sophisticated, and outgoing man who saw something in me that I hadn't yet learned to see in myself. What followed was a whirlwind romance that lasted exactly two weeks—intense, transformative, and ultimately brief. It was the relationship I would always measure others against, the one that left me wondering "what if" long after it ended, knowing I would never have the answer.

Recently, over dinner with friends, we found ourselves sharing stories of these formative relationships—the soulmates and Mr. Rights who somehow never quite became permanent fixtures in our lives. Each of us had tales of connections derailed by bad timing, terrible luck, or simply the stubborn blindness of youth. We spoke of loves that were always "almost" but never quite, of people who became lifelong friends because romance had proved impossible, of relationships that didn't get away but didn't stay either.

It was during that conversation that the idea for this story was born. I realized that these experiences—the crush I never pursued, the whirlwind romance that changed me, the universal pattern of "almost" that seemed to define so many meaningful connections—weren't just personal anecdotes. They were the building blocks of a larger story about how we love, how we lose, and how we sometimes find our way back to what matters most.

*Almost Always* draws from those memories, weaving together elements of my own experience with the shared stories we all carry —the ones about perfect timing that wasn't quite perfect, about courage that came too late, about the magnetic pull between two people who recognize something essential in each other but can't quite figure out how to make it work. It's about the person you call "your best friend" because you could never make the romance stick, even though you both knew it was something deeper.

My characters, Patrick and David's story spans decades and

cities, but at its heart, it's about those moments we all recognize: standing in a club at two in the morning, feeling completely seen by someone you've just met; making promises you can't keep; learning that love doesn't always conquer all, but sometimes conquers just enough.

This novel is for everyone who has loved across distance and time, who has waited in the space between "almost" and "always," and who understands that some of the most important relationships in our lives are defined not by their duration, but by their depth—and by the way they teach us who we're capable of becoming.

The club is gone now, making way for something more practical. But the music plays on, and the memories remain, transformed into something I hope will resonate with anyone who has ever wondered about the road not taken, the love not quite captured, the perfect moment that slipped away only to return, years later, when you're finally ready to receive it.

*Michael Mansoca*
  *Los Angeles, 2025*

# PART
## One

# CHAPTER
*One*

PATRICK'S EYES were greener than the stained glass windows of St. Bartholomew's on Easter morning, and just as likely to make you believe in miracles—though at the moment, they were wide with terror as Kelly Campbell approached him with a tube of black eyeliner.

"Oh, fuck no," Patrick said, scrambling backward on his narrow dorm bed until his shoulders hit the cinder block wall. It was one of the few times profanity felt necessary, and Kelly's delighted cackle told him she appreciated the effort.

"Oh, fuck yes," she shot back, brandishing the eyeliner like a weapon. "You're twenty-two years old, O'Brien, and you spend Friday nights color-coding your sociology notes. That shit ends tonight."

She'd burst into his room twenty minutes earlier carrying what looked like a grocery bag from Jewel-Osco, her dark hair escaping from a hastily constructed ponytail and her cheeks flushed pink from the February cold. Her own outfit was already assembled for whatever mayhem she had planned—ripped black tights under a leather mini skirt, combat boots that added three inches to her height, and a vintage Ramones t-shirt that looked like it had survived actual concerts. Multiple silver chains hung around her neck, and her dark eyes were already rimmed with the kind of dramatic makeup that made her look dangerous and glamorous, all at once.

Patrick had known trouble was coming the moment she'd kicked the door shut behind her with unnecessary force.

"Kelly, whatever you're thinking—"

"I'm not thinking anything, sweetheart. I'm doing, and so are you." She set the bag down with a suspicious rustling sound and began pulling out items that made Patrick's stomach flip: black jeans that looked several sizes too small, a studded belt, what appeared to be at least three different shirts in colors he'd never wear, and—his eyes widened—a small arsenal of makeup containers.

His roommate had taken the Friday afternoon train down to Champaign to visit his girlfriend, leaving Patrick with the rare luxury of a quiet weekend on campus. He'd been perfectly content with his textbooks and highlighted articles about media consolidation, the comfortable chaos of academic work spread across his bed, the radiator clanking its familiar rhythm against the cold.

"There's a place called Medusa's," Kelly announced, shaking the black jeans at him. "And we're going dancing."

"I don't dance."

"Bullshit. Everyone dances. Some people just need the right outfit first." She held up the jeans and squinted at his frame. "These are going to look fucking amazing on you."

Patrick stared at the clothes spread across his roommate's bed like evidence of some crime he hadn't yet committed. The sensible part of his brain—which was most of his brain—catalogued all the reasons this was a terrible idea. He didn't know how to dress like that. He'd never worn makeup. He'd certainly never been to a gay club, which is obviously what Medusa's was, even if Kelly hadn't said so explicitly.

But there was another part of him, smaller and quieter, that was curious. That wondered what it would feel like to be someone else for a night. Someone who didn't overthink every decision, who didn't catalog every social interaction for later analysis.

"I don't even know how to put on eyeliner," he said weakly.

Kelly's grin was triumphant. "Lucky for you, I'm a fucking artist."

The next hour passed in a blur of fabric and fumbling. The black jeans were indeed too tight, hugging his thin frame in ways that made him hyperaware of his own body. The studded belt felt like costume jewelry, but Kelly assured him it looked "perfectly punk rock." The shirt—shirts, actually, because she'd layered a mesh thing over something purple and shimmery—made him feel exposed and ridiculous.

"Stop looking in the mirror like someone died," Kelly commanded, approaching him with a hair spray bottle filled with something blue. "You look good. Different, but good."

"I look like I'm going to a costume party dressed as someone I've never met."

"Exactly." She began spritzing sections of his red hair with the blue mixture, and Patrick tried not to think about how his mother would react. "That's the whole fucking point. Tonight, you're not Patrick O'Brien from Arlington Heights who does all his homework three days early. Tonight, you're just... Patrick. The Patrick who might surprise himself."

The makeup came last. Kelly worked with the focused concentration of an artist, tilting his chin this way and that, telling him to close his eyes, to look up, to hold still damn it. The eyeliner felt strange and heavy on his lids, and he had to resist the urge to blink constantly. But when she finally turned him toward the mirror, Patrick barely recognized himself.

His green eyes, always his best feature according to his mother, seemed enormous and luminous. The blue streaks in his hair caught the harsh dorm lighting and somehow made his pale skin look porcelain rather than sickly. The clothes, which had felt like a costume minutes before, now seemed to belong to this new version of himself.

"I look like..." He paused, searching for the right comparison.

"Like a cross between a leprechaun and the lead singer of The Cure," Kelly finished cheerfully. "It's a good look on you, trust me."

Patrick turned away from the mirror, suddenly overwhelmed. This was too much—the clothes, the makeup, the person staring back at him who looked confident and mysterious and nothing like the boy who spent Friday nights reorganizing his class notes.

"Kelly, I can't do this. I can't go to some club looking like this. What if someone sees me? What if—"

"What if what?" Kelly's voice was gentler now, the profanity dropping away as she sat down on the bed beside him. "What if you have fun? What if you meet someone interesting? What if you discover that maybe you're braver than you think you are?"

Patrick looked down at his hands, noting how strange they looked emerging from the mesh sleeves. "What if I'm not?"

"Then we come home, you wash your face, and you go back to your textbooks. But Patrick..." She waited until he met her eyes, and for a moment, beneath all the chains and makeup, she looked almost maternal. "What if you are?"

Outside, the February wind rattled the windows, and someone in the hallway was laughing about something—the kind of easy, careless laughter that Patrick had always envied but never quite managed himself. He thought about the questions his family would ask when he went home, about the careful ways he'd learned to deflect and redirect. He thought about the part of himself he kept hidden, even from Kelly, even from himself most of the time.

"One night," he said finally.

"One night," Kelly agreed, but her smile suggested she knew better.

They took the Red Line El to Belmont, Kelly chattering excitedly about the club while Patrick caught glimpses of himself in the dark train windows—each reflection a small shock, as if he were glimpsing a stranger who happened to be wearing his face. The closer they got to their destination, the more animated Kelly became.

"Fair warning," she said as they climbed the stairs from the station, "if I meet someone decent tonight, you might be taking the El back alone. Think you can handle that, sweetheart?"

Patrick felt a flutter of panic. The idea of navigating his way back to campus alone, dressed like this, in the middle of the night, made his stomach clench. "Kelly—"

"Relax. I'm not going to abandon you on your first night out. But if some gorgeous woman wants to take me home..." She shrugged, grinning. "A girl's got to have her priorities."

The cold hit them like a slap when they emerged onto Belmont Avenue. Snow was beginning to fall, light flakes that caught in Kelly's dark hair and made Patrick's newly blue-streaked locks feel instantly damp. He wrapped his arms around himself, already missing the warmth of the train.

"I'm fucking freezing," he said through chattering teeth.

"Beauty is pain, O'Brien. Deal with it." Kelly had refused to let him bring a coat at all, insisting that their outfits were too perfect to be hidden under bulky winter wear. "We didn't spend an hour putting this look together just to cover it up with some puffy jacket."

They walked the few blocks to the club, Patrick's teeth chattering despite his attempts to look casual. Kelly seemed immune to the cold, her combat boots clicking confidently on the sidewalk as she navigated patches of ice with practiced ease. Other people were heading in the same direction—couples holding hands, groups of friends laughing loudly, individuals walking alone with purpose. Most were dressed as dramatically as Kelly, though Patrick noticed he wasn't the only one who looked like he might be visiting from another planet.

Medusa's entrance was on the ground floor of a narrow building squeezed between a vintage clothing store and a late-night diner. A small crowd had gathered outside the entrance, stamping their feet and breathing clouds of vapor into the frigid air. The bouncer—a massive man in a leather jacket that looked warm enough to survive an arctic expedition—was checking IDs with methodical patience.

"This is it," Kelly announced, joining the line behind two

women who looked like they'd stepped out of a Robert Palmer video. "You ready for this shit?"

Patrick looked up at the club's neon sign, its serpentine letters casting pink and blue shadows on the snow-covered sidewalk. His heart was beating so fast he was sure Kelly could hear it over the muffled bass line seeping through the building's walls. The makeup felt heavy on his face, the tight clothes restrictive, the blue streaks in his hair like a flag announcing his participation in something he didn't fully understand.

But he was here. Despite every instinct telling him to turn around and catch the next train back to campus, despite the voice in his head that sounded suspiciously like his father asking what the hell he thought he was doing, he was here.

"Yeah," he said, surprising himself with how steady his voice sounded. "I think I am."

Kelly squeezed his arm through the mesh sleeve, her rings cold against his skin. "That's my boy."

The line moved forward, and Patrick shivered in the falling snow, watching the neon light dance across the faces of strangers who seemed to know exactly who they were and what they wanted. In a few minutes, he would be inside. In a few minutes, everything would change.

He just didn't know how much.

# CHAPTER
## *Two*

WHAT THE FUCK am I doing here?

The thought slammed into Patrick's mind the moment the bouncer waved them through, his flashlight beam having passed over their IDs with practiced indifference. The heavy black doors swung shut behind them with a finality that made Patrick's stomach drop, and suddenly they were facing a narrow staircase that disappeared upward into darkness.

The walls were black. The stairs were black. Everything was black except for the colored lights that flickered and flashed somewhere above them, spilling down like water through the darkness. The music wasn't just louder here—it was alive, growing stronger with each step up, a bass line that seemed to be calling from some electronic underworld.

Kelly grabbed his hand and pulled him forward, her rings digging into his palm. "Come on, sweetheart, don't chicken out now."

But Patrick couldn't have turned back if he'd wanted to. Bodies pressed behind them, pushing the whole crowd slowly upward like some strange pilgrimage. In the narrow stairwell, he could smell everything at once—leather and cigarettes and perfume and sweat and something else, something electric and dangerous that made his pulse race.

The steps were slick under his feet, worn smooth by thousands of club-goers before him. Each footfall brought the music closer, until he could feel it vibrating through the walls, through the handrail, through his bones. The person behind him was breathing on his neck, and the person in front of Kelly was pressed so close Patrick could see the individual studs on his leather jacket catching the light from above.

*Claustrophobic. I'm going to have a panic attack right here on these stairs.*

"Kelly, I can't—"

"Yes, you can." Her voice was fierce, protective. "We're almost there. Trust me."

The ascent felt endless, but then suddenly they crested the top step and the world exploded into view.

The dance floor stretched out before them like some alternate universe—two stories tall, the ceiling lost in darkness and disco balls that fractured light into a million moving pieces. Patrick's eyes struggled to process it all at once: the enormous space packed wall-to-wall with bodies, the balcony that wrapped around the entire perimeter like some Roman colosseum, figures leaning against the railing looking down at the crowd below with predatory interest.

To his left, another black staircase spiraled upward, this one open to the dance floor so you could see people climbing toward what looked like a bar tucked back into the balcony level. The main floor stretched out in front of them—a central dance area surrounded by bars and seating areas tucked under the balcony's overhang. Several raised platforms, like cubes or pedestals, dotted the space, with dancers elevated above the crowd, their bodies silhouetted against the spinning lights.

The DJ was positioned somewhere behind them, invisible but omnipresent, the source of the relentless beat that made the air itself seem to pulse. And everywhere, everywhere, there were people—more people than Patrick had imagined could fit in any space, and still more kept streaming up the stairs behind them.

"Holy shit," he breathed, forgetting to be self-conscious about the profanity.

"I fucking love this place," Kelly shouted directly into his ear, her voice barely cutting through the wall of sound.

The bass line didn't just play—it lived in Patrick's chest, a second heartbeat that made his ribs vibrate and his lungs struggle to find their rhythm. Colored lights swept the space in dizzying arcs—red, blue, green, purple—each beam cutting through a haze of cigarette smoke and dry ice that made the air taste metallic and sweet.

*Too much. This is all too much.*

The lights hit the crowd in fragments: a flash of bleached hair, the glint of metal studs, lips moving in conversation he couldn't hear, eyes that caught the strobes and threw them back like mirrors. The press of strangers surrounded him—some in full leather, others in torn denim, a few in clothes that left little to the imagination.

Kelly tugged him forward into the chaos, her combat boots somehow finding purchase on floors that felt sticky under Patrick's feet. Bodies pressed against him from all sides—leather and denim and bare skin slick with sweat, the smell of cologne and cigarettes and something alive and electric that he couldn't name. They pushed through clusters of people, each group its own microclimate of sensation. Here, the sweet smell of someone's fruity drink mixing with hairspray and perfume. There, the heat radiating from bodies packed together, the air so thick it was like breathing soup.

"There's Jake Morrison!" Kelly suddenly squealed, spotting someone across the room. "Holy shit, I haven't seen him since high school!"

Patrick turned to follow her gaze, but in the strobing lights, faces became abstract—a nose here, a smile there, eyes that belonged to no one and everyone. The crowd shifted and swayed like a living thing, and he lost sight of Kelly for a moment, panic rising in his throat.

"Kelly—"

But when he turned back, she was already moving away, pulled into the orbit of a tall guy with spiked hair and a leather jacket. Patrick watched her disappear into a knot of people, her laugh echoing back to him through the music, and suddenly he was alone.

Completely, utterly alone.

The realization hit him like cold water. He stood frozen in the middle of the dance floor as bodies moved around him, through him, past him. The music pounded in his skull—something with synthesizers and a driving beat that seemed designed to make thinking impossible. People danced with abandon, arms raised, heads thrown back, lost in the rhythm in ways Patrick had never imagined possible.

*I don't belong here. I should leave. I should find Kelly and tell her I'm sick and we need to go home.*

But his feet wouldn't move. Something about the chaos was hypnotic, even as it overwhelmed him. The lights painted everything in otherworldly colors, making the ordinary magical and strange. A woman with platinum hair danced nearby, her movements liquid and confident, and when the lights hit her she looked like she was made of silver. Two men pressed close together moved as one body, their eyes closed, completely absorbed in each other and the music.

The song changed—something with an infectious beat and familiar synthesizer line—and something shifted in Patrick's chest. Around him, the crowd responded with renewed energy, voices joining in on the chorus, arms pumping in unison.

Patrick found his shoulders beginning to move, almost involuntarily. The beat was simple, repetitive, hypnotic. His body wanted to respond even as his mind catalogued all the reasons he should run. The tight jeans that had felt like a costume now seemed to help him find his rhythm, the studded belt catching the lights as his hips began to sway.

He looked ridiculous, he was sure of it. He had no idea what he was doing, no sense of rhythm or style. But something about the anonymity of the crowd, the way the strobing lights made everyone into fragments and shadows, gave him permission to try.

His feet started to move, small steps in place at first, then something bolder. The mesh shirt caught the air as he raised his arms, and he could feel eyes on him—but in the darkness and chaos, he couldn't tell if they were judging or approving. The bass line thrummed through his body, and for the first time since entering the club, he felt like he might be able to breathe.

The eyeliner Kelly had applied felt heavy on his lids, but when he caught glimpses of himself in the mirrored walls, he looked like he belonged. The blue streaks in his hair caught the colored lights, and his pale skin looked ethereal rather than washed out. He was still Patrick O'Brien from Arlington Heights, still the boy who organized his textbooks by subject and publication date, but he was also something else. Someone else.

The crowd pressed closer as the song built to its climax, and Patrick let himself be carried by the music, by the energy of all these bodies moving together in the dark. His heart was still racing, but it felt different now—not panic, but possibility. The sensory overload that had threatened to crush him was becoming something else: a baptism of sound and light and motion that was washing away every careful boundary he'd built around himself.

He was dancing. Badly, probably, but dancing. And somewhere up on the balcony, someone was watching.

# CHAPTER
## *Three*

DAVID CHEN WAS the kind of beautiful that cautioned rooms of their existence, pulling air from life choices and setting prose adrift across tranquil waters that would make even Walden flutter.

Even leaning against the balcony railing in the strobing chaos of Medusa's, nursing his third vodka tonic and looking thoroughly bored, he commanded attention. His friends had learned to position themselves strategically around him—close enough to bask in the overflow of interest he attracted, far enough away to catch the ones he inevitably rejected.

"There," said Marcus, nudging David's shoulder and pointing toward a group near the main bar. "Blond guy in the tank top. He's been staring at you for twenty minutes."

David followed his gaze with the lazy indifference of someone who'd heard this announcement a hundred times before. The guy was handsome enough—broad shoulders, confident stance, the kind of obvious masculinity that telegraphed itself across a crowded room. Six months ago, David might have been interested. Tonight, he looked like every other guy who'd ever bought David a drink.

"Not feeling it," David said, taking another sip and turning back to survey the dance floor below.

His friends exchanged glances. David's pickiness had become legendary, even by Fire Island standards. It wasn't that he had impossibly high standards—well, maybe he did—but lately, nothing seemed to catch his interest for more than five minutes. Beautiful men threw themselves at him with increasing desperation, and David remained unmoved, polite but distant, as if he were watching it all happen to someone else.

"You're impossible," laughed Trevor, a regular fixture in their group who'd been trying unsuccessfully to set David up for months. "What exactly are you looking for? Because at this rate, you're going to die alone with your trust fund and your perfect cheekbones."

David smiled, the expression that had graced a dozen party photos in genre magazines, but his attention was already drifting. The crowd below moved like a living kaleidoscope, bodies appearing and disappearing in the sweep of colored lights. From up here, the dance floor looked like some primitive ritual—all that pulsing energy and desperate connection, people losing themselves in music and darkness and each other.

He'd been coming to Medusa's for three years now, ever since transferring to University of Chicago, and he could read the patterns like sheet music. The veterans who moved with practiced confidence. The tourists wide-eyed and overdressed. The couples marking territory. The predators circling. The lost souls looking for something they couldn't name.

And then there were the projects.

David's eyes snagged on something—someone—moving through the crowd near the entrance to the main floor. A flash of red hair streaked with blue, pale skin made ethereal by the strobing lights, clothes that looked like they'd been assembled by committee. Even from thirty feet up, David could tell this was someone's makeover project, probably some friend's well-meaning attempt to drag a wallflower into the light.

The figure disappeared behind a cluster of dancers, and David found himself leaning forward slightly, waiting for another glimpse.

"Earth to David," Marcus was saying. "You're not even listening."

But David was listening—to something else entirely. The music had shifted, something with a driving beat that seemed to pulse in sync with his heartbeat. The crowd responded with renewed energy, and there—there he was again.

The redhead was alone now, standing frozen in the middle of the dance floor like a deer caught in headlights. David could see the exact moment when panic set in, the way the boy's shoulders tensed, how he looked around desperately for whoever had brought him here. Classic abandonment scenario. His friend had probably spotted someone more interesting and vanished, leaving him stranded in enemy territory.

David should have felt sympathy. Instead, he felt something else entirely—a pull of recognition that made no sense. He didn't know this person. Had never seen him before. But something about the way the boy stood there, vulnerable and overwhelmed but not quite broken, made David's chest tighten.

"Who is that?" he found himself asking.

"Who's what?" Trevor followed David's gaze. "Oh, the Halloween reject down there? Someone's science project, by the look of it. Probably some fag hag's charity case."

But David barely heard him. The boy was moving now—tentatively at first, just shoulders swaying to the beat. The clothes that had looked like a costume from above suddenly seemed to fit him perfectly, the mesh shirt catching the light as he raised his arms, the tight jeans following the line of his narrow hips.

He looked ridiculous. He looked beautiful. He looked like he was discovering his own body for the first time.

"David." Marcus snapped his fingers in front of David's face. "You're staring."

"Am I?" David's voice sounded distant, even to himself.

The lights swept across the dance floor again, red and blue and gold, and for just a moment they caught the boy full-on. David saw him clearly—green eyes wide with concentration, pale skin flushed with effort and embarrassment, blue-streaked hair damp with sweat. He was trying so hard to find the rhythm, to belong, to transform himself into someone who deserved to be here.

And in that instant, David saw something else. Beneath the awkward clothes and amateur makeup, beneath the obvious terror and desperate hope, there was something real. Something authentic and unguarded that David hadn't seen in years of beautiful, confident men who knew exactly what they wanted and how to get it.

The boy stumbled slightly, caught himself, kept dancing. A laugh escaped him—David couldn't hear it over the music, but he could see it in the boy's face, surprised and delighted, as if he'd just discovered something wonderful about himself.

David's friends were still talking, but their voices had become background noise. The entire club had become background noise. There was only the figure moving on the dance floor below, only the way the lights caught in his red hair, only the magnetic pull that seemed to be drawing every molecule in David's body toward the edge of the balcony.

"I have to go," David said suddenly, pushing away from the railing.

"Go where?" Trevor called after him. "David, you just got here!"

But David was already moving toward the stairs, his heart beating in rhythm with the bass line below. He didn't have a plan. He never needed a plan. But this felt different—urgent and inevitable in a way that made his usual confidence seem irrelevant.

Halfway down the spiraling staircase, he caught another glimpse of the redhead through the crowd. The boy was really dancing now, lost enough in the music to let his body move naturally, unconscious of how beautiful he looked in his uncertainty.

David paused on the stairs, gripping the railing, and felt something shift inside his chest. It was like recognition—not of a face or a voice, but of something deeper. As if he'd been searching for something he couldn't name, and suddenly there it was, spinning under disco balls and strobing lights, wearing clothes that didn't quite fit and makeup applied by amateur hands.

The song changed to something slower, more hypnotic, and David watched the boy close his eyes and sway to the rhythm. In the shifting colored light, he looked like something from a dream —otherworldly and fragile and completely, heartbreakingly real.

David took the rest of the stairs two at a time.

The story was beginning.

Patrick had stopped thinking.

Somewhere between the third song and the fourth, between the moment his shoulders found the rhythm and his hips remembered they could move, his mind had finally quieted. The eyeliner felt natural now, the mesh shirt like a second skin, the blue streaks in his hair catching the lights as he turned his head to the beat.

He caught a glimpse of himself in one of the mirrored walls and barely recognized the figure moving there. This stranger with his face—confident, sensual, free—smiled back at him with an expression he'd never seen in his own reflection. *If my friends could see me now,* he thought, and the idea should have terrified him. This wasn't him. The good Catholic boy from Arlington Heights didn't move his hips like that, didn't close his eyes and let his body follow rhythms he'd never known existed.

But wasn't it him? Wasn't this exactly who he'd been all along, buried under layers of expectation and propriety and the constant, exhausting effort to be perfect?

The crowd pressed around him, but instead of claustrophobia, he felt held. Anonymous. Free to let his soul escape his body for the first time in twenty-two years, to stop worrying about what others might think, to stop being the responsible one, the careful one, the one who never made waves. His body moved without permission from his brain, finding patterns in the music he'd never known he could hear.

A woman in silver spun past him, her laugh like wind chimes, and Patrick found himself smiling back without the usual careful calculation of appropriateness. A couple near the platform moved together like water, and he didn't look away in embarrassment—he watched, curious, learning. The fear was still there, humming beneath his skin, but it was quieter now, drowned out by something larger and more insistent.

He raised his arms above his head and let the music wash over him, through him. For the first time in his life, he was just *being* instead of *becoming* something else for someone else's comfort.

He didn't notice the figure moving steadily through the crowd toward him.


"What the hell just happened?" Trevor stared at the empty space where David had been standing moments before, his voice tight with something that sounded dangerously close to jealousy. "Did he seriously just abandon us for some random guy on the dance floor?"

Marcus leaned against the balcony railing, scanning the crowd below. He'd been in David's orbit the longest, ever since David transferred to University of Chicago, and he knew better than most how this worked. They'd all gravitated toward David thinking they could conquer him, add him to their collection of beautiful conquests like they had since high school. Instead, David had flipped them completely—taking them to bed one by one, staying in control, being the one who called the shots. They'd all begged for more, and they'd all learned to accept their place in his orbit, grateful for whatever attention he chose to give them.

"There," Marcus pointed, trying to keep his voice neutral. "Red hair, looks like he's having some kind of religious experience."

"That's what broke the David Chen spell?" Trevor's voice cracked slightly, and he cleared his throat to cover it. He'd been fighting his feelings for David for two years now, pretending the casual hookups were enough, that he didn't spend sleepless nights replaying every conversation, every touch. "I mean, he's cute in a lost-puppy kind of way, but David usually goes for the obvious tens. Guys who look like they stepped out of magazines."

Trevor hated how desperate he sounded, but he couldn't help it. David had never looked at any of them the way he was looking at the stranger below.

"Maybe that's the point," said Jake, David's roommate, who'd been quietly nursing his beer while the others gossiped. Jake was the only one who'd never slept with David, the only one who could still think clearly around him. "When was the last time you saw David actually interested in someone? Like, really interested, not just killing time?"

They watched as David's unmistakable silhouette moved through the crowd below, cutting a path toward the redhead with the kind of focused determination they'd never seen from him. Usually David waited for people to come to him—and they always did. David knew about Trevor's feelings, of course. David knew everything. But he'd never acknowledged them directly, never looked Trevor in the eye when he turned him down for dinner or drinks or anything that might resemble a date. Not because he couldn't, but because David was kind enough not to let Trevor's heart shatter completely. He had no use for a puppy following him around.

"This is different," Marcus said, almost to himself.

Trevor snorted, but it sounded hollow. "Different how? It's probably just the thrill of the hunt. David loves a challenge."

But Jake was shaking his head. "Look at him move. That's not hunting. That's..."

"Homing," Marcus finished quietly.

They fell silent, watching their beautiful, unattainable friend navigate the chaos below like he was following some invisible thread. In three years of knowing David, none of them had ever seen him look so certain about anything. And none of them had ever felt quite so invisible.

The music shifted—something slower but more intense, bass notes that seemed to vibrate in David's bones as he moved through the crowd. Each step brought him closer to the figure spinning under the lights, and with each step, his certainty grew.

This was insane. He didn't approach strangers on dance floors. He didn't chase after lost-looking boys in amateur makeup. He was David Chen—people came to him, not the other way around.

But none of his usual rules seemed to apply tonight.

The redhead was twenty feet away now, then fifteen, then ten. David could see the concentration on his face, the way he'd given himself over completely to the music. There was something pure about it, unguarded in a way that made David's chest tighten.

Five feet.

David reached out and tapped the boy's shoulder, gentle but insistent. Time seemed to slow as the figure turned, green eyes wide with surprise, lips slightly parted as if he'd been about to say something to the music itself.

And then their eyes met.

Everything stopped.

The disco balls kept spinning, the bass kept pounding, hundreds of bodies kept moving around them, but David felt like he'd stepped outside of time itself. Those green eyes—impossibly green, like stained glass windows or deep forest pools—looked directly into him, and David felt something fundamental shift in his understanding of the world.

This wasn't attraction. This wasn't even desire, though both of those were there too. This was recognition. As if some part of his soul had been calling out across the darkness, and finally, impossibly, something had answered back.

"Hi," David said, but the music swallowed his voice completely. The boy's eyebrows drew together in confusion, and David realized he hadn't heard a word.

David leaned in closer, his hand settling on the boy's shoulder to steady himself against the press of the crowd. The moment his palm made contact, electricity shot through both of them—David could see it in the way the boy's eyes widened, could feel it in the slight tremor that ran through that narrow frame.

"I'm David," he said, his mouth close to the boy's ear, his breath warm against sensitive skin.

The boy shivered—actually shivered—and David felt something primal and possessive stir in his chest. The delicate ear, the way the boy's breath caught, the unconscious way he leaned slightly into David's touch... David filed it all away, some instinct telling him this information would be important later.

"Patrick," the boy breathed back, his voice barely audible but somehow perfectly clear.

David pulled back just enough to meet those green eyes again, his hand still resting on Patrick's shoulder. "Patrick," he repeated, and the name felt like something he'd been waiting his whole life to say.

And just like that, David Chen's perfectly controlled world tilted off its axis and began spinning in an entirely new direction.

# CHAPTER
## *Four*

INNOCENCE HAD NEVER FELT SO MUCH like a weapon until someone finally taught him how to wield it.

Patrick stood frozen under David's gaze, suddenly aware that everything about him—his wide green eyes, his uncertain smile, the way he trembled slightly under that confident touch—was having an effect he'd never imagined possible. David's hand rested on his shoulder with the casual confidence of someone who knew exactly what he wanted, and Patrick found himself leaning into that touch despite every rational thought screaming that this was happening too fast, too intensely, too impossibly. The warmth of David's palm seemed to burn through the mesh of his shirt, and when David had spoken into his ear—that breath, that closeness— Patrick's entire body had responded in ways he didn't know were possible.

"Patrick," David repeated, pulling back just enough to meet his eyes again, and the way he said the name made Patrick feel like he'd never heard it before. Like it belonged to someone braver than he'd ever imagined himself to be.

Patrick tried to respond, but the music swallowed his voice completely. He gestured helplessly at his ears, shaking his head, and David's face broke into a grin that could have powered the entire club. Without warning, David leaned in again, his lips so close to Patrick's ear that Patrick could feel them brush against his skin.

"Can't hear a damn thing," David said, and Patrick shivered again at the sensation. "Want to go somewhere we can actually talk?"

The question should have terrified him. Following a stranger— a devastatingly beautiful stranger who looked like he belonged on magazine covers—somewhere quieter implied things Patrick wasn't sure he was ready for. But when David pulled back to gauge his reaction, those dark eyes held something Patrick recognized: genuine interest, not just predatory hunger.

Patrick nodded before his brain could object.

David's grin widened, and then he was taking Patrick's hand— actually taking his hand, fingers intertwining like they'd done this a thousand times before—and leading him through the crowd. Patrick's heart hammered against his ribs as they moved, not just from the bass line that surrounded them but from the simple, overwhelming fact that he was holding hands with another man for the first time in his life.

David's hand was warm and slightly callused, strong enough to guide Patrick confidently through the press of bodies without being demanding. Patrick found himself studying their joined hands in the strobing lights—David's tan fingers against his pale ones, the easy way David held on without gripping too tightly, as if he understood that Patrick might need to bolt at any moment but was hoping he wouldn't.

They navigated toward the spiral staircase Patrick had noticed earlier, the one that led up to the balcony level. As they started to climb, David stayed a step ahead, his free hand trailing along the railing while he pulled Patrick gently upward. The music grew slightly less overwhelming as they ascended, though Patrick could still feel it vibrating through the metal steps.

Halfway up, Patrick caught a glimpse of Kelly through the crowd below. She was pressed against the guy with spiked hair, her hands tangled in his leather jacket, but something made her look up. Their eyes met for just a moment across the chaos, and Patrick saw her face transform—surprise, then delight, then something that looked almost like pride.

She mouthed something that might have been "Holy shit!" and gave him an exaggerated thumbs up before her attention was reclaimed by Spiked Hair Guy. But Patrick caught her expression in that last second before she turned away: pure happiness. As if she'd been waiting his entire life for this moment, for him to finally let loose and surprise himself.

*He needed to,* Kelly had said earlier, and now Patrick understood what she meant.

The balcony level was marginally quieter, though the music still pounded through the floor and walls. David led him toward a small bar tucked into an alcove, past clusters of people who seemed to be having the conversations that were impossible on the main floor. Most barely glanced at them, too absorbed in their own dramas and connections, but Patrick noticed a few eyes tracking David's movement through the space.

Particularly a group of guys near the main railing who were openly staring. Patrick caught glimpses of their faces in the strobing lights—attractive, well-dressed, the kind of people who clearly belonged in places like this. But there was something in their expressions as they watched David pass, something that looked like recognition mixed with surprise. And maybe jealousy.

David seemed oblivious to their attention, or maybe just used to it. He moved like he owned the place, like he'd been born knowing exactly how to navigate spaces like this, completely focused on leading Patrick toward their destination.

They found two empty stools at the far end of the bar, somewhat sheltered from the worst of the noise by a curved wall that created a small pocket of relative quiet. David released Patrick's hand to flag down the bartender, and Patrick immediately missed the contact. He flexed his fingers, still feeling the phantom warmth of David's touch.

"What can I get you?" David asked, leaning close enough that

Patrick could hear him without the intimate proximity of before. Somehow, this felt almost more dangerous—being able to have an actual conversation, to look directly into David's face without the excuse of shouting over music.

"I... I don't really drink much," Patrick admitted, feeling immediately ridiculous. Here he was, in a gay club, wearing makeup and mesh, and he sounded like he was ordering at a church potluck.

But David's expression didn't change, except for the slightest softening around his eyes. "That's okay. Beer? Coke? Something with enough sugar to keep you standing after all that dancing?"

The fact that David had been watching him dance sent heat flooding through Patrick's chest. "Coke sounds good."

David ordered a Coke for Patrick and another vodka tonic for himself, then turned to face him fully. In the slightly better lighting of the bar area, Patrick could see David clearly for the first time—and the sight nearly knocked him off his stool.

David was beautiful in the way that classical sculptures were beautiful, all clean lines and perfect proportions. His black hair fell in a way that suggested it naturally looked effortless, and his dark eyes held depths that made Patrick want to dive in and never surface. He was wearing clothes that probably cost more than Patrick's textbooks—a simple black shirt that fit like it had been made for him, jeans that managed to be both casual and somehow elegant.

But it was David's smile that undid him completely. Not the polished grin Patrick had glimpsed on the dance floor, but something smaller and more real, as if David was letting his guard down just slightly.

"So," David said, his voice now audible over the muffled music. "Patrick. Tell me something true."

The question caught Patrick completely off guard. Not 'What's your major?' or 'Where are you from?' but something that demanded actual honesty. Patrick found himself staring into David's eyes, searching for the right answer, and realized he had no idea how to be anything but truthful with this person.

"This is the first time I've ever been to a place like this," Patrick said. "Actually, this is the first time I've been anywhere like this. My friend Kelly—she basically dressed me up like a doll and dragged me here because she said I needed to stop hiding."

"And were you? Hiding?"

Patrick considered the question, really considered it. "Yeah. I think I was. From a lot of things."

David nodded slowly, as if this answer made perfect sense. "What made you stop? Tonight, I mean."

"I don't know if I have stopped," Patrick said honestly. "Maybe I'm just... pausing. Trying to figure out who I am when I'm not trying to be who everyone else wants me to be."

David's smile grew warmer. "That's a hell of a place to start figuring it out."

"What about you?" Patrick asked, emboldened by David's openness. "Is this who you really are, or are you trying to figure something out too?"

The question seemed to surprise David, and for a moment, something flickered across his face—vulnerability, maybe, or recognition. "That's... that's a really good question. I'm not sure anyone's ever asked me that before."

They stared at each other across the small space between their stools, and Patrick felt that magnetic pull again, stronger now that they could actually see each other clearly. David's eyes seemed to be cataloguing every detail of Patrick's face, and Patrick found himself doing the same—noting the way David's eyebrows drew together slightly when he was thinking, the small scar near his left temple, the way his lips curved when he was deciding whether to smile.

"Can I ask you something?" David said.

"Sure."

"The outfit. It's not really you, is it? I mean, it looks incredible on you," he added quickly, "but it's not how you usually dress."

Patrick felt heat flood his cheeks. "Is it that obvious?"

"Only because I've been watching people play dress-up in places like this for years. You wear it well, but you move like you're not quite sure it belongs to you." David's expression was gentle, curious rather than judgmental. "Kelly's project?"

"Complete makeover. She said I looked like I spent Friday nights color-coding my sociology notes."

"Do you?"

"Usually, yeah."

David laughed—a real laugh, not the polished sound Patrick had heard from the balcony. "I love that. Most people I meet here are trying so hard to be someone else that they've forgotten who they actually are underneath."

"And you?" Patrick found himself asking. "Who are you underneath?"

David's laugh faded, and for a moment, he looked almost surprised by the question. "I'm not sure I remember anymore. It's been a while since anyone bothered to ask."

The admission hung between them, honest and a little raw, and Patrick felt something shift in his chest. This wasn't just attraction anymore, wasn't just the thrill of being noticed by someone beautiful. This felt like the beginning of something real.

"Tell me something true," Patrick said, echoing David's earlier request.

David was quiet for a long moment, studying Patrick's face as if trying to decide how much honesty he could handle. Finally, he said, "I came down from the balcony because I couldn't stop watching you dance. I've never done that before—approached someone like that. Usually people come to me."

"Why me?"

"Because you looked like you were discovering yourself for the first time. And I..." David paused, his cheeks coloring slightly. "I realized I've been waiting my whole life to see what that looks like."

The words settled between them like a confession, and Patrick felt his breath catch. In the strobing lights filtering up from the dance floor below, David looked young and uncertain and completely, devastatingly beautiful.

Patrick reached across the small space between them and

touched David's hand where it rested on the bar. The contact sent electricity shooting up his arm, but this time, he didn't pull away.

"I'm glad you came down," he said simply.

David turned his hand palm up, catching Patrick's fingers in his, and smiled. "So am I."

# CHAPTER
## *Five*

CONQUEST AND SEDUCTION were throwaway currencies, but this boy demanded something far more precious in exchange.

David sat across from Patrick, watching him nurse his Coke like it was communion wine, and realized he was witnessing something he'd never encountered before: someone who couldn't be bought with charm or conquered with confidence. Patrick's green eyes grew impossibly wider when he was thinking hard about a question, and David found himself cataloguing these details not as tactical advantages, but as treasures he wanted to protect. The unconscious way he touched his bottom lip when he was deciding whether to say something honest. The fact that his pale skin flushed pink all the way down his neck when David leaned in closer.

"Tell me something true," David had said, expecting the usual careful answers—something calculated to impress or seduce. Instead, Patrick had given him vulnerability wrapped in words so honest they felt like weapons.

*This is the first time I've ever been to a place like this.*

David had been coming to clubs since he was seventeen, had perfected the art of reading people's desires and giving them just enough to keep them wanting more. He knew how to play the game—the careful dance of advance and retreat, the strategic deployment of charm and distance. But Patrick wasn't playing any game David recognized.

"What about you?" Patrick asked, and David realized he'd been staring in silence for thirty seconds. "Is this who you really are, or are you trying to figure something out too?"

The question hit David like cold water. When was the last time someone had asked him who he was underneath? Most people were too busy trying to get his attention, or his body, or his number to bother with actual curiosity about his inner life.

"That's... that's a really good question," David heard himself say, and the admission felt dangerous. "I'm not sure anyone's ever asked me that before."

Patrick's expression shifted—not surprise, exactly, but something sadder. Recognition, maybe. As if he understood what it meant to be seen as a surface instead of a person.

"Can I ask you something?" David said, needing to regain some equilibrium.

"Sure."

"The outfit. It's not really you, is it?" David had spotted makeover projects before, but something about Patrick made him want to know the real person underneath the costume. "I mean, it looks incredible on you, but it's not how you usually dress."

Patrick's blush deepened, and David felt something possessive stir in his chest. He wanted to be the only one who could make Patrick turn that particular shade of pink.

"Is it that obvious?"

"Only because I've been watching people play dress-up in places like this for years." David leaned forward slightly, drawn by Patrick's openness. "You wear it well, but you move like you're not quite sure it belongs to you. Kelly's project?"

"Complete makeover. She said I looked like I spent Friday nights color-coding my sociology notes."

"Do you?"

"Usually, yeah."

David laughed—really laughed, not the practiced sound he usually made in social situations. There was something so refreshingly honest about Patrick's admission, so free of pretense. "I love that. Most people I meet here are trying so hard to be someone else that they've forgotten who they actually are underneath."

"And you?" Patrick asked, turning David's own question back on him. "Who are you underneath?"

The question landed like a punch to the chest. David opened his mouth to give some smooth deflection, the kind of non-answer that usually satisfied people, but Patrick's green eyes were so earnest, so genuinely curious, that David found himself telling the truth instead.

"I'm not sure I remember anymore. It's been a while since anyone bothered to ask."

The admission hung between them, raw and more honest than David had intended. He waited for Patrick to look away, to get uncomfortable with the sudden depth, to change the subject to something safer. Instead, Patrick reached across the small space between them and touched David's hand where it rested on the bar.

The contact was electric, but more than that—it was gentle. Comforting. No one had touched David like that in years, as if he might need comfort rather than conquest.

"Tell me something true," Patrick said softly, echoing David's earlier words.

David stared down at their joined hands—Patrick's pale fingers against his darker ones, so much smaller but somehow steadier than his own. The music pounded around them, people laughed and flirted and played their endless games, but in this small pocket of space, David felt like he was seeing clearly for the first time in years.

"I came down from the balcony because I couldn't stop watching you dance," he said, the words spilling out before he could stop them. "I've never done that before—approached someone like that. Usually people come to me."

"Why me?"

David looked up into those impossible green eyes and felt something fundamental shift in his chest. "Because you looked like you were discovering yourself for the first time. And I..." He paused, suddenly understanding something about himself he'd never articulated before. "I realized I've been waiting my whole life to see what that looks like."

Patrick's breath caught, and David watched something beautiful happen to his face—surprise melting into something softer, warmer. Understanding, maybe. Or recognition.

"I'm glad you came down," Patrick said simply.

David turned his hand palm up, catching Patrick's fingers properly in his own, and felt like he was holding something precious. Something that could break if he wasn't careful. "So am I."

The music shifted below them—something slower, more hypnotic. New Order, one of David's favorites, though he'd never paid attention to the lyrics before. Tonight, with Patrick's hand in his, the song seemed to be speaking directly to him.

"Dance with me," David said, the words surprising him as much as they seemed to surprise Patrick.

"I don't really know how—"

"Neither do I," David lied, because the truth was that he'd never danced the way he wanted to dance with Patrick. He'd never wanted to hold someone and move slowly while the world spun wildly around them.

They made their way back down to the main floor, David leading but letting Patrick set the pace. The crowd pressed around them, but David found himself moving protectively, using his body to shield Patrick from the worst of the chaos. It was an unfamiliar instinct—usually David expected others to navigate around him, not the other way around.

He'd learned early that his looks were a currency most men wanted to trade in. At seventeen, he'd gone looking for love with the earnest hope of every teenager who believed in fairy tales. Instead, he'd found conquest after conquest, men who wanted to possess his beauty, to add him to their collection of pretty things.

The disillusionment had been swift and brutal. If that was what dating and romance were—just games of domination and power—then he'd decided to perfect the game and become the one who always won. He'd built his persona like armor, becoming the alpha who did the conquering instead of being conquered.

But Patrick was stripping all of that away, peeling back years of careful construction with nothing but honesty and trust. This green-eyed boy was reminding David of what he'd really wanted at seventeen, before the world had taught him that wanting anything real was dangerous.

The dance floor was packed, bodies moving frantically to the driving beat, but David pulled Patrick into a small pocket of space and held out his arms. Patrick stepped into them hesitantly, and David felt that electric shock again, stronger now that they were pressed close together.

"Just move with me," David murmured into Patrick's ear, and felt Patrick shiver at the contact.

They swayed together, completely out of sync with the frantic energy around them, creating their own rhythm in the chaos. Patrick was tense at first, clearly self-conscious, but gradually David felt him relax, his body molding against David's as if they'd been made to fit together.

When Patrick finally let his head rest against David's chest, David felt something break open inside him. This wasn't seduction or conquest or any of the games he was used to playing. This was trust, pure and simple, offered without calculation or expectation. Patrick was giving him something precious—his uncertainty, his vulnerability, his hope—and David felt the weight of that responsibility settle over him like a blessing.

Above them on the balcony, Trevor's audible gasp cut through the music before he turned away sharply, unable to watch anymore. Marcus caught the glassy shine in Trevor's eyes and felt his own chest tighten with recognition of what they were all witnessing: David being gentle with someone. David choosing tenderness over dominance. It was like watching their entire understanding of him crumble in real time.

David tightened his arms around Patrick's narrow frame, oblivious to his friends' emotional turmoil above. All he could feel was the steady rhythm of Patrick's breathing, the trust implicit in the way Patrick melted against him. For the first time in years, David felt more at peace than he had since he was seventeen and still believed in love.

The song played on, and David closed his eyes, breathing in the scent of Patrick's hair, feeling the steady rhythm of his breathing. Around them, the club pulsed with its relentless energy, but in this small circle of trust they'd created, David felt more at peace than he had in longer than he could remember.

He was falling, David realized. Not just into attraction or desire, but into something deeper and more terrifying. Into the possibility of caring about someone else's happiness more than his own satisfaction.

Into love, though he wasn't ready to name it yet.

But as Patrick's arms tightened around him and they swayed together in the strobing darkness, David found he didn't care about the fall.

He just wanted to see where it would take them.

# CHAPTER
## *Six*

SOME NIGHTS YOU PLAYED WINGMAN, and some nights
you witnessed a fucking miracle.

Kelly Campbell pushed away from Jake Morrison's wandering
hands and scanned the dance floor below, her lipstick smeared and
her hair even wilder than when she'd started the evening. Jake had
turned out to be all leather jacket and no substance—decent
enough for some heavy petting against the wall, but his idea of
conversation consisted mainly of grunting and asking if she
wanted to see his motorcycle.

*Jesus Christ, Patrick was right about guys like this.*

She'd lost track of her project somewhere around 11:30, caught
that brief glimpse of him heading upstairs with some gorgeous
guy who looked like he'd stepped out of a magazine, and figured
her work was done. Patrick was a big boy. He could handle
himself for a few hours while she got her own needs met.

Except now it was past 2am, Jake had proved himself to be
exactly as boring as his conversation suggested, and Kelly was
starting to worry. She'd brought Patrick here to get him out of his
shell, not to abandon him to whatever predator had caught his
scent.

She made her excuses to Jake—something about needing to find her friend—and started pushing through the thinning crowd. The club was starting to empty out, the hardcore dancers and the truly desperate the only ones left standing. The music had shifted to something slower, more hypnotic, and the lights seemed less frantic now, more like the aurora borealis than a seizure-inducing strobe show.

And then she saw them.

Holy fucking shit.

Patrick—her sweet, innocent, color-coding-his-notes Patrick—was wrapped around some stunning dark-haired guy like they were the only two people in the universe. But it wasn't just the physical closeness that made Kelly stop dead in her tracks. It was the way Patrick's entire body had melted into this stranger's arms, the way his head rested on the guy's chest like he'd found home, the way they swayed together completely out of sync with the music around them.

Kelly had seen Patrick nervous, seen him overthinking, seen him carefully calculating every social interaction. She'd never seen him surrender.

The guy—and Christ, he was beautiful, all sharp cheekbones and perfect bone structure—held Patrick like he was made of spun glass. One hand tangled gently in Patrick's red hair, the other spread protectively across his back, and his eyes were closed like he was memorizing the moment. This wasn't some club hookup. This wasn't even just attraction.

This was the kind of shit that happened in romance novels.

Kelly felt her throat tighten with something she wasn't expecting. Pride, maybe. Or recognition. She'd known Patrick needed this—needed someone to see past his careful walls to the person underneath. She just hadn't expected it to happen so fast, or so completely.

She watched them sway together for another minute, noting the way other people instinctively gave them space, as if everyone could sense they were witnessing something sacred. Even in a place designed for casual encounters and forgettable nights,

Patrick and his mysterious stranger had created their own bubble of intimacy.

*Patrick needed to do this,* she thought, remembering her words from earlier in the evening. *He needed to stop hiding.*

And apparently, he had.

Kelly waited until the song ended and they reluctantly pulled apart before making her approach. She could see the moment Patrick spotted her—his face lighting up with a mixture of relief and embarrassment, like he'd been caught doing something wonderful and terrible at the same time.

"Well, well, well," she called out as she got closer, making sure her voice carried over the music. "Look what the cat dragged in."

Patrick's face went three shades of red, but he was smiling—really smiling, not the careful, polite expression he usually wore in social situations. "Kelly, this is David. David, this is Kelly, my friend who basically kidnapped me tonight."

David extended his hand with the kind of confidence that suggested he was used to making good first impressions. "The famous Kelly. Patrick's told me a lot about you."

"Has he now?" Kelly studied David's face as they shook hands, looking for the telltale signs of someone just looking to get laid. Instead, she found genuine warmth, and something else—possessiveness, maybe, or protectiveness. The way David's free hand stayed at the small of Patrick's back, the way his attention kept drifting back to Patrick even while talking to her.

*Holy shit. This guy's already half in love with him.*

"I hope you've been taking good care of my boy here," Kelly said, making it sound like a joke but watching David's reaction carefully.

"I'm trying to," David said, and the sincerity in his voice made Kelly's estimation of him jump several notches. "Though I think he's been taking better care of me."

Patrick made a sound that might have been a protest, but David just smiled and pulled him closer, and Kelly watched Patrick melt into the contact like butter on warm toast.

*Jesus. They're both gone.*

"So," Kelly said, because someone had to be the adult here, "what's the plan? Because this place is about to close, and I'm pretty sure neither of you has thought past the next five minutes."

Patrick and David looked at each other, and Kelly could practically see the panic setting in. The magic of the club was one thing, but what happened when the lights came up and reality reasserted itself?

"There's an all-night diner a few blocks from here," Kelly said, taking pity on them. "Melrose. Best pancakes in the city, and they don't ask questions about why you look like you've been dragged through a hedge backwards."

"That sounds perfect," David said, but he was looking at Patrick when he said it, like he was asking permission.

Patrick nodded, and Kelly caught the way his hand found David's without conscious thought, fingers intertwining like they'd been doing it for years instead of hours.

*Well, fuck me sideways. Patrick O'Brien's got himself a boyfriend.*

They gathered their things—what little they had—and headed for the exit. Kelly walked slightly behind them, watching the way they moved together, how David unconsciously adjusted his pace to match Patrick's, how Patrick leaned into David's warmth as they descended the stairs toward the exit.

As they passed the balcony level, Kelly caught sight of a group of guys pressed against the railing, staring down at them with expressions ranging from shock to something that looked like devastation. One of them—a blond who looked like he'd been crying—raised his hand in what might have been a wave, but David didn't even glance up. His entire attention was focused on Patrick, one hand protective on his back as they navigated through the crowd.

Kelly had seen David's type before—the kind of guy who collected admirers like trophies. But watching him now, completely oblivious to the heartbreak he was leaving in his wake, she realized this was different. David wasn't ignoring his friends out of cruelty. He literally didn't see anyone else in the room.

*Poor bastards,* Kelly thought, feeling a flicker of sympathy for the guys on the balcony. *They just watched their god fall to earth.*

The cold Chicago air hit them like a slap, and Kelly watched Patrick shiver in his mesh shirt and inadequate clothes. Without hesitation, David shrugged out of his jacket and draped it around Patrick's shoulders, and Kelly had to bite back a smile at Patrick's expression—surprised gratitude mixed with something that looked dangerously close to adoration.

*You beautiful, innocent disaster,* Kelly thought affectionately. *You have no idea what you've gotten yourself into.*

But as they walked through the empty streets toward the diner, Patrick practically glowing under David's attention, Kelly realized that maybe—just maybe—Patrick knew exactly what he was doing.

And maybe, for the first time in his careful, controlled life, he was exactly where he belonged.

# CHAPTER
## *Seven*

CHICAGO NIGHTS COULD FREEZE your soul and snow
could bury your dreams, but none of that shit could touch what
Kelly was watching unfold between these two lovesick fools.

The three of them walked through the empty Chicago streets
like survivors of some beautiful disaster, their breath creating
clouds in the frigid February air. Patrick was swimming in David's
jacket—a black leather thing that looked like it came from somewhere Patrick couldn't even pronounce—but the way he clutched
it around himself suggested he was holding onto more than just
warmth.

"Jesus, it's fucking freezing," Kelly muttered, wrapping her
arms around herself. She was regretting her decision to forbid
coats—their outfits had looked too perfect to cover up, but
hypothermia was starting to seem like a real possibility.

Patrick immediately started to shrug out of the jacket. "Here,
take—" Then he stopped, his face flushing as he realized it wasn't
his to offer. "I mean, it's not mine, it's David's—"

"Hey," David said gently, taking the jacket from Patrick's shoulders and draping it around Kelly instead. "Problem solved."

Kelly felt her heart do something complicated as warmth

enveloped her—not just from the leather, but from the genuine kindness of the gesture. "Thanks," she managed, and meant it.

David wrapped his arms around Patrick, pulling him close as they hurried toward the diner's neon glow. "Besides," he murmured into Patrick's ear, "this gives me an excuse."

Kelly watched them move together, David's body shielding Patrick from the worst of the wind, and shook her head in amazement. Another point in David's favor. She kept collecting these little moments—his protectiveness, his thoughtfulness, the way he seemed to anticipate Patrick's needs without being asked. This whole night felt surreal. She'd dragged Patrick out hoping he'd get laid, maybe gain some confidence. She'd never expected to witness something that looked suspiciously like love at first sight.

Even in their hurried dash to escape the cold, Kelly couldn't help but notice how David moved with Patrick—one arm wrapped protectively around him, adjusting his pace, using his body as a windbreak. She'd seen plenty of guys stake their claim after a club hookup, but this felt different. Protective rather than possessive.

The diner's neon sign cast pink light across the snow-covered sidewalk, and Kelly pushed through the door with relief. The blast of warm air and the smell of coffee and bacon grease felt like salvation after the frozen wasteland outside.

Melrose was exactly what you'd expect from a 3am diner— cracked vinyl booths, fluorescent lighting that made everyone look like they were dying, and a waitress who looked like she'd seen everything twice and wasn't impressed by any of it. Perfect for three people who looked like they'd been dragged through a nightclub and spit out the other side.

"Booth in the back," Kelly said, leading them past a trucker nursing coffee and a couple having what looked like a breakup conversation in hushed, angry whispers.

Patrick slid into the booth first, and David followed without hesitation, immediately wrapping an arm around Patrick's shoulders to share warmth. Kelly took the seat across from them, shrugging out of David's jacket and offering it back, but David waved her off. She tried not to smile at the way they naturally gravitated toward each other, David's thigh pressed against Patrick's, Patrick's hand somehow finding David's on the table between them.

"Well," Kelly said, opening her menu with theatrical flair, "this is fucking adorable."

Patrick turned approximately the color of a fire truck. "Kelly—"

"What? I'm just saying, if I'd known all it would take was some eyeliner and tight jeans to get you to stop being such a hermit, I would have dragged you out months ago."

David was watching this exchange with fascination, like he was seeing Patrick through new eyes. "How long have you two been friends?"

"Since freshman year," Kelly said, settling in for what she privately thought of as her interview. She'd perfected the art of vetting Patrick's potential disasters, though to be fair, most of them had been hypothetical. "Found him in the library at midnight, reorganizing the sociology section because some asshole had put Durkheim in the wrong place."

"You reorganized the library?" David's voice held something that sounded dangerously close to affection.

"Just that one section," Patrick mumbled, but Kelly caught the way David's thumb traced across his knuckles, and the way Patrick's whole body seemed to relax under that simple touch.

The waitress appeared—Božena, according to her name tag—looking like she'd rather be anywhere else. "What can I get you kids?"

"Coffee," Kelly said. "And pancakes. Lots of pancakes."

"Same," David said, then looked at Patrick. "You hungry?"

"I don't usually eat this late—"

"Pancakes," Kelly interrupted. "Trust me, sweetheart, you're going to need the carbs."

As Božena shuffled away, muttering something about college kids in what sounded like Polish, Kelly leaned back in the booth and studied David more carefully. Up close, in the harsh diner lighting, he was still devastating—sharp cheekbones, perfect bone structure, the kind of face that belonged on magazine covers. But there was something else there too, something softer when he looked at Patrick.

"So," Kelly said, because someone had to ask the hard questions, "what's your story, David? Because no offense, but guys who look like you don't usually approach guys who look like they're having a nervous breakdown on the dance floor."

"Kelly," Patrick protested, but David was laughing.

"Fair question," David said. "Honestly? I don't know what happened tonight. I saw Patrick dancing and..." He paused, searching for words. "It was like seeing someone discover fire. I couldn't look away."

Kelly felt something shift in her chest. Most guys would have given her some bullshit line about instant attraction or physical chemistry. David was talking about Patrick like he was a work of art.

"And now?"

David's hand tightened around Patrick's. "Now I'm hoping he'll let me see him again when we're both sober and not covered in club sweat."

Patrick made a sound that might have been a laugh or a whimper. "I'm sober. I had one Coke."

"I'm not talking about alcohol," David said quietly, and Kelly felt like she was witnessing something private and profound.

The coffee arrived, along with a stack of pancakes that could have fed a small army. Kelly watched Patrick fumble with the syrup—his hands were shaking slightly, whether from cold or nerves or something else entirely—and David gently took the bottle from him, drizzling syrup over Patrick's pancakes with the kind of careful attention usually reserved for surgery.

"Thanks," Patrick whispered, and the way he looked at David made Kelly's throat tight.

They ate in comfortable silence for a while, the kind of quiet that comes after everything important has been said. Kelly found herself cataloguing details: the way David cut his pancakes into neat squares, the way Patrick ate slowly, savoring each bite, the way they both kept stealing glances at each other like they couldn't quite believe this was real.

"So what happens now?" Kelly asked eventually, because someone had to be practical.

Patrick and David looked at each other, and Kelly could practically see the panic setting in. The magic of the night was one thing, but dawn was only a few hours away, and with it would come the harsh light of reality.

"I..." Patrick started, then stopped, looking lost.

"I'd like to see you again," David said simply. "If you want to."

"Yes," Patrick said, so quickly that Kelly had to bite back a grin. "I mean, if you want to. I don't really know how this works."

"Neither do I," David admitted. "But I'd like to figure it out. With you."

Kelly felt her heart do something complicated in her chest. She'd brought Patrick here to get him out of his shell, maybe have a little fun, gain some confidence. She hadn't expected to play witness to what looked like destiny unfolding in real time.

"Well," she said, signaling Božena for the check, "I hate to break up this Hallmark moment, but it's almost four in the morning, and some of us have class on Monday."

They paid the check—David insisting on covering it despite Patrick's protests—and started to bundle back into the cold.

"Wait," David said suddenly, stopping them at the door. "You guys took the El, right? You don't have to go all the way back to Belmont in this weather. I drove."

Kelly raised an eyebrow. "You have a car?"

"BMW," David said, almost apologetically. "It's parked down on Halsted. We're all going back to campus anyway—I'm just in a different dorm."

Patrick looked relieved at the prospect of not facing the frozen train platform again. "Are you sure? I mean, what about your friends?"

Something flickered across David's face. "My friends?"

"The guys on the balcony," Kelly said. "The ones who looked like you'd just kicked their puppy when we left."

David ran a hand through his hair. "Shit. I drove them here. I didn't even think..." He looked genuinely distressed. "They'll have to find their own way back."

"We should go check on them," Patrick said immediately, and Kelly watched David's expression soften completely at Patrick's concern for people he'd never even met.

"You want to check on my friends?" David asked, something like wonder in his voice.

"Well, yeah. I feel bad that they're stranded because of me."

Kelly felt her heart do another complicated flip. *Jesus, Patrick. You're going to ruin this man completely.*

"Okay," David said, looking at Patrick like he'd just offered to cure cancer. "Let's go see if they're still there."

They walked down to Halsted, where David's black BMW sat looking ridiculously expensive among the other cars. The heated seats were a revelation after the frozen Chicago night, and soon they were pulling up outside Medusa's again.

Sure enough, Trevor, Marcus, and Jake were huddled outside the club, looking cold and slightly abandoned.

"There they are," David muttered, rolling down his window. "Hey! Need a ride?"

The relief on their faces was immediate, though Kelly caught the way Trevor's expression tightened when he saw Patrick in the front seat. They all piled in—Marcus and Jake in the back, Trevor behind Patrick, and Kelly finding herself perched on Jake's lap.

"Hope you don't mind," she said to Jake with a grin. "I'm equal opportunity when it comes to laps."

Jake laughed. "Sorry to disappoint, but I'm more interested in the guy driving than the girl on my lap."

"Story of my life," Kelly said cheerfully, but she was watching the dynamics in the car more carefully now.

David had unconsciously reached over to trace Patrick's fingers where they rested on the center console, and Marcus was observing this intimate gesture with fascination. But it was Trevor who caught Kelly's attention—staring resolutely out the window, his jaw tight, refusing to look at the gentle way David touched Patrick.

*Oh, honey,* Kelly thought, recognizing heartbreak when she saw it. *You've got it bad, and he doesn't even know you exist.*

The drive back to campus was quiet, filled with unspoken tensions and the weight of a night that had changed everything for some of them, and left others feeling more invisible than ever.

At the entrance to Patrick's dorm, Kelly turned to say good-night and found them standing close together, David's hands on Patrick's shoulders, both of them looking like they were about to say goodbye to something precious.

"I'll, um, I'll see you..." Patrick started.

"Tomorrow," David said firmly. "Today, I mean. Later today."

# CHAPTER
## *Eight*

PATRICK HAD NEVER WANTED to stop time until someone made forever feel like not nearly long enough.

The BMW pulled up outside his dorm, its engine purring to a stop in the sudden quiet of early morning Chicago. Through the windshield, Patrick could see the familiar brick building where he'd lived for three years, where his textbooks waited in careful stacks and his sociology notes lay color-coded on his desk. It looked exactly the same as when he'd left six hours ago, but Patrick felt like he was returning from another planet entirely.

David's friends began the awkward shuffle of goodbyes and thank-yous from the back seat, but Patrick barely heard them. All his attention was focused on the way this incredible night was about to end, and how desperately he didn't want it to.

They all climbed out of the car, Kelly offering David his jacket back with a grateful smile. Patrick watched David shrug back into the leather and felt something twist in his chest at the reality that this magical night was actually ending.

In the back seat, Trevor felt his stomach drop as Kelly walked away toward the dorm entrance. He knew what was coming next —David saying goodbye to Patrick, probably kissing him—and even though he wanted to look away, he found himself unable to move, trapped in his own masochistic need to witness his heart breaking in real time.

"I should probably get these guys back to their dorm," David said, glancing toward his friends who were clearly ready to leave.

"Of course," Patrick said quickly. "Thank you for... for everything tonight."

"You don't have to thank me," David said softly, stepping closer.

At the entrance to his dorm, Patrick found himself standing close to David, feeling David's hands settle gently on his shoulders. They looked at each other in the falling snow, and Patrick felt like they were about to say goodbye to something precious and irreplaceable.

"I'll, um, I'll see you..." Patrick started, not wanting to assume anything, not wanting to seem too eager or presumptuous.

"Tomorrow," David said firmly. "Today, I mean. Later today."

Behind them, Kelly cleared her throat. "I'm going to go upstairs and pretend I don't see whatever's about to happen down here."

She pushed through the door and climbed halfway up the first flight of stairs, then stopped and listened. Through the glass doors, she could see their silhouettes—David pulling Patrick into the small vestibule between the outer and inner doors, the way Patrick melted against him, the careful tenderness of what was obviously Patrick's first real kiss.

Kelly smiled and continued up the stairs, thinking about transformation and magic and the way some nights could change everything.

Patrick O'Brien was going to be just fine.

———

Patrick felt his face flush as Kelly pushed through the outer door, but David just smiled and gently pulled him toward the building's entrance.

"Come here," David said softly, drawing Patrick into the small vestibule between the outer and inner doors.

Suddenly they were alone in a pocket of relative warmth, the sounds from the street muffled by glass and brick. David reached up and gently brushed snow from Patrick's hair, his fingers lingering against Patrick's cheek.

"You're freezing," David murmured.

"I'm okay," Patrick whispered, though he wasn't sure if that was true. He felt like every nerve ending in his body had suddenly come alive.

"Patrick," David said, his voice barely audible. "Can I...?"

Patrick nodded, not trusting himself to speak.

David stepped closer, one hand cupping Patrick's cheek while the other settled at the small of his back, and Patrick felt his breath catch.

"I want this to be perfect for you," David whispered against his lips.

Then David's mouth was on his, soft and warm and impossibly gentle, and Patrick understood for the first time why people wrote songs about kissing. David tasted like vodka and promise, like everything Patrick had been afraid to want and everything he'd never known he needed. The kiss was careful at first, almost reverent, as if David understood exactly how precious and terrifying this moment was for Patrick.

Through the car window, Trevor watched David pull Patrick into the vestibule, watched them move together in the dim light behind the glass doors, and felt something die inside his chest. David was kissing Patrick with a tenderness Trevor had only dreamed of receiving, holding him like he was something precious and breakable. Marcus, sitting beside him, noticed the way Trevor's hands had clenched into fists, the way his breathing had gone shallow and pained.

When Patrick's lips parted on a soft gasp, David deepened the kiss just slightly, and Patrick felt something fundamental shift inside him. His hands found David's jacket, clutching the leather like an anchor as the world tilted and rearranged itself around this single point of contact. He melted against David completely, giving himself over to this moment, to this person who had appeared in his life like magic and changed everything in the space of a single night.

Time stopped. The cold disappeared. The fear that had lived in Patrick's chest for twenty-two years quietly packed its bags and left without saying goodbye.

When they finally broke apart, both breathing hard, Patrick kept his eyes closed for a long moment, afraid that opening them might make the magic disappear.

"Look at me," David said softly.

Patrick opened his eyes to find David watching him with an expression so tender it made his throat tight.

"How was that?" David asked, a small smile playing at the corners of his mouth.

"Perfect," Patrick breathed, and meant it completely.

They pulled apart slowly, neither wanting to be the first to break the connection. Through the glass doors, Patrick could see David's friends waiting by the car, and he knew this moment had to end.

"I'll see you today," David said, not quite a question.

"Yes," Patrick said, smiling. "Definitely yes."

Patrick watched through the glass as David jogged back to the car and drove away into the snowy Chicago night. Only when the taillights disappeared did he finally push through the inner doors and begin the climb to his room, his lips still tingling and his heart full of the terrifying, wonderful knowledge that his carefully controlled life had just been turned completely upside down.

And for the first time in twenty-two years, Patrick O'Brien couldn't wait to see what happened next.

# CHAPTER
## *Nine*

DAVID CHEN HAD NEVER BEEN UNDONE by someone's laughter until Patrick made joy sound like music.

They sat in the ice cream shop window, snow falling steadily outside, and David watched Patrick take another bite of vanilla while shaking his head in amazement. "I still can't believe you made me eat ice cream in twenty-degree weather," Patrick said, but he was grinning, that wide, unguarded smile that made David's chest tight with something he didn't have words for yet.

"Says the guy who ordered vanilla," David shot back, gesturing with his spoon. "After sampling half the shop."

"Hey, you're the one who insisted on trying everything. 'Just one more sample,'" Patrick mimicked in an exaggerated voice. "'I need to make sure the strawberry doesn't have chunks.'"

David felt heat climb his neck. "It was a legitimate concern."

"You asked for seven samples, David. Seven. That poor kid behind the counter thought you were having some kind of crisis."

The memory made David laugh despite his embarrassment. He'd never done anything like that before—acting like a kid in a candy store, literally. But something about Patrick's presence made him want to be silly, to let go of the careful control he usually maintained. When Patrick had started taking bites from each sample spoon, turning it into a game, David had felt something loosen in his chest that he hadn't even realized was wound tight.

"Besides," Patrick continued, scraping the bottom of his cup, "we both ended up with the most boring flavors possible. Chocolate and vanilla. We're like the Wonder Bread of ice cream choices."

"Speak for yourself. This is premium vanilla."

"Oh, excuse me, Mr. Sophisticated Palate."

They fell into comfortable silence, watching the snow accumulate on the sidewalk outside. The shop was nearly empty—who else would be crazy enough to eat ice cream in a blizzard?—and David found himself cataloguing details the way he had that first night at the club. The way Patrick tucked his red hair behind his ear when he was thinking. How he ate ice cream slowly, savoring each bite instead of rushing through it. The unconscious way he'd started leaning closer to David as they talked, like he was drawn by some invisible force.

It had been three days since that first night at Medusa's. Three days of discovering that the sweet, nervous boy from the dance floor was also wickedly funny when he relaxed, surprisingly stubborn about his opinions, and completely devastating when he smiled like that.

They'd met for dinner yesterday at a little sandwich shop near campus, and David had reached across the table to take Patrick's hand without thinking about it. Patrick had gone pink but hadn't pulled away, and they'd sat there for an hour just talking, fingers intertwined like they'd been doing it for years instead of days.

"Can I ask you something?" Patrick said suddenly, his voice quieter than before.

"Sure."

Patrick set down his spoon and looked directly at David, those green eyes serious now. "Why me?"

The question hit David like a physical blow. He opened his mouth to give some casual answer, something smooth and deflecting, but Patrick's expression stopped him. This wasn't casual

curiosity. This was Patrick genuinely trying to understand something that mattered to him.

"I..." David started, then stopped. Why Patrick? It was a simple
question with no simple answer. "I don't know."

Patrick's face fell slightly, and David realized how that
sounded.

"No, I mean—I don't know because it's not... it's not logical."
David set down his own spoon, searching for words. "It's a feeling.
A lot of feelings, actually. Things I've never..." He paused, feeling
exposed in a way that usually made him want to run. "Things I've
never felt before."

Patrick's expression softened. "Good feelings?"

"Terrifying feelings," David said honestly. "But yeah. Good."

They stared at each other across the small table, and David felt
that familiar pull, that magnetic force that seemed to draw him
toward Patrick without his permission. In the harsh fluorescent
lighting of the ice cream shop, Patrick looked young and hopeful
and completely beautiful, and David wanted to tell him everything
—about the way his chest tightened when Patrick smiled, about
how he'd started looking forward to things for the first time in
years, about the growing certainty that whatever this was between
them, it was the most real thing he'd ever experienced.

"Are we..." Patrick started, then stopped, his cheeks coloring.
"Never mind."

"What?"

"It's stupid. We've only known each other a few days."

"Patrick. What?"

Patrick fidgeted with his spoon, not meeting David's eyes. "Are
we... I mean, what are we? Are we..." He trailed off, unable to
finish the question.

David felt something warm spread through his chest. Patrick
wanted to ask if they were boyfriends—David could see it in his
face, hear it in the careful way he wasn't saying the words. It
should have terrified him. Three days ago, the idea of being
anyone's boyfriend would have sent him running. Now, looking at
Patrick's nervous expression, all David wanted to do was say yes.

"We're figuring it out," David said gently. "Is that okay?"

Patrick's smile was radiant. "Yeah. That's okay."

"Good. Because I was thinking..." David grinned. "Tomorrow I could pick you up and we could go somewhere. Maybe that mall you mentioned? Old Orchard?"

"You want to go to a suburban mall?" Patrick looked skeptical. "It's not exactly your scene."

"You are my scene," David said without thinking, then felt his face burn at how that sounded. "I mean—"

"I know what you meant," Patrick said softly. "And yes. I'd love that."

They finished their ice cream in comfortable silence, and David found himself thinking about tomorrow, about spending a whole day with Patrick, about the growing certainty that this sweet, funny, complicated boy was changing everything he thought he knew about himself.

"Hey, Pat," he said as they bundled back into their coats.

Patrick went suddenly still. "What did you say?"

David caught the shift in Patrick's tone immediately. "I said Pat. Is that...? What's wrong?"

"Nothing's wrong, it's just..." Patrick's voice was quiet, almost distant. "Only my grandmother ever called me that. She died when I was twelve."

David felt like he'd stepped on something precious. "Shit. Patrick, I'm sorry, I didn't know—"

"It's okay," Patrick said quickly. "It's just... I know it's irrational, but I like to keep that just for her, you know?"

David nodded, understanding completely. "Of course. I won't—"

"Actually," Patrick interrupted, a small smile returning to his face, "maybe you could call me something else? If you want to, I mean. Something that's just... ours?"

David felt his heart do something complicated in his chest. Something that was just theirs. The idea of having a private language with Patrick, even something as simple as a nickname, made him feel possessive and tender in equal measure.

"Let me think..." David studied Patrick's face, taking in the hopeful expression, the way his green eyes lit up when he was excited about something. "You know what? You look like a Packy."

"Packy?!" Patrick burst into laughter. "Where did you get that from?"

"I don't know," David grinned. "You just look like a Packy. It suits you."

"Packy," Patrick repeated, testing it out. "I love it."

The following Saturday, David picked Patrick up in the BMW and they drove north to Old Orchard Mall. Patrick gave directions from the passenger seat, pointing out landmarks from his childhood, and David found himself storing away every detail. The elementary school where Patrick had learned to read. The park where he'd broken his arm falling off the monkey bars. The house where his best friend from third grade had lived.

"You really grew up around here," David said as they pulled into the mall parking lot.

"Born and raised in Arlington Heights," Patrick confirmed. "Population: boring."

"I don't think anything about you is boring."

Patrick's blush was immediate and adorable. "You say things like that and I forget how to think."

David parked the car and turned to face Patrick fully. "Good. I like you better when you're not overthinking everything."

They walked toward the mall entrance, and David noticed the way Patrick kept glancing at their hands, clearly wanting to reach for him but holding back. When they passed through the automatic doors into the warmth of the mall, Patrick leaned closer.

"Just so you know," he whispered, "I wouldn't normally... I mean, in public..."

David understood immediately. Without hesitation, he reached over and took Patrick's hand, interlacing their fingers and continuing to walk as if nothing had happened.

"David," Patrick hissed, his face flaming. "People will see."

"So?"

"So... I..." Patrick looked around nervously, but he didn't let go of David's hand. After a few minutes of walking, David felt Patrick's grip relax, his shoulders lose their tension. Some people noticed them—a few stares, one disapproving look from an older woman—but most just went about their business.

"How does it feel?" David asked quietly.

"Terrifying," Patrick admitted. "But also... right. Really right."

David squeezed his hand, feeling something warm settle in his chest. This was new for him too, though he suspected Patrick didn't realize it. David had never held hands with someone in public, never been part of a couple that walked through malls together on Saturday afternoons. It should have felt ordinary, boring even. Instead, it felt revolutionary.

They wandered through the shops, Patrick pointing out stores he'd frequented as a teenager, David content to follow his lead. But when they passed Marshall Field's, David spotted something in the window that made him stop.

"Hold on," he said, pulling Patrick into the store.

"What are we—"

David headed straight for the sunglasses display and picked up a pair of tortoiseshell wayfarers. Without asking permission, he slipped them onto Patrick's face and stepped back to assess the effect.

"Jesus," David breathed.

The sunglasses transformed Patrick completely. They made his cheekbones look sharper, his jaw more defined, turned him from sweet and innocent into something approaching dangerous. David felt his mouth go dry.

"How do I look?" Patrick asked, clearly amused by David's reaction.

"Like trouble," David said honestly. "Come on, I have an idea."

He pulled Patrick toward the men's department, his mind already forming a plan. Patrick needed new clothes—not the costume Kelly had put together, but something that was actually him. Something that would show the world what David saw when he looked at Patrick.

"David, what are we doing?"

"Trust me," David said, already pulling items off racks. "You said you wanted to go back to Medusa's, right? But this time, you should go as yourself."

Patrick looked skeptical but followed David to the fitting room. David handed him piece after piece—dark jeans that would hug his frame properly, a soft gray henley that would bring out his eyes, a black leather jacket that was simpler and more classic than David's own.

"Try these," David said, pushing Patrick into the fitting room.

"All of it?"

"All of it."

Twenty minutes later, Patrick emerged from the fitting room looking like he'd stepped out of David's dreams. The clothes fit him perfectly, emphasizing his lean frame without overwhelming it. The gray henley made his red hair look like fire, and the leather jacket gave him an edge that made David's pulse quicken.

"How do I look?" Patrick asked, clearly self-conscious.

"Perfect," David said, his voice rougher than he'd intended. "You look perfect."

Patrick studied himself in the mirror, turning slightly to see the full effect. "I do look different, don't I? More... grown up."

"You look like yourself," David said. "The version of yourself you've been hiding."

Patrick met David's eyes in the mirror. "I'll wear this to Medusa's, but only if you agree to something."

"What?"

"Come with me to the Art Institute first. There's a painting I want to show you. My favorite."

David raised an eyebrow. It seemed like an odd request—he'd never been particularly interested in art—but the hopeful expression on Patrick's face made the answer easy.

"Sure. We could have lunch there too, if you want."

Patrick's smile was radiant. "Really? Next Saturday then? Lunch at the Art Institute, then Medusa's?"

"It's a date," David said, and meant it completely.

"A date," Patrick repeated, like he was testing the words.

"Is that okay?"

"More than okay," Patrick said, still looking at himself in the mirror. "It's perfect."

David bought the entire outfit without letting Patrick see the total, ignoring his protests about the cost. As they walked back to the car, Patrick wearing his new sunglasses and looking more confident than David had ever seen him, David realized something had shifted between them. They weren't just figuring things out anymore. They were building something real.

And for the first time in his life, David wanted to see where it would lead.

# CHAPTER
## *Ten*

WHEN THE ART Institute of Chicago opened in 1893, people like David wouldn't have been allowed through its doors, though their money would have been welcomed with open arms.

The irony wasn't lost on him as he climbed the marble steps beside Patrick, passing between the two massive bronze lions that guarded the entrance like ancient sentries. David Chen could now afford to buy half the paintings in this place, could write checks that would fund entire exhibitions, could have his name etched in brass on any wall he chose. His mother would be thrilled to hear he was "in attendance" at such a prestigious institution, though she'd be politely puzzled that he'd come to actually see the art rather than attend some gala or fundraiser.

Growing up, David had learned to think of places like this the way his parents did—as institutions that people like them were supposed to fund once they were established, attend like all well-off people did. Not so much for the art itself, that was a side benefit if you were into that sort of thing. Rather, these were gifts by the elite to the commoners, markers that set them apart from those who could only visit on free admission days.

But this was David's first chance to see something like this through the eyes of someone who obviously had a real connection here, a genuine passion that had nothing to do with social obligation or tax write-offs. It was intriguing.

Patrick's entire demeanor had changed the moment they'd passed through the entrance. Gone was the careful, reserved boy who measured every step and calculated every social interaction. In his place was someone David had only glimpsed in fleeting moments—animated, confident, completely at ease in his own skin. Patrick's eyes were bright with excitement as he practically bounced on his toes, scanning the information boards and directional signs like a navigator plotting a course to buried treasure.

"This way," Patrick said, grabbing David's hand without hesitation and pulling him toward a grand staircase that swept upward into the heart of the museum. "You have to see it. I mean, I know you probably know it already, everyone does, but seeing it in person is completely different."

David allowed himself to be led up the marble steps, amused by this side of Patrick he'd never seen before. It was like watching a kid drag his parent toward Santa at the mall, pure enthusiasm unburdened by self-consciousness. Around them, the museum breathed with a kind of secular reverence—people speaking in hushed tones while pointing at paintings, debating meanings and artistic merit, moving through the galleries with the careful respect usually reserved for churches.

The enormity and weight of the place struck David as they climbed higher. Original masterpieces hung on every wall, centuries of human creativity and genius collected under one roof. He'd seen reproductions of these works his entire life—in textbooks, on postcards, in his parents' coffee table books—but being surrounded by the actual canvases, the real brushstrokes, the authentic colors that had emerged from some artist's vision decades or centuries ago, was overwhelming in a way he hadn't expected.

Patrick navigated the galleries with the confidence of someone who'd walked these halls hundreds of times, turning left and right without consulting maps or signs, David's hand still firmly clasped in his. They passed through rooms of Impressionists and Post-Impressionists, Medieval manuscripts and modern sculptures, Patrick occasionally slowing to point out a particular favorite but clearly focused on a specific destination.

And then they turned a corner, and Patrick stopped dead in his tracks.

The painting dominated the entire wall—enormous, maybe ten feet across and six feet tall, a sprawling scene of people scattered across what looked like a riverside park. Even from across the room, David could see the distinctive technique, thousands of tiny dots of color that somehow resolved into figures and trees and water when viewed from a distance.

"There it is," Patrick breathed, and David realized he was witnessing something deeply personal.

David knew the piece, if only vaguely—the same way he knew the Mona Lisa or the ceiling of the Sistine Chapel, cultural touchstones he'd absorbed through osmosis rather than study. Georges Seurat's "A Sunday on La Grande Jatte." But watching Patrick's face as they approached the massive canvas, David understood that his knowledge was superficial compared to the profound connection Patrick obviously felt.

"Sunday on La Grande Jatte," Patrick said softly, his voice taking on the tone of someone sharing a sacred secret. "1884 to 1886. Seurat spent two years working on it, using a technique called pointillism—all those tiny dots of pure color. He was only twenty-six when he finished it."

They moved closer, and David could see what Patrick meant. Up close, the painting dissolved into thousands of individual brushstrokes, each one a deliberate choice of color and placement. But step back, and the dots merged into a coherent scene of Parisians enjoying a lazy afternoon by the Seine.

"I first saw this on a school field trip in sixth grade," Patrick continued, his arm sliding around David's back with an unconscious intimacy that made David's heart skip. "I stood right here—well, probably about where we are now—and just stared. I'd never seen anything like it. The teacher had to practically drag me away."

David watched Patrick's face as he spoke, noting the way his features softened, how his usual careful guardedness had completely evaporated. This was Patrick in his element, sharing something that mattered to him more than David had realized anything could matter to someone his age.

"What got to you about it?" David asked, genuinely curious.

Patrick was quiet for a moment, his fingers unconsciously tracing small circles on David's back as he studied the painting. "I think it was the first time I realized there was a whole world beyond Arlington Heights and Chicago. All these people, having their perfect Sunday afternoon in some beautiful place in France. I wanted to be one of them, you know? To be the guy in the top hat, or one of the women with the parasols. To be part of something that elegant and timeless."

David felt something shift in his chest as he listened. This wasn't just about art appreciation or cultural sophistication. This was about a lonely kid from the suburbs discovering that beauty and wonder existed beyond the boundaries of his small world.

"Plus," Patrick added with a grin, "it came to Chicago of all places. How crazy is that? This incredible piece of Paris, just sitting here in the Midwest where a kid like me could stumble across it on a random Tuesday in sixth grade."

Patrick turned to face David fully, his eyes bright with the kind of passion David rarely saw in anyone, let alone someone discussing a painting. "Do you see how he captured the light? The way it filters through the trees and reflects off the water? And look at the woman in the foreground with the monkey—there's something mysterious about her, like she's keeping a secret."

As Patrick pointed out details, his hand drifted from David's back to gesture toward the canvas, then returned to rest at David's waist, fingers playing absently with the fabric of his shirt. The casual intimacy was unlike anything David had seen from Patrick before—no self-consciousness, no careful calculation of appropriate boundaries. Just pure, unguarded enthusiasm shared with someone he trusted completely.

David found himself leaning in closer, not just to see the

painting better but to study Patrick's face as he spoke. Those green eyes were completely alive, and when Patrick turned to meet his gaze, David felt like he was seeing straight through to Patrick's soul. There was no awkwardness, no nervous glancing away. Just two people sharing something beautiful.

"You really love this," David said quietly.

"I do," Patrick admitted. "I know it probably sounds silly—"

"It doesn't sound silly at all." David reached up to brush a strand of red hair from Patrick's forehead. "It sounds like passion. Real passion. I don't think I've ever felt that way about anything."

Patrick's expression softened even further. "You will. When you find the right thing."

Without thinking, David heard himself say, "Maybe I already have."

They stared at each other in front of the massive painting, surrounded by other museum visitors but completely absorbed in their own private moment. David realized that something had shifted not just in how he saw Patrick, but in how he thought about their relationship. This wasn't casual dating anymore. This wasn't figuring things out.

*Boyfriend,* David thought, and the word felt right in a way that should have terrified him but somehow didn't. *Patrick is my boyfriend.*

"Excuse me," a security guard said politely, approaching them with a gentle smile. "I'm going to need you gentlemen to step back just a bit. Museum policy."

Patrick immediately flushed red and stepped backward, the spell broken as his usual self-consciousness reasserted itself. "Sorry," he mumbled, suddenly aware that they'd been standing closer to the painting than was probably appropriate, and definitely closer to each other than he would normally allow in public.

"No problem at all," the guard said kindly. "Happens all the time with that one. It has a way of drawing people in."

David watched Patrick retreat into himself slightly, the magical openness of the past few minutes dimming as public awareness returned. But something had been revealed here, something precious that David suspected few people had ever been invited to see.

"Come on," Patrick said, his hand finding David's again but with less of the earlier abandon. "Let me show you the courtyard downstairs. There's a Chagall window that's incredible, and we can get lunch."

As they made their way back through the galleries toward the lower level, David reflected on what he'd just witnessed. Patrick had shared his most intimate world with him—not just a favorite painting, but the source of dreams and wonder that had shaped how he saw beauty itself. David wondered if anyone else had ever been given this glimpse into what made Patrick who he was beneath all his careful layers.

The courtyard restaurant was tucked beneath soaring windows of brilliant blue stained glass, Chagall's ethereal figures floating in jewel-toned light that painted everything in the room with an otherworldly glow. Small tables surrounded a central fountain, the sound of water mixing with the quiet conversations of other diners.

"I had no idea any of this existed," David admitted as they settled at a table near the fountain, finger sandwiches and a glass of wine each—certainly not burgers and fries, but perfect in its own elegant way.

"Most people don't, unless they're really into museums," Patrick said, some of his earlier confidence returning as he relaxed into his chair. "I used to come here sometimes when I needed to think. Or when I wanted to remember that there's more to the world than whatever was stressing me out."

David looked around at the light filtering through the Chagall windows, the fountain, the quiet sophistication of the space, and realized he was seeing Chicago through completely different eyes. "How many times can someone say they've had lunch next to a fountain in the middle of a world-class art museum?"

"Not many," Patrick agreed with a smile.

"It's perfect," David said, and he wasn't just talking about the setting. "You're perfect."

Patrick's blush was immediate and beautiful, but instead of deflecting or changing the subject, he held David's gaze. "I'm really glad you came with me today."

"So am I," David said, reaching across the table to take Patrick's hand. "Thank you for sharing this with me. For trusting me with something that matters to you this much."

Patrick's smile was radiant. "There's a lot more I want to share with you."

The promise in those words made David's pulse quicken, but it wasn't just desire—though that was certainly there. It was the recognition that Patrick was offering him something rare and precious: access to the real person beneath all the careful construction, the dreams and passions and vulnerabilities that Patrick kept hidden from almost everyone else.

As they finished lunch beneath the blue glow of the Chagall windows, David felt the last of his emotional defenses quietly surrender. Whatever this was between them, wherever it was heading, he was all in.

He just hoped they'd have enough time to figure out what came next.

# CHAPTER
## *Eleven*

DAVID HAD SEEN beautiful men in expensive clothes before, but he'd never seen someone wear confidence like Patrick was wearing it tonight.

They sat at the same tucked-away table in the upstairs bar where they'd first talked nearly two weeks ago, but everything had changed. Patrick looked radiant in the clothes they'd chosen together—the gray henley bringing out his eyes, the leather jacket giving him an edge that made David's pulse quicken. But more than the clothes, there was something in Patrick's eyes that burned a hole straight through David's heart. A spark of self-assurance, a comfort in his own skin that transformed his shy grin into something genuinely alluring.

"I still can't believe you told your mother about me," Patrick said, taking another sip of his Sprite with a splash of white wine—David had ordered for both of them, knowing Patrick didn't drink much, but wanting him to have something special tonight.

David swirled his vodka tonic, remembering the phone call he'd made after dropping Patrick off earlier to change. "I called her when I got back to my dorm. Told her I'd spent the day at the Art Institute."

"And?"

"She was thrilled. You know how mothers get about 'refined cultural experiences.'" David smiled at the memory. "She started going on about how wonderful it was that I was developing an appreciation for the arts, how it would serve me well in business circles, all that."

Patrick leaned forward, clearly fascinated. "Then what?"

"Then I told her it was a date. With a boy named Patrick." David watched Patrick's face carefully as he continued. "She went quiet for a minute. She's still... adjusting to my 'lifestyle choices,' as she calls them. But I didn't care. I was proud to tell her your name."

Patrick's eyes widened. "You were proud?"

"I've never done that before," David admitted. "Given my mother a name, I mean. She knows I date, but I've never acknowledged anyone specific. She pretends my hookups don't exist, and I let her."

"But this time was different?"

"This time was different." David reached across the table to trace Patrick's fingers where they rested on the dark wood. "I think she's curious about you now. She asked if you come from money."

Patrick nearly choked on his drink. "What did you tell her?"

"That you're worth more than money could buy." David's voice was soft, sincere. "I think she's starting to wonder if this Patrick character might be... different. More refined. Someone serious."

Patrick stared at him, something like wonder in his green eyes. "She wants to know about me?"

"She does. And honestly? I think she's relieved that I'm dating someone who takes me to art museums instead of just..." David gestured vaguely.

"Instead of just what?"

"Instead of just looking for hookups and a good time." David felt heat climb his neck. "I've never brought substance to anything I've done with another guy. You make me want to..." He paused.

"What?" Patrick asked softly.

David reflected, nearly not completing his thought—part

embarrassment, part uncertainty about how to articulate the feeling. "You make me want to... stop pretending. To mean something... to someone... like you."

Patrick's blush was immediate and beautiful. "I can't believe you told her my name."

David could see how much it meant to Patrick, this simple acknowledgment of his existence in David's family life. It was touching in a way that made David's chest tight—no one had ever cared this much about whether his mother approved of them.

"Ready to go show off those new clothes on the dance floor?" David asked, finishing his drink.

Patrick grinned, the shy uncertainty of two weeks ago replaced by genuine excitement. "Let's see if I remember how to do this."

The main floor was just as chaotic as David remembered—strobing lights, bodies pressed together, the relentless pulse of music that seemed to live in your chest. But this time, instead of watching Patrick from the balcony, David was beside him as they found their place in the crowd.

A Siouxsie and the Banshees song was playing, something neither of them recognized, but they moved together with the mass of dancers, Patrick no longer the terrified boy in Kelly's costume but someone who belonged here, who had earned his place on this floor.

Then something unexpected happened. The song ended, and instead of the usual New Wave or alternative track, Madonna's voice filled the space, commercial and bright and completely out of place at Medusa's.

The crowd responded with surprised delight, energy levels spiking as the familiar pop melody took over. David raised an eyebrow—Madonna was way too mainstream for this crowd, but whoever was DJing tonight was either new or someone had made a mistake.

Patrick's face lit up like Christmas morning. "I love this song!"

David watched, fascinated, as Patrick began to really move, not just following the beat but engaging with the music on a deeper level. While everyone else was just dancing to the rhythm,

Patrick was listening to the words, his lips moving along with the lyrics.

He started laughing suddenly, a sound of pure joy that made David's heart skip.

"What's funny?" David called over the music.

Patrick leaned in close, his breath warm against David's ear. "Not funny, just... I just realized something. Music is poetry set to a tune."

David pulled back to look at Patrick's face, seeing that spark of intellectual curiosity even here, even while dancing in a crowded club. Most people would just move mindlessly to the beat, but Patrick's brain was actively engaging with every element of the experience, finding meaning and beauty even in a Madonna song at a gay club.

"I love that about you," David said, and he meant it completely. Patrick's eagerness to understand everything, to find depth and significance in moments that others might dismiss as trivial, was one of the things that made him extraordinary.

As the song progressed, Patrick moved closer, his earlier inhibitions completely forgotten. David could see Patrick's lips moving with the lyrics, quietly at first, but David reached out and lifted Patrick's chin, encouraging him to let go completely.

The result was beautiful—Patrick practically serenading David right there on the dance floor, singing along with Madonna's words about opening hearts and taking chances, his green eyes locked on David's face with an intensity that made the rest of the world disappear.

When Patrick reached the chorus, encouraging David to open his heart, David felt something fundamental shift inside his chest.

"Maybe I have," David replied, giving Patrick that smile that had charmed countless others but had never felt this genuine before. This wasn't about conquest or seduction. This was pure, uncontrollable happiness.

Patrick took the initiative then, leaning in for a kiss that was awkward and unpracticed but passionate in its simplicity and pure joy. David felt something click into place, a certainty that had been building for two weeks finally crystallizing into absolute clarity.

He was in love. Completely, irrevocably in love.

When they broke apart, both breathing hard, Patrick's face was flushed and beautiful in the strobing lights.

"David?" Patrick said, having to raise his voice over the music. "Can we go to that same diner again?"

David glanced at his Tissot—12:30 already. "You want to go now?"

Patrick nodded. "I'm kind of hungry, and... it's loud."

It was loud, but David suspected Patrick wanted something more than just a quieter environment. The diner felt like their place now, somewhere they could make their own. A place where they could talk about what was happening between them without the chaos of the club.

"Let's go," David said, taking Patrick's hand.

They made their way down the stairs and out onto Halsted, where the February air hit them like a physical force. Even though Patrick had his new leather jacket, David immediately shrugged out of his own and wrapped it around Patrick's shoulders, needing to make sure his boyfriend was as warm as possible. Then he pulled him close as they walked the few blocks to Melrose.

God, he was falling. Had fallen. Was drowning in feelings he'd never experienced before and never wanted to surface from.

As they walked through the snowy Chicago night toward their diner, David realized that whatever happened next, whatever they talked about over coffee and pie at 1 AM, his life had been permanently changed by this red-haired boy who saw poetry in pop songs and magic in pointillist paintings.

And for the first time in his life, David Chen was exactly where he wanted to be.

# CHAPTER
## *Twelve*

PATRICK HAD NEVER BEEN SO terrified of three little words in his life.

They sat in the same booth at Melrose where Kelly had brought them two weeks ago, but everything felt different now. More intimate. More charged. David kept fidgeting with his napkin, tearing small pieces off the edge in a way that was completely unlike his usual composed self. It was making Patrick nervous too, a restless energy bouncing between them like electricity.

"The museum was incredible today," David said, his voice slightly strained. "And dancing was fun. Madonna, huh? Who would have thought Medusa's would go mainstream."

"Yeah," Patrick agreed, trying to match David's casual tone. "The whole day was... perfect."

But the conversation felt forced, like they were both dancing around something enormous sitting between them on the table. Patrick suspected he knew what it was—the same thing that had been keeping him awake at night, the words that kept forming in his mind every time David smiled at him or took his hand or looked at him like he was something precious.

*I love you.*

The thought had been there since their first kiss in the dorm vestibule, growing stronger every day they spent together. But saying it out loud felt impossible. What if David didn't feel the same way? What if it was too soon? What if Patrick was just naive about these things?

David cleared his throat. "Patrick, there's something I've been wanting to—"

"Well, well, well," a familiar voice interrupted. "Look who's back! Where's your third wheel tonight?"

Božena, their waitress from before, stood beside their table with her hands on her hips, looking pleased to see them. Patrick felt relief and frustration in equal measure—saved from whatever awkward conversation they were about to have, but also disappointed that the moment was broken.

"Just the two of us tonight," David said, recovering his composure quickly.

"Ah, so this is a date then," Božena said, but it wasn't really a question. "Good for you boys. About time. What can I get you?"

Patrick felt his face burn, but he couldn't help smiling at her directness. They ordered—coffee and pie for both of them—and watched her bustle away with obvious approval written all over her face.

"She's something else," Patrick said, and they both started laughing, some of the tension finally breaking.

As they ate, they fell into easier conversation—David asking about Patrick's plans after graduation, Patrick wondering about David's career goals. Both being honest but carefully avoiding the real question hovering between them: what did this mean for them? For whatever this was they were building together?

Patrick found himself studying David's face as he talked, cataloguing details he wanted to remember forever. The way David's eyes lit up when he was passionate about something. How his voice got softer when he said Patrick's name. The unconscious way he reached across the table to touch Patrick's hand whenever he was making a point.

*I love you*, Patrick thought again, the words so clear in his mind he was amazed they weren't audible.

Finally, David seemed to steel himself, setting down his fork with deliberate precision. "Listen, Patrick, there's something I was thinking of telling you, but—"

"More coffee, boys?" Božena was back, pot in hand, interrupting again with perfect timing. She topped off their cups while chattering about the weather, completely oblivious to the moment she'd just shattered.

David's jaw tightened slightly, but he managed a polite smile until she left. Patrick wanted to reach for his hand, to tell him to continue, but before he could speak, the diner's bell chimed and three familiar figures walked through the door.

Marcus, Jake, and Trevor. David's friends from that first night.

Patrick's stomach dropped as they spotted their booth and began walking over. David's expression shifted, his usual confident mask sliding back into place, but Patrick caught the flash of annoyance in his eyes.

"Well, look what we have here," Marcus said with a grin that didn't quite reach his eyes. "The mysterious Patrick. We haven't seen you in two weeks, David. Wonder why that could be."

The comment stung, even though Patrick knew it wasn't entirely meant to be cruel. He watched David's posture change, becoming more commanding, more like the person Patrick had first seen on the balcony at Medusa's—beautiful and untouchable and in complete control.

"Marcus, Jake, Trevor," David said smoothly. "What brings you to this fine establishment?"

"Late-night munchies," Jake said, but his attention was already shifting to Patrick. "Mind if we join you? I feel like we never got properly introduced."

Before either Patrick or David could object, they were sliding into the booth across from them, Trevor taking the spot directly across from Patrick. Patrick tried to smile politely, but something about Trevor's intense stare made him uncomfortable. Not hostile, exactly, but searching, like he was trying to solve some puzzle Patrick represented.

"So, Patrick," Marcus said, clearly taking charge of the conversation. "Tell us about yourself. What's your major? What do you plan to do with your life? And most importantly—" he grinned "—why do you like this jerk?"

Patrick laughed despite his nervousness. "He's not a jerk. He's..." He glanced at David, who was watching him with an unreadable expression. "He's wonderful."

The simple honesty of the statement seemed to surprise everyone at the table, including David. Patrick saw something soft flicker across David's face before he reached over to take Patrick's hand, a gesture that was both possessive and tender.

"Are you guys going to eat?" David asked his friends, but there was an edge to his voice that suggested he wanted them to leave.

The conversation continued, the friends asking Patrick about his classes, his family, his interests. Patrick answered as best he could, trying to be friendly while feeling increasingly out of his depth. These were David's people, his world, and Patrick felt like an intruder despite David's reassuring presence beside him.

After about twenty minutes, David excused himself to use the restroom, and Marcus and Jake immediately followed, making jokes about going as a group. Patrick managed a polite laugh, but his attention was caught by Trevor, who remained seated and was watching the others disappear down the corridor with an unreadable expression.

When they were out of sight, Trevor shuffled in his booth, and Patrick felt his pulse quicken. There had been something about Trevor all evening—the way he'd barely spoken, the intense looks, the careful distance he maintained from the group's banter.

"I..." Trevor started, then stopped, running a hand through his blond hair. "I don't really know what to say."

Patrick remained quiet, sensing that whatever was coming needed space to emerge. He folded his hands in his lap and tried to look approachable, even though his heart was racing.

"This isn't normal for me," Trevor continued, his voice barely above a whisper. "I'm usually... confident. Part of the 'club,' you know? I get what I want. Except..." He looked directly at Patrick for the first time all evening. "Except with David."

Patrick's breath caught. He thought he might know where this was going, but he waited for Trevor to continue.

"It's been two weeks since I've seen David do something I've always wanted him to do but could never ask for." Trevor's voice was getting shakier. "Fall for someone. I just... I always hoped it would be me."

The confession hung between them, raw and painful. Patrick watched Trevor's carefully constructed composure crumble, saw the tears gathering in his eyes, and felt his heart break for this stranger who was carrying such a heavy secret.

"But seeing you," Trevor continued, "so different from everyone David's ever... hunted, conquered, whatever. You're so... vulnerable, but also welcoming. Accepting. And I can see why he chose you. It just..." His voice cracked. "It hurts."

Without thinking, Patrick slid around to Trevor's side of the booth and put his arm around his shoulders. Trevor immediately broke down, crying silently into Patrick's shoulder while Patrick offered his napkin and simply held space for the pain.

"I'm so embarrassed," Trevor whispered. "This is stupid. I'm being stupid."

"No," Patrick said firmly. "You're not stupid, and don't ever think that. It's brave that you shared this with me."

"But I don't want to cause problems between you two—"

"You're not." Patrick's voice was gentle but certain. "But I think you need to be honest with David."

Trevor pulled back, wiping his eyes. "I can't do that. Not now that he has you. I just need to forget about it."

Patrick moved back to his side of the booth and pushed a glass of water toward Trevor. "Don't try to forget it. It's better to admit your feelings and work toward something you can actually do with them."

Something about Patrick's calm acceptance seemed to unlock something in Trevor. "Can I ask you something? About David?"

Patrick nodded.

"Are you... do you love him?"

The question hit Patrick like a physical blow. Here was Trevor, David's friend who'd been secretly in love with him, asking Patrick to admit the very thing he'd been too scared to say out loud.

"Yes," Patrick whispered, the word escaping before he could stop it. "I do. I have since... since our first kiss. But I haven't told him."

"Why not?"

"Because I'm terrified," Patrick admitted. "This is all new to me. Everything with David is a first—holding hands, kissing, feeling this way about someone. What if it's too soon? What if he doesn't feel the same way?"

Trevor leaned forward, something shifting in his expression. "Patrick, can I tell you something about David? He's not just the confident guy everyone sees. He has a heart. A real one. And the way he looks at you..." Trevor shook his head. "I've known him for three years, and I've never seen him look at anyone the way he looks at you."

"Really?"

"Really. And if you love him, you should tell him. Life's too short to be embarrassed about loving someone, even if you're worried they won't feel the same way. It's better to love than to wonder."

Patrick stared at Trevor, amazed by the generosity of spirit it took to encourage him to pursue the person Trevor wanted for himself. "You're an incredible person, you know that?"

Trevor managed a watery smile. "So are you. I can see why David fell for you. You're his soulmate."

The word hit Patrick with surprising force. Soulmate. Was that what this was?

"You should tell him tonight," Trevor continued. "All those things you just told me—tell David. He needs to hear them."

Before Patrick could respond, he heard laughter echoing from the corridor. David and the others were returning. Trevor quickly slid back to his original seat, wiping his face with the napkin Patrick had given him.

"What's this?" Marcus asked as they approached, taking in Trevor's slightly red eyes and Patrick's protective posture.

"Nothing," Trevor said with a shaky grin. "Just telling Patrick what a piece of shit David is."

David's face darkened, clearly ready to take offense, but Patrick quickly reached for his arm. "Actually, we had a great conversation getting to know each other while you three were off doing... whatever took you so long in the bathroom."

Trevor shot Patrick a grateful look, and David's expression softened, though Patrick could see the curiosity in his eyes. They'd definitely talk about this later.

The rest of the meal passed more smoothly. The friends seemed to relax, seeing David in a different light—more human, more vulnerable when he was with Patrick. And Patrick found himself actually enjoying their company now that the initial tension had broken.

When it was time to leave, David offered to give everyone a ride back to campus. As they piled into the BMW, Trevor managed to hug Patrick awkwardly from the back seat and whisper in his ear: "Remember what we talked about. Tell him."

"What was that about?" David asked as they drove away from his friends' dorm.

Patrick smiled, feeling lighter than he had all evening. "I'll tell you later. But David? Your friends are really good people."

David glanced at him with surprise and something that looked like pride. "I'm glad you think so. They seem to really like you too."

As they pulled into the campus parking lot, Patrick felt Trevor's words echoing in his mind. *Tell him. Life's too short to wonder.*

Maybe it was time to stop being afraid.

# CHAPTER
## *Thirteen*

PATRICK HAD NEVER FELT READIER for anything in his life until someone was about to take it all away.

As they pulled into the campus parking lot, David seemed lost in thought, his fingers drumming against the steering wheel in a nervous rhythm that Patrick had never seen before. The conversation with Trevor kept echoing in Patrick's mind—*Tell him. Life's too short to wonder.*—and Patrick felt something shift inside his chest. Maybe it was time to stop being afraid.

David turned off the engine but didn't move to get out of the car. In the sudden quiet, Patrick could hear his own heartbeat, could feel the weight of everything they hadn't said to each other pressing down on the space between them.

"Patrick," David said quietly, not looking at him. "I was wondering... I mean, if you wanted to..." He stopped, running a hand through his hair. "This is going to sound stupid."

"What?" Patrick asked, turning to face him fully.

David finally met his eyes, and Patrick saw something vulnerable there, something that looked almost like fear. "Would you maybe want to come back to my room with me? Not for... I mean,

I'm not trying to pressure you into anything. I just thought maybe we could... cuddle? Sleep together. Just sleep."

The words hung between them, and Patrick felt his heart do something complicated in his chest. This was it. The moment he'd been wondering about, worrying about, dreaming about for two weeks. David was asking him to stay over, and even though he'd made it clear there were no expectations, Patrick could feel the significance of the offer.

He was still a virgin. David wasn't. That fact had been sitting in the back of Patrick's mind for days now, not exactly anxiety but awareness. He'd wondered when this conversation would come up, how it would happen, what he would say. After all their talks and fun times together, this was the first time the possibility of physical intimacy had been directly addressed.

Patrick remained quiet for a moment, mulling over what to say. Part of him had been wondering if it was time to discuss being physical with David. The past two weeks had been a constant education in desire—learning what it felt like to want someone so completely, to crave their touch, to fall asleep thinking about David's hands and lips and what it would mean to truly be together.

David must have taken his silence as hesitation, because he started to backtrack. "It's silly, I know. Too soon and all that. I don't want to push—"

"I'd like that," Patrick said simply, cutting off David's apology. "Cuddling."

David's face transformed, relief and happiness flooding his features. "Really?"

"Really." Patrick smiled, feeling some of his nervousness ease. "I'd like that a lot."

They climbed out of the car and walked across campus together, their breath creating clouds in the frigid air. David stayed close, occasionally bumping Patrick's shoulder with his own, and Patrick could feel the anticipation radiating from both of them. This felt different from their other goodnights, charged with the careful caress of tempered passion and the promise of the unknown.

"Just so you know," Patrick said as they approached David's dorm, "I've never... I mean, I've never spent the night with anyone before."

David stopped walking and turned to face him. "Never?"

"Never." Patrick felt heat climb his neck. "So if I'm weird about anything, or if I don't know what I'm doing—"

"Hey." David reached out and took Patrick's hand. "There's no wrong way to do this. We'll figure it out together, okay?"

Patrick nodded, feeling that familiar flutter of trust and safety that David always seemed to inspire in him. They climbed the steps to David's building, and Patrick found himself cataloguing details—the way David's key turned in the lock, the sound of their footsteps echoing in the hallway, the fact that in a few minutes he would be in David's bed, in David's arms, closer than they'd ever been before.

They were almost at David's door when David stopped short, his hand freezing on his keys.

"What?" Patrick asked, following David's gaze.

There, taped to David's door, was a piece of paper with "EMER-GENCY" written in large black letters across the top. Below it, Patrick could see text instructing David to see the RA immediately, no matter what time of night.

David's face went pale as he ripped the tape off and read the note. Patrick watched his eyes scan the page, saw the exact moment when the urgency registered, when David's expression shifted to worry and fear.

"What is it?" Patrick asked, though part of him already knew he didn't want to hear the answer.

They found the RA's room and David pounded on the door until a sleepy voice answered. When the door opened, the RA immediately gestured them inside.

"David, come in," he said, stepping aside. Patrick hesitated, but David pulled him along, and the RA noticed but said nothing.

"I got your note," David said, holding up the paper with shaking hands.

"Right. You need to call home immediately," the RA said, gesturing toward his desk phone. "Family emergency."

"What kind of emergency?" David pressed, his voice tight with fear. "What happened?"

The RA shook his head. "I don't know anything more than that. The dean contacted me and said there was a family situation that required you to call home right away. That's all I was told."

David sank onto the RA's desk chair like his legs had given out. Patrick hovered behind him, wanting to offer comfort but not knowing what would help, not understanding what was happening but knowing with absolute certainty that their world was about to change forever.

The RA handed David the phone, and Patrick watched David's hands shake as he dialed. The wait seemed endless—ring after ring after ring—until finally someone picked up.

"Dad?" David's voice was barely a whisper. "I got the message. What's—"

Patrick couldn't hear the other side of the conversation, but he could see David's face crumple, could see the exact moment when whatever his father was telling him hit home. David doubled over like he'd been punched, a sound escaping him that was somewhere between a sob and a scream.

"No," David said into the phone. "No, that can't... when? How?"

Patrick felt tears spring to his own eyes, not knowing what had happened but knowing that David was breaking apart in front of him. He moved closer, putting a hand on David's shoulder, feeling helpless and terrified.

"I'll be on the first flight," David said, his voice thick with tears. "Tell Mom I'm coming. Tell her I'll be there as soon as I can."

He hung up the phone and sat there for a moment, staring at nothing, his breathing shallow and ragged.

"David?" Patrick said softly. "What happened?"

David looked up at him, and Patrick had never seen such raw pain in another person's eyes. "My brother," David whispered.

"Steve. He was driving home from a party and a drunk driver... he's dead, Patrick. My brother is dead."

The words hit Patrick like a physical blow. He sank to his knees beside David's chair, wrapping his arms around him as David finally broke down completely, sobbing into Patrick's shoulder while Patrick held him and whispered meaningless comfort and tried not to think about what this meant for them, for their future, for the perfect night that had just turned into a nightmare.

Outside, snow continued to fall on the University of Chicago campus, blanketing their world in white silence while inside, everything Patrick had dared to hope for quietly crumbled to dust.

# CHAPTER
## *Fourteen*

PATRICK HAD NEVER WATCHED someone's heart break in real time until he saw David crumble at the sound of his father's voice.

The next few hours passed in a blur of frantic motion and terrible silence. David hung up the phone and sat motionless for what felt like an eternity, staring at nothing while tears rolled down his cheeks. When he finally spoke, his voice was hollow, mechanical: "I have to get home. I have to catch the first flight to San Francisco."

Patrick wanted to say something—anything—that might provide comfort, but what words existed for this? How do you console someone whose world has just shattered? Instead, he simply followed David back to his place, staying close as David moved through his room like a sleepwalker, throwing clothes into a duffel bag with no apparent system or thought.

"Do you need help packing?" Patrick asked softly.

David looked at him as if he'd forgotten Patrick was there. "I... what do I pack for a funeral? For my brother's funeral?" His voice cracked on the last word, and Patrick felt his own throat tighten in response.

"Just the basics," Patrick said gently. "A suit. Some comfortable clothes. You can figure out the rest when you get there."

David nodded and continued his robotic packing. Patrick watched helplessly as David pulled items from drawers and his closet—a black suit, dress shirts, toiletries—everything that would transform him back into the California boy from money, leaving behind the college student who'd fallen in love at a Chicago nightclub.

"The airline says there's a 7 AM flight," David said suddenly, checking his watch. It was nearly 5 AM. "If I leave now, I can make it."

Patrick felt something cold settle in his stomach. "I'll come with you. To the airport, I mean."

David stopped packing and looked at him. "You don't have to—"

"I want to," Patrick said, and meant it completely. The thought of David making this terrible journey alone was unbearable.

They loaded David's bag into the BMW in the pre-dawn darkness, the campus eerily quiet around them. Patrick had never seen Chicago this empty, this still. Even the snow had stopped falling, leaving everything blanketed in pristine white that reflected the streetlights like scattered diamonds.

The drive to O'Hare took forty-five minutes through empty highways, and they barely spoke. David gripped the steering wheel so tightly his knuckles were white, his jaw clenched against tears that kept threatening to fall. Patrick wanted to reach over and take his hand, wanted to offer some gesture of comfort, but something about David's rigid posture warned him away.

"Tell me about Steve," Patrick said finally, needing to break the awful silence.

David was quiet for so long that Patrick thought he hadn't heard. Then, softly: "He was six years older than me. Always looked out for me, especially when I was little and kids would..." He gestured vaguely at his face, his heritage. "He taught me how to fight back. How to stand up for myself."

Patrick felt his chest tighten. He'd never thought about David facing that kind of cruelty, but of course he had. The confidence David wore so naturally had been hard-won.

"He was the one who helped me understand that being gay wasn't something to be ashamed of," David continued. "When I came out in high school, he just shrugged and asked if I wanted him to beat up anyone who gave me trouble about it." David's voice broke slightly. "He was... he was a good brother."

"He sounds like an amazing person," Patrick said softly.

"He was supposed to see me graduate," David whispered. "In three months. He was going to drive up from LA with his girl-friend. We were going to..." He stopped, unable to finish.

They pulled into the airport's departure area just as the sun was beginning to rise, painting the sky in shades of pink and gold that felt obscene in their beauty. How could the world look so lovely when something so terrible had happened?

David parked in a loading zone and turned off the engine. For a moment, they sat in the sudden quiet, both staring at the terminal building where their perfect two weeks would officially come to an end.

"I don't know when I'll be back," David said finally.

"That's okay," Patrick replied, though his heart was breaking. "You need to be with your family."

"Patrick, I..." David turned to face him, and Patrick could see him struggling with words that wouldn't come. "This timing is so—"

"Don't," Patrick said gently. "Don't apologize for grief. Don't apologize for loving your brother."

David's eyes filled with fresh tears. "But we were just starting to—"

"We'll figure it out," Patrick said, trying to sound more confident than he felt. "When you're ready. When you've had time to..."

But even as he said the words, Patrick felt the fragility of what they'd built together. Two weeks of magic against a lifetime of separate histories, different worlds, and now this catastrophic interruption. How did love survive something like this?

David reached for his bag in the back seat, and Patrick felt panic rise in his throat. This was it. David was really leaving, and Patrick had no idea when—or if—he'd see him again.

They walked to the terminal entrance together, Patrick carrying David's bag because David's hands were shaking too badly to manage it. The automatic doors slid open, revealing the bustling early-morning energy of travelers, flight announcements echoing overhead, the sterile brightness of departure gates.

At the security checkpoint, they stopped. This was as far as Patrick could go.

"I should..." David gestured toward the gates beyond security.

"Yeah," Patrick agreed, though every instinct in his body was screaming at him to hold on, to not let David walk away.

They faced each other in the busy corridor, people streaming around them like water around stones. David looked lost, younger than his twenty-two years, and Patrick wanted desperately to make this easier for him somehow.

"Patrick," David said, his voice urgent now, as if he'd suddenly realized their time was running out. "I need you to know—"

"I know," Patrick said softly, understanding. "I know, and I... I feel the same way."

David's face crumpled with relief and fresh grief. "I was going to tell you tonight. After we... I was going to say it."

"I was going to say it too," Patrick admitted. "I've been wanting to for days."

They stared at each other, both finally acknowledging what had been building between them, what they'd been too scared to name. But even this moment of recognition felt hollow, overshadowed by the terrible reason David had to leave.

"I have to go," David whispered, glancing at the departure boards. "If I miss this flight..."

"Go," Patrick said, stepping back even though it felt like tearing away part of himself. "Go be with your family."

David shouldered his bag and started toward security, then stopped and turned back. For a moment, Patrick thought he might run back, might choose to stay, but David just stood there looking at him with an expression of such profound loss that Patrick had to look away.

"I'll call you," David said.

"Okay," Patrick replied, though he wondered if that was true. How do you make plans for the future when the present has just exploded?

Patrick watched as David showed his ID to the security agent, as he disappeared into the maze of metal detectors and X-ray machines. At the last moment, David turned and looked back through the checkpoint, his eyes finding Patrick's across the distance.

They raised their hands in identical waves—small, inadequate gestures that carried the weight of everything they couldn't say. Then David was gone, swallowed up by the crowd of travelers heading to their gates, and Patrick was left standing alone in the bright, impersonal space of the airport, feeling like his heart had just been ripped from his chest.

He drove David's car back to campus—David had pressed the keys into his hand at the last minute, saying he'd figure out what to do about it later—and returned to his dorm room as his roommate was waking up.

"Where have you been?" his roommate asked sleepily.

"At the airport," Patrick said, which was true but explained nothing.

He lay down on his narrow bed, still wearing the clothes from their perfect evening at Medusa's, and stared at the ceiling. The room felt impossibly quiet after the constant noise of the airport, and in that silence, Patrick finally let himself feel the full weight of what had just happened.

David was gone. The person who had changed everything about how Patrick saw himself, who had made him feel brave and beautiful and worthy of love, was three thousand miles away dealing with unimaginable grief. And Patrick had no idea if what they'd built together was strong enough to survive the distance, the time, the terrible circumstances that had torn them apart just when they were finally ready to say the words that mattered most.

Outside his window, the University of Chicago campus was waking up to a normal Saturday morning. Students were heading to breakfast, making plans for the weekend, living their ordinary lives. But for Patrick, everything had changed. In the space of a few hours, he had fallen completely in love and lost that love to forces beyond his control.

He closed his eyes and tried to remember the feeling of David's hand in his, the sound of his laughter, the way he'd looked in the strobing lights of Medusa's when time had stopped and anything had seemed possible.

David would be back soon. A week, maybe two at most—just long enough for the funeral and to help his family with the immediate arrangements. Then he'd return to finish the semester, and they would pick up where they'd left off. They would finally say those three words that had been interrupted by tragedy. They would have that conversation about cuddling, about what came next between them.

Patrick held onto that hope as tightly as he held David's jacket, breathing in the faint scent of expensive cologne and warmth. The timing was terrible, but it didn't have to be the end of their story. People survived tragedies and came back stronger. Love could wait a few weeks.

But as Patrick lay there in the growing daylight, a small voice in the back of his mind whispered warnings he wasn't ready to hear. What if grief changed David? What if family obligations in California became more complicated than expected? What if the distance gave David time to realize that what they'd shared was just a beautiful moment, not the beginning of something lasting?

Patrick pushed those fears away and focused on the certainty that David would call soon, that his voice would sound the same, that they would make plans for his return. Some things were strong enough to survive interruption. What they had felt like one of those things.

At least, Patrick desperately hoped it was.

# CHAPTER
## *Fifteen*

PATRICK HAD NEVER REALIZED how many assumptions people made about your life until he tried to explain why the person everyone expected to see him with had simply vanished.

Three weeks had passed since David left for California, and Patrick felt like he was living in a strange state of suspended animation. Classes continued, final exams loomed, and graduation preparations buzzed around campus with relentless normalcy, but everything felt muted, like he was experiencing it all through thick glass. He attended lectures and took notes, but couldn't remember what he'd learned. He ate meals but couldn't taste them. He slept but woke exhausted.

The worst part was the questions. Not the obvious ones—those he could handle with simple deflection. "David had a family emergency," he'd say when people asked where his constant companion had gone. "He had to go home to California." True enough, and most people were satisfied with that explanation.

It was the subtle questions that cut deeper. The way people looked at him sitting alone at lunch, the careful way Kelly asked if he'd heard from David, the obvious concern from professors who'd grown accustomed to seeing him and David together around campus. Even his roommate had started hovering with awkward teenage compassion, bringing him extra snacks from the dining hall and offering to let Patrick borrow his television during study hours.

The phone calls had started three days after David left. Late at night, usually after midnight, when the grief and exhaustion finally overwhelmed David's careful composure. Patrick would answer on the first ring, having learned to sleep lightly, waiting for David's voice to cut through the darkness of his dorm room. They would talk for hours sometimes—David's voice raw and broken, Patrick whispering comfort into the receiver while his roommate slept fitfully across the room.

David would tell him about the funeral arrangements, about his parents' devastating grief, about the terrible logistics of sudden death. But mostly he would just cry, and Patrick would listen, his ear pressed to the phone, his heart breaking for this person he loved but couldn't reach. Sometimes David would fall asleep on the line, and Patrick would stay awake listening to his breathing, reluctant to hang up and break their only connection.

He understood. Of course he understood. David was dealing with the unimaginable—planning his brother's funeral, supporting his devastated parents, managing the logistics of a sudden death. But being David's lifeline, his emotional anchor during the worst period of his life, was taking its own toll on Patrick. The late-night calls left him exhausted, and the weight of David's grief combined with his own sense of loss made everything feel impossibly heavy. Understanding didn't make the burden any lighter.

It was on a Thursday evening in early May, when the Chicago spring had finally decided to show up and the campus was golden with late sunlight, that Patrick found himself sitting alone in their coffee shop on Michigan Avenue. He'd come here without really thinking about it, drawn by muscle memory and the ridiculous hope that somehow David might be there, that this whole nightmare might have been some kind of elaborate misunderstanding.

Instead, he sat at their usual table with a cup of coffee growing cold in front of him, staring at the empty chair across from him and trying not to think about graduation next week. About sitting alone at commencement while David's seat remained empty. About moving back to his parents' house in the suburbs while David's life unfolded three thousand miles away.

"Patrick?"

He looked up to find Trevor standing beside his table, holding his own coffee cup and looking uncertain. Patrick blinked, momentarily disoriented. He'd been so lost in his own thoughts that he hadn't noticed anyone approaching.

"Hi," Patrick said, trying to summon a polite smile. "Trevor, right?"

"Right." Trevor gestured to the empty chair across from Patrick. "Mind if I sit? You look like you could use some company."

Patrick hesitated. The last time he'd seen Trevor, it had been at the diner with David, during that intense conversation where Trevor had revealed his feelings and encouraged Patrick to tell David he loved him. They'd parted on good terms that night, but that felt like a lifetime ago now. Still, the coffee shop felt too empty, and Trevor's expression held none of the sharp-edged jealousy Patrick remembered from their first meeting.

"Sure," Patrick said, gesturing to the chair.

Trevor sat down and took a sip of his coffee, studying Patrick's face with undisguised concern. "You look like hell," he said finally, but his tone was gentle rather than critical.

Patrick managed a weak laugh. "Thanks. That's exactly what I was going for."

"Sorry." Trevor ran a hand through his blond hair, a gesture Patrick remembered from that night at the diner. "I just meant... you look tired. And sad. Which makes sense, given everything."

Patrick felt something twist in his chest at the kindness in Trevor's voice. "You heard about David's brother?"

"Jake told me." Trevor's expression darkened. "God, Patrick, I'm so sorry. Steve was... David talked about him sometimes. He really loved him."

"Yeah," Patrick said quietly, staring down at his untouched coffee. "He did."

They sat in silence for a moment, and Patrick found himself oddly grateful for Trevor's presence. Most people who'd heard about David's family emergency didn't seem to understand the magnitude of what had happened, or why Patrick seemed so affected by it. But Trevor knew David, had seen them together, understood the depth of what had been interrupted.

"Can I ask you something?" Trevor said finally. "And you can tell me to mind my own business if you want."

Patrick nodded.

"Are you okay? I mean, really okay? Because you've been... I don't know how to put this without sounding like a stalker, but I've noticed you around campus these past few weeks, and you look like someone who's lost something important."

The simple recognition of his pain hit Patrick harder than he'd expected. His throat tightened, and for a moment he couldn't speak. When he finally found his voice, it came out rougher than he'd intended.

"I don't know how to answer that," Patrick admitted. "I mean, I'm fine. David's the one who lost his brother. David's the one dealing with real tragedy. I just..." He trailed off, unable to finish the sentence without revealing more than he was ready to share.

"You just fell in love with someone who had to leave at the worst possible moment," Trevor said quietly.

Patrick's head snapped up, startled by Trevor's directness. "How did you—"

"That night at the diner," Trevor said with a small, sad smile. "When we talked while David and the others were in the bathroom. You told me you loved him. And the way you both looked at each other..." He shook his head. "It was pretty obvious you'd both finally figured it out. And then this happened."

Patrick felt heat rise in his cheeks. He'd almost forgotten that he'd admitted his feelings to Trevor that night, had been so focused on Trevor's own confession that he'd barely processed his own vulnerability.

"I'm sorry," Patrick said. "That night, when you told me about your feelings for David, I should have been more... I don't know. Sensitive. Understanding."

"Don't apologize," Trevor said firmly. "You were perfect that night. You listened without judging, you were kind when you could have been cruel, and you gave me advice that I really needed to hear." He paused, studying Patrick's face. "Actually, that's sort of why I wanted to talk to you."

"What do you mean?"

Trevor leaned back in his chair, seeming to gather his thoughts. "That night, you told me that it was better to admit my feelings and work toward something I could actually do with them, rather than trying to forget about them. You said I shouldn't try to forget about loving David."

Patrick nodded, remembering.

"Well, I've been thinking about that a lot these past few weeks. About what you said, and about what I could actually do with my feelings for David that would be healthy instead of destructive." Trevor met Patrick's eyes. "And I realized that one thing I could do was take care of the person David loves when he can't be here to do it himself."

Patrick stared at Trevor, speechless. The generosity of the gesture, the emotional intelligence it represented, was overwhelming. This was the same person who'd seemed so hostile and jealous just weeks ago.

"Trevor," Patrick said finally, "you don't have to—"

"I want to," Trevor interrupted. "Look, I'm not going to pretend this is entirely altruistic. Taking care of you feels like taking care of David, in a way. And maybe that helps me deal with my own feelings about him being gone. But it's also..." He paused, seeming to search for the right words. "You were good to me that night. You didn't have to be. You could have been petty or territorial or any number of things, but instead you were kind. You made me feel less alone with something I'd never told anyone before."

Patrick felt tears prick at his eyes. "You're an incredible person," he said, echoing the words he'd spoken to Trevor at the diner.

"So are you," Trevor replied. "Which is why you shouldn't have to sit in coffee shops by yourself looking like your world ended. Even if it feels like it did."

They talked for another hour, and Patrick found himself relaxing for the first time in weeks. Trevor was easier to talk to than Patrick had expected—funny and self-deprecating and surprisingly insightful. He told Patrick about his own struggles with unrequited love, about the way seeing Patrick and David together had forced him to confront what he actually wanted in a relationship rather than just fixating on what he couldn't have.

"I'm starting graduate school at Northwestern in the fall," Trevor said as they prepared to leave. "I need a fresh start, somewhere David's shadow isn't everywhere I look."

"That sounds like a good idea," Patrick said. "Healthy."

"Yeah, well, you taught me that sometimes the healthy choice and the easy choice aren't the same thing." Trevor stood up and shouldered his backpack. "Listen, graduation's next week. I know David won't be there, and I know that's going to be hard. If you want someone to sit with, someone who gets why his empty seat matters, I'll be there."

Patrick felt his throat tighten again. "Thank you," he managed. "That would... that would mean a lot."

"Good." Trevor grinned, and for the first time Patrick could see the confident, charming person Trevor had always been underneath the pain and jealousy. "Plus, my parents are coming, and they're dying to meet David's 'friend' that I've mentioned. They'll have to settle for meeting David's boyfriend instead."

Patrick blushed at the word—boyfriend—but didn't correct him. It felt good to have someone acknowledge what he and David had been building, even if it felt impossibly fragile now.

As they walked to the El station together, Trevor chatting easily about his graduate school plans and his hopes for a fresh start, Patrick felt something loosen in his chest. The grief was still there, the uncertainty about David's return, the fear that what they'd built together might not survive the distance and tragedy. But for the first time in weeks, he didn't feel completely alone with it.

Trevor had been wrong about one thing, though. This wasn't

just about taking care of Patrick for David's sake, or about Trevor managing his own feelings. This was about friendship—real, genuine friendship between two people who'd found something valuable in each other despite starting as rivals.

And maybe, Patrick thought as they reached the campus quad where students were setting up for graduation festivities, that was exactly what he needed to get through whatever came next. Not a substitute for David or a consolation prize, but proof that kindness could create unexpected connections, that empathy could transform enemies into allies, and that sometimes the people who understood your pain best were the ones who'd experienced their own version of the same loss.

The sun was setting behind the downtown buildings, painting the busy street in warm golden light. Graduation was in five days. David's seat would be empty, but Patrick wouldn't be sitting alone. And for now, that felt like enough.

# PART
## *Two*

# CHAPTER

## Sixteen

FOUR YEARS COULD RESHAPE A HEART, but some connections refused to be redrawn.

Patrick O'Brien sat in his cramped cubicle at Meridian Press, squinting at the green text glowing on his computer monitor in the fluorescent wasteland of downtown Chicago's financial district. The morning coffee had gone cold hours ago, and the stack of manuscripts on his desk seemed to grow taller every time he looked away. But when the familiar chime of incoming email cut through the ambient hum of office life, his pulse quickened in a way that still caught him off guard.

```
From: 76543,2109@compuserve.com
To: 84729,1156@compuserve.com
Subject: Finally found THE
apartment

Packy,
```

You're not going to believe this place. It's a fourth-floor walk-up in the Village that probably violates seventeen building codes, but it has CHARACTER. And by character, I mean the radiator sounds like someone's dismantling a motorcycle, and I'm pretty sure the previous tenant was either a very large cat or a very small horse.

But here's the thing - it has two bedrooms! One for sleeping, and one that could be an office or... I don't know, a place for visitors who might want to help their friend move boxes up four flights of stairs while I provide pizza and questionable wine.

I'm kidding about the questionable wine. I've learned things since college.

Seriously though, you should come see New York. I know I've been saying that for years, but I mean it. When was the last time you left Chicago? And before you say "last Christmas when I visited my aunt in Milwaukee," that doesn't count.

Think about it. You could see the city, we could catch up properly (not just these late-night phone calls where one of us is always half-asleep), and I promise I won't make you carry anything heavier than a lamp.

Let me know.

David

Patrick leaned back in his desk chair, a smile tugging at the corners of his mouth despite the familiar ache that always accompanied David's emails. Four years of these messages, scattered like bread-crumbs across the distance between them. Four years of almost-plans and could-be-visits that never quite materialized.

He closed his eyes and let himself remember those first awful weeks after David had left for California. The late-night phone calls that came like clockwork, David's voice raw with grief and exhaustion, sometimes just needing someone to listen while he cried three thousand miles away. Patrick had spent countless nights with his ear pressed to the receiver, whispering comfort into the darkness while his heart broke for this person he loved but couldn't reach.

The guilt still twisted in his stomach when he thought about Steve's funeral. He'd stared at his savings account balance for hours, calculating airfare to San Francisco, imagining himself somehow finding the church, sitting in the back, being there for David when he needed him most. But what would he have said to David's parents? *Hi, I'm the boy your son was falling in love with before tragedy struck?* David had mentioned his mother's struggles with his "lifestyle," and Patrick couldn't bear the thought of adding more chaos to an already devastated family.

So he'd stayed in Chicago, answering David's calls, photo-copying textbooks and Federal Expressing them to California, spending evenings reading David's class notes aloud over long-distance lines because there wasn't time to mail them. Watching helplessly as David finished his degree remotely, walking across the graduation stage alone while David's seat remained empty in the audience.

That June evening, when David had called from JFK airport to say he'd landed in New York, that he was really doing it, really starting over, Patrick had hung up the phone and cried for the first time since that morning at O'Hare. Not just for David, but for the future they'd almost had, the words they'd never said, the life that had been interrupted before it could truly begin.

But then life had moved forward, as life stubbornly insisted on doing. Patrick had started at Meridian Press, found his rhythm in the publishing world, discovered he had a talent for recognizing good writing buried in amateur manuscripts. David had thrown himself into the financial world with the kind of intensity that suggested he was running from something. They'd learned about CompuServe, bought their first computers, figured out this new thing called email that let them stay connected without the weight of hearing each other's voices.

And still, somehow, they'd never managed to be in the same place at the same time.

David would suggest Patrick come to New York just as Patrick got swamped with a major project. Patrick would hint about David visiting Chicago right when David was traveling for work. It was as if the universe had decided they'd had their chance and lost it, and now they were destined to orbit each other at a safe distance forever.

Patrick had actually made a list once, sitting at his parents' kitchen table on a rainy Sunday afternoon. Pros and cons of moving to New York, written in his careful handwriting on a sheet of typewriter paper. The pros column had been longer: New York was the heart of publishing, more opportunities, museums, culture, energy... and David. Always David, though he'd been too proud to write that down.

The cons were simpler but heavier: leaving family, leaving home, leaving the Midwest identity that felt as essential to him as breathing. Chicago was in his bones. Even living in his childhood bedroom to save money for a Lincoln Park condo felt more right than the idea of starting over in some overpriced Manhattan shoebox.

"Working hard or hardly working?"

Patrick jumped, quickly closing the message as his cubicle neighbor Mark leaned against the partition wall. Mark Hoffman was one of the few bright spots at Meridian Press—mixed German and Vietnamese heritage, same age as David, with an easy humor that had gradually worn down Patrick's professional reserve.

"Just checking messages," Patrick said, trying to look busy with the manuscript on his desk.

"Ah, the mysterious email correspondent." Mark grinned. "Let me guess—your college friend from New York again?"

Patrick felt heat climb his neck. He'd mentioned David a few times, carefully casual, never quite explaining the full story. "Something like that."

"You know, most people just pick up the phone."

"It's complicated."

Mark studied his face with the kind of perception that made Patrick nervous. "It's always complicated with the ones that matter. But Patrick? Life's short. Maybe it's time to uncomplicate it."

Before Patrick could respond, Mark was gone, heading back to his own cubicle with the kind of easy confidence Patrick envied. Patrick stared at his blank computer screen, David's words still echoing in his mind, and felt something shift inside his chest.

> When was the last time you left
> Chicago?

The truth was, Patrick couldn't remember. Not for anything that mattered, anyway. He'd become so careful, so settled in his routines, so afraid of disrupting the safe life he'd built. But what was he protecting, really? His evenings alone in his childhood bedroom? His weekend trips to the Art Institute by himself? The growing certainty that he was becoming exactly the kind of person he'd never wanted to be—safe, predictable, alone?

David was offering him an adventure. A long weekend in New York, helping his friend move, seeing the city through the eyes of someone who'd actually built a life there. What was the worst that could happen? They'd be awkward with each other? They'd realize too much time had passed? They'd finally have the conversation they'd been avoiding for four years?

Maybe it was time to stop being afraid.

Patrick pulled up a new email and started typing before he could change his mind:

```
From: 84729,1156@compuserve.com
To: 76543,2109@compuserve.com
Subject: RE: Finally found THE
apartment
```

David,

You're right - I can't remember the
last time I left Chicago for
anything more exciting than a
family obligation. And you're also
right that late-night phone calls
where one of us is half-asleep
aren't exactly quality time.

I called American Airlines. I could
come next Thursday evening if you
can pick me up at JFK - I have no
idea how to navigate New York
public transportation and I'd
rather not end up in New Jersey by
accident.

Round-trip is $127, which seems
reasonable for my first real
vacation in... embarrassingly long.

Fair warning: I have no idea what
I'm doing when it comes to cities
bigger than Chicago, so you'll have
to be patient with your small-town
friend.

Let me know if Thursday works.

Packy

P.S. - I promise I'm stronger than
I look. I can handle more than a
lamp.

He hit send before he could second-guess himself, then sat back
in his chair with a mixture of excitement and terror racing through

his veins. Somewhere in New York, David would open this email and know that Patrick was finally ready to bridge the distance between them.

The response came back so quickly Patrick wondered if David had been sitting at his computer waiting:

```
From: 76543,2109@compuserve.com
To: 84729,1156@compuserve.com
Subject: RE: RE: Finally found THE
apartment

I can't believe you're coming! I'm
so happy! Thursday is perfect.
Flight details, please - I'll be
there with bells on. Well, not
literally bells. That would be
weird. You know what I mean.

This is going to be great, Packy.
I've missed you.

David
```

Patrick stared at those last words until they blurred on the screen.

```
I've missed you.
```

Such simple words for such a complicated truth. He'd missed David too—missed him in ways he'd never learned how to articulate, missed him like a phantom limb, missed him every time he heard a song that reminded him of dancing at Medusa's or saw a couple holding hands in Boystown or walked past the Art Institute and remembered sharing something beautiful with someone who understood.

But now, for the first time in four years, they were going to be in the same city. The same room. Close enough to touch.

Patrick wasn't sure if he was ready for that, but he was finally ready to find out.

# CHAPTER
## *Seventeen*

PATRICK HAD IMAGINED this moment a thousand times, but nothing had prepared him for the reality of seeing David's face in a crowd after four years of separation.

The flight from O'Hare had been turbulent—not just the air pockets over Pennsylvania, but Patrick's nerves, which had been building steadily since he'd boarded the plane in Chicago. What if they were awkward with each other? What if David looked different, sounded different, had become someone Patrick didn't recognize? What if four years of phone calls and emails had created an illusion of closeness that couldn't survive being in the same room?

Patrick clutched his small duffel bag—the same one David had used that terrible morning at O'Hare—and followed the stream of passengers through the maze of JFK's corridors. The airport was enormous, nothing like the manageable chaos of O'Hare, and Patrick felt overwhelmed by the sheer volume of people rushing past him speaking a dozen different languages.

*What am I doing here?* he thought, the same panic that had hit him that first night at Medusa's washing over him. *I don't belong in New York. I'm going to embarrass myself.*

But then he rounded the corner into the arrivals area, scanning the crowd of waiting faces, and there he was.

David.

Patrick's breath caught in his throat. David looked older—not just four years older, but more polished, more sophisticated. His hair was shorter, styled in a way that probably cost more than Patrick spent on groceries in a month. He wore a navy blazer over dark jeans that fit perfectly, and even from across the crowded terminal, Patrick could see the confidence that radiated from him like heat.

This was David the Wall Street professional, David the New Yorker, David who belonged in a world Patrick had only seen in movies. For a moment, Patrick felt like that nervous boy in Kelly's costume again, completely out of his depth.

But then David spotted him, and his face transformed. The polished professional mask fell away, replaced by pure joy—the same expression Patrick remembered from their ice cream shop conversation, from dancing at Medusa's, from that last morning in the dorm vestibule. David's whole body seemed to light up as he started moving through the crowd, and Patrick felt his doubts melt away.

This was still David. His David.

They met somewhere in the middle of the chaos, David reaching him first and pulling him into a hug that lifted Patrick's feet off the ground. Patrick wrapped his arms around David's neck and breathed in the scent he remembered—expensive cologne and warmth and something indefinably David that no amount of time or distance could change.

"I can't believe you're actually here," David said into Patrick's ear, his voice thick with emotion. "I kept thinking you'd change your mind."

"I almost did," Patrick admitted, and when they pulled back to look at each other, they stayed close, faces only inches apart. Patrick could feel David's breath, could see the flecks of gold in his dark eyes, and suddenly the air between them was charged with four years of unspoken words.

David's gaze dropped to Patrick's lips, lingering there for a heartbeat too long. Patrick felt himself leaning closer, drawn by muscle memory and longing, his eyes fluttering closed as the distance between them narrowed to almost nothing. For a moment, it felt inevitable—four years of separation about to be erased with a single kiss.

But then David's eyes flicked around the busy terminal, reality crashing back. They both stepped back at the same time, the spell broken but the tension still humming between them like a live wire. Patrick felt his cheeks flush—had he misread the moment? Was he still the same person who fell in love with David Chen, or had four years changed everything?

David cleared his throat, running a hand through his perfectly styled hair, looking as unsettled as Patrick felt. "You look..." He paused, searching for words, and Patrick held his breath. "You look like yourself. More yourself, if that makes sense."

Patrick knew what he meant. The shy uncertainty of college had settled into something steadier, more grounded. Patrick had learned to be comfortable in his own skin, even if he was still the same person who preferred quiet evenings and organized book-shelves to crowded parties.

"So do you," Patrick said. "I mean, different, but—"

"Yeah." David grinned, the expression so familiar it made Patrick's chest tight. "Come on, let's get out of here. I want to show you everything."

They walked toward the exit together, David's hand resting on the small of Patrick's back in a gesture so natural it was as if no time had passed at all. Patrick felt some of his airport anxiety fade, replaced by a different kind of nervousness—the awareness that this weekend would either prove their connection could survive anything, or show them both that some things were better left as beautiful memories.

"Fair warning," David said as they approached the sliding doors to the outside world, "New York is going to hit you like a freight train. It's not Chicago."

"I figured," Patrick said, adjusting his grip on his bag. "I'm ready."

David looked at him with something that might have been admiration. "Yeah," he said softly. "I think you are."

The doors opened, and Patrick got his first taste of New York City—the noise, the smell of exhaust and hot dogs and something indefinably urban, the sheer scale of everything towering above them. It was overwhelming and exhilarating and completely foreign.

But David was beside him, solid and warm and real, and for the first time in four years, Patrick felt like he might finally be exactly where he belonged.

# CHAPTER
## *Eighteen*

PATRICK HAD NEVER FELT SO SIMULTANEOUSLY at home and out of place in his life.

David's apartment was exactly what Patrick had imagined New York living would be—a fourth-floor walk-up with narrow stairs that creaked under their weight, thin walls that barely muffled the sounds of neighbors arguing in what sounded like three different languages, and windows that looked out onto a fire escape and the brick wall of the building next door. But it was also unmistakably David's space, filled with small touches that made Patrick's chest tight with recognition.

"Sorry about the climb," David said, slightly out of breath as he fumbled with his keys. "The real estate agent called it 'charming vintage character.' I call it 'my daily cardio routine.'"

Patrick laughed, setting down his duffel bag as David finally got the door open. "It's perfect. Very... New York."

The apartment itself was smaller than Patrick's childhood bedroom, but David had made it work. A narrow living room with a worn leather couch that Patrick suspected had been inherited from someone's older brother, bookshelves made from boards and cinder blocks that held an eclectic mix of finance textbooks and novels, and a kitchen that was really just a corner with a refrigerator, stove, and sink clustered together like they were having a meeting.

But it was the details that caught Patrick's attention. The Seurat print from the Art Institute hanging above the couch—the same painting Patrick had shown David that day that felt like a lifetime ago. A small framed photo on the bookshelf that Patrick recognized as David and his brother Steve, both grinning at the camera with their arms around each other's shoulders. A stack of CompuServe printouts on the coffee table that Patrick suspected were their email exchanges.

"You kept the painting," Patrick said, walking over to the Seurat print.

David's voice was soft when he answered. "It reminds me of that day. Of you explaining why it mattered to you." He paused, and Patrick could feel him watching. "I think about that afternoon a lot, actually."

Patrick turned around, and there was that charged air between them again, the same electricity that had sparked at the airport. They were alone now, no crowds to break the spell, no public space to remind them to be careful. Just Patrick and David and four years of unfinished conversations hanging in the air between them.

"So," David said, clearing his throat and gesturing around the small space. "This is it. Home sweet extremely expensive home." He was nervous, Patrick realized. This confident Wall Street professional was actually nervous about showing Patrick his apartment.

"I love it," Patrick said honestly. "It feels like you."

David's smile was grateful and a little surprised. "Really? I sometimes feel like I'm playing dress-up, pretending to be a real New Yorker. Like someone's going to figure out I'm just a kid from California who doesn't know what he's doing."

It was such an unexpectedly vulnerable admission that Patrick felt something shift inside his chest. This was the David he remembered from college—not the polished facade, but the person underneath who second-guessed himself and worried about belonging.

"Well, you're doing a pretty convincing job of fooling everyone," Patrick said. "Including me."

They stood there looking at each other, and Patrick felt the weight of everything they hadn't said over the past four years pressing down on them. There were so many questions he wanted to ask. How was David really doing? Did he still think about those two weeks at college? Had there been other relationships, other people who'd tried to fill the space Patrick had left behind?

But before he could figure out how to voice any of those thoughts, David was moving again, the moment broken by his need to keep busy.

"You must be starving," David said, heading toward the kitchen corner. "I know it's late, but I thought we could grab dinner somewhere in the neighborhood. There's this little Italian place that's nothing fancy, but the pasta is incredible, and—"

"David," Patrick interrupted gently.

David stopped mid-sentence, his hands frozen halfway to the refrigerator handle. "Yeah?"

"I'm here. We have all weekend. You don't have to entertain me every second."

David's shoulders sagged slightly, and Patrick realized he'd been holding himself rigid since they'd arrived. "I just... I want this to be good. I want you to like it here. To like..." He gestured vaguely around the apartment, but Patrick suspected he meant something broader than just the physical space.

"I already do," Patrick said simply.

For a moment, David just looked at him, something unguarded and hopeful flickering across his face. Then he nodded, some of the tension leaving his body.

"Okay," David said. "Okay, good. So... dinner? There's actually a farmers market a few blocks away that runs late on Thursdays. We could walk around, pick up some things, cook here if you want. It's not exactly Chicago, but—"

"I'd love that," Patrick said, cutting off what was clearly going to be another nervous ramble. "Lead the way."

They grabbed David's keys and headed back down the four flights of stairs, but this time the mood felt different. Lighter. Less fraught with the weight of four years and more like two friends— two people who cared about each other—figuring out how to spend an evening together.

The farmers market was nothing like the sprawling suburban affairs Patrick knew from home, but it had its own charm. Vendors had set up tables along two blocks of closed street, selling everything from fresh pasta to late-season tomatoes to bread that smelled like heaven. David moved through the stalls with the easy confidence of someone who belonged here, greeting a few vendors by name, sampling offerings with the kind of casual intimacy that spoke of routine.

"You come here a lot," Patrick observed, watching David chat with an elderly Italian woman about her olive oil selection.

"Every Thursday after work," David confirmed, handing the woman a five-dollar bill and accepting a small bottle in return. "It's one of the things that makes this place feel like home instead of just where I happen to live."

They wandered through the market, David buying ingredients for what he promised would be "the world's simplest pasta with the world's best tomatoes," while Patrick took in the energy around them. It was so different from Chicago—more intense, more crowded, everyone moving with a purpose that seemed urgent and exciting. But there was also an intimacy to it, neighbors chatting with vendors, families with small children weaving between the stalls, couples holding hands while they debated between different types of cheese.

"What are you thinking?" David asked, catching Patrick staring at a young couple who were feeding each other samples of honey.

"Just... this is nice," Patrick said. "Different from what I expected."

"What did you expect?"

Patrick considered the question as they walked back toward

David's building, their arms occasionally brushing as they navigated the narrow sidewalks. "I don't know. Something more... impersonal, I guess. More like what you see in movies. All business suits and taxi cabs and people who don't have time to talk to each other."

"Oh, that exists too," David said with a laugh. "Believe me. But this part of the city... it feels more like a neighborhood. Like a place where people actually live instead of just work."

Back in David's apartment, they fell into an easy rhythm preparing dinner. David handled the pasta while Patrick dealt with the tomatoes, their movements coordinated in a way that felt natural despite the small kitchen. They talked about work, about their families, about books they'd been reading—safe topics that let them relearn each other's rhythms without venturing into dangerous territory.

But Patrick was hyperaware of every accidental brush of David's hand against his, every moment when David leaned close to reach for something and Patrick caught that familiar scent. The physical space was so small that they couldn't help but be in each other's orbit, and the casual intimacy of cooking together felt both completely natural and charged with possibility.

"Wine?" David asked, producing a bottle of red from somewhere. "Fair warning—my knowledge of wine comes entirely from asking the guy at the corner store what goes with pasta."

"Perfect," Patrick said, accepting the glass David handed him. Their fingers touched briefly during the exchange, and Patrick felt that same electric jolt from the airport.

They ate sitting on David's couch, plates balanced on their knees, talking and laughing in a way that made Patrick remember why he'd fallen for David in the first place. Not just because he was beautiful—though he was still that, even more so now with the confidence that came from building a life in a city like New York—but because he was funny and thoughtful and genuinely interested in Patrick's stories about work and his family and his quiet life in Chicago.

"I'm glad you came," David said suddenly, during a lull in the conversation.

"So am I," Patrick replied, and meant it completely.

They sat there in comfortable silence for a moment, the weight of the day and the wine and four years of separation settling over them. Patrick was acutely aware that they hadn't talked about sleeping arrangements, about where exactly he would be spending the night in David's tiny apartment. The couch was comfortable enough, but narrow, and Patrick couldn't help but wonder...

"So," David said, apparently thinking along the same lines, "I should probably mention that the second bedroom is more of a generous closet with delusions of grandeur. But the couch is actually pretty comfortable, or..." He trailed off, leaving the sentence hanging.

"Or?" Patrick prompted, his heart beating faster.

David looked at him directly, and Patrick saw something vulnerable and hopeful in his eyes. "Or you could... I mean, the bed is big enough for two. If you want. Just sleeping," he added quickly. "I don't want you to think I'm assuming anything."

Patrick felt something warm spread through his chest. This was David offering intimacy without pressure, closeness without expectations. It was exactly what Patrick would have hoped for, if he'd been brave enough to hope for anything.

"I'd like that," Patrick said softly. "Just sleeping."

David's smile was radiant. "Good. Great. I just... I've missed having you close."

The words hung in the air between them, honest and uncomplicated, and Patrick felt something he'd been holding tight in his chest for four years finally begin to unclench.

Maybe this weekend would be exactly what they both needed. Maybe some connections were strong enough to survive anything, even time and distance and all the ways people changed.

Maybe they were finally ready to find out.

# CHAPTER

## *Nineteen*

PATRICK HAD NEVER BEEN SO aware of another person's breathing in his life.

They stood at opposite ends of David's small bedroom, both suddenly awkward after the easy intimacy of dinner and conversation. The room felt charged with an energy neither knew existed. Patrick's duffel bag sat on the floor like a question mark, and he found himself studying David's space instead of looking directly at him.

The bedroom was as carefully curated as the living room—a double bed with simple white sheets, a dresser topped with cologne bottles and loose change, a small desk by the window where Patrick could see more CompuServe printouts. On the nightstand was another photo of David and Steve, this one from what looked like a family vacation, both brothers tan and grinning in front of some California landmark.

"I should..." Patrick gestured vaguely toward his bag, then began pulling out a t-shirt and shorts for sleeping. His hands were shaking slightly, and he hoped David wouldn't notice.

"Yeah, me too," David said, moving to his dresser and pulling out similar clothes.

They stood there for another awkward moment before Patrick took the initiative, turning away and beginning to unbutton his shirt. He could feel David's eyes on him, could hear the soft sounds of David following suit behind him. The intimacy of undressing in the same space, even with their backs to each other, felt both thrilling and terrifying.

When they'd both changed into sleeping clothes, David cleared his throat. "Bathroom's down the hall if you want to..."

"Sure," Patrick said, grateful for the momentary escape.

They took turns brushing their teeth at the small sink, standing close enough that their elbows bumped occasionally. Patrick caught David's eye in the mirror once and felt that familiar jolt of electricity. This was so domestic, so normal, and yet charged with four years of separation and longing.

"Here," David said when they returned to the bedroom, handing Patrick a glass of water. "In case you get thirsty in the night."

"Thanks," Patrick said, accepting the glass and using the moment to look around the room again. He imagined himself here more often, imagined his clothes mixed with David's in the dresser, imagined mornings where he didn't have to leave. The thought both thrilled and terrified him.

He wondered if David had brought other men here, if this bed had seen other reunions, other passionate nights. The thought sent an unexpected stab of jealousy through his chest, which he tried to push down. They'd had no obligations to each other, no promises. Of course David had probably been with other people. He was beautiful, successful, living in New York. Patrick had no right to expect anything else.

David caught him looking around and raised an eyebrow. "What are you thinking?"

"Just... taking it all in," Patrick said, which was true if incomplete.

They climbed into bed from opposite sides, the mattress dipping as they settled under the covers. David reached over to turn off the bedside lamp, plunging them into darkness broken only by the flicker of lights from the street outside and the distant sounds of the city that never slept.

They lay there in the dark, both on their backs, careful not to touch despite the relatively small space. Patrick was hyperaware of David's warmth beside him, of the sound of his breathing, of how easy it would be to just roll over and...

"This is nice," David said softly.

"Yeah," Patrick agreed. "Different from Chicago. The sounds, I mean."

"You'll get used to it. The sirens become white noise after a while."

They talked about small things—the differences between Chicago and New York, David's work schedule, Patrick's commute from Arlington Heights. Safe topics that kept them from addressing the elephant in the room: what this weekend meant, what they were to each other now, what they wanted from each other.

Finally, Patrick gathered his courage. "David? Can I ask you something?"

"Of course."

Patrick turned onto his side to face David, though he could barely make out his features in the darkness. "Did you... I mean... well... are we...?" He stopped, frustrated by his inability to form the words.

David turned to face him too, and now they were close enough that Patrick could feel his breath. "Do you want to be?" David's voice was soft, uncertain. "I mean... I would... well... I don't want to presume..."

"Yes!" Patrick said, perhaps too quickly, then felt his face burn. "I mean... only if you..."

And that was it. The crack in the wall that had been holding back four years of suppressed emotion suddenly split wide open.

They lay there facing each other, still not quite touching, but the words began to flow. Patrick told David how much he'd missed him, how he'd hoped but hadn't expected anything because he

didn't know where they stood, how he'd assumed David had probably been with lots of other men...

"I haven't," David interrupted softly.

"What?"

"I haven't been with anyone. Not one guy since I left for the
funeral."

Patrick's breath caught. "But... why? I mean, you could have
anyone you wanted."

David was quiet for a moment. "Because... this is embarrassing
to admit... but because of you."

"Me?"

"Yes."

"Why?"

"Because when I left that night all those years ago, we were
going to... well... I hoped we would..."

"Sleep together?" Patrick's voice was barely a whisper.

"Well..."

"Yes?"

"I... hoped."

Patrick's heart was pounding now. "Like sleep-sleep? Or sleep,
you know?"

Patrick turned more fully toward David, and his excitement
betrayed him as his body pressed against David's leg. But instead
of pulling away, David smiled and turned to face Patrick
completely, their faces now inches apart in the darkness. Patrick
could feel David's body responding to their closeness, and
suddenly it was like being transported back to that night four
years ago, before the phone call, before everything changed.

And then Patrick felt David's lips on his.

All the passion he'd never realized he'd been holding back—
four years of longing and love and desire—poured out of him.
David was gentle but sure, leading them both into territory that
was new for Patrick but felt as natural as breathing.

What followed was everything Patrick had imagined and
nothing he could have prepared for. David's hands mapping his
body with reverent care, whispered endearments and soft gasps,

the overwhelming sensation of finally, finally being complete. It was Patrick's first time, but David made it perfect—patient and tender and passionate all at once.

Afterward, they lay tangled together, skin against skin, David's fingers tracing lazy patterns on Patrick's chest while Patrick marveled at the feel of David's heartbeat under his palm. The messy hair, the gentle caresses, the way they fit together so perfectly—it all felt right and safe and exactly what Patrick had been missing without even knowing it.

"Was that...?" David asked softly, pressing a kiss to Patrick's temple.

"Perfect," Patrick breathed. "It was perfect."

"Good," David murmured, pulling him closer. "Because I've been waiting four years to show you how much I love you."

The words hung in the air between them, finally spoken after all this time. Patrick lifted his head to look at David, seeing the truth of it written in his eyes even in the darkness.

"I love you too," Patrick whispered back. "I never stopped."

And as they held each other in the flickering light from the New York streets outside, Patrick finally understood what home really meant. It wasn't a place at all. It was this—David's arms around him, their hearts beating in sync, and the knowledge that some connections really were strong enough to survive anything.

Even four years of separation, grief, and fear couldn't break what they had. They were finally exactly where they belonged.

# CHAPTER

## *Twenty*

DAVID HAD NEVER UNDERSTOOD the word "tender" until he woke at 3 AM with Patrick curled against his chest like a secret.

The pale light from the street filtered through his bedroom window, casting shadows across Patrick's sleeping face. His red hair was tousled from their earlier passion, his lips slightly parted, one hand resting over David's heart as if even in sleep he needed to feel it beating. David had never seen anything more beautiful in his life.

In all his sexual encounters—and there had been many before he'd left from California—David had perfected the art of satisfaction without attachment. Quick, efficient, pleasurable, done. He'd never wanted anyone to stay over, never craved the messy intimacy of waking up together, never understood why some people talked about cuddling like it was essential rather than optional.

But this—Patrick's warm weight against him, the steady rhythm of his breathing, the absolute trust implicit in the way he'd fallen asleep in David's arms—this was a revelation. David carefully adjusted his position, not wanting to wake Patrick but needing to see his face more clearly. When Patrick unconsciously nuzzled closer, making a small sound of contentment, David felt something break open in his chest.

*This is what I've been missing,* he thought, pressing his lips to the top of Patrick's head. *This is what all those other encounters were trying to be.*

David let himself study Patrick's sleeping form—the elegant curve of his neck, the scattered freckles across his pale shoulders, the way his eyelashes cast shadows on his cheeks. Four years of wondering what might have been, four years of measuring every potential partner against the memory of green eyes and honest laughter, and now Patrick was here, real and warm and completely his.

David rested his own head on Patrick's chest, listening to the steady heartbeat beneath his ear, and fell back into the deepest sleep he'd had in years.

Patrick woke to sensation he'd never imagined possible.

The morning light was soft through David's bedroom window, and for a moment Patrick was disoriented, not remembering where he was or why his body felt so languid and satisfied. Then David's mouth moved against him in a way that made Patrick's eyes flutter shut and his breath catch, and suddenly he was wide awake and completely overwhelmed.

"David," he gasped, his hands fisting in the sheets as pleasure built in ways his body had never experienced. "What are you—oh God—"

David lifted his head just enough to meet Patrick's eyes, his dark hair tousled and his lips curved in a smile that was equal parts wicked and tender. "Good morning, Packy," he said softly, before returning his attention to the task at hand.

Patrick had thought about this—of course he had, what twenty-six-year-old virgin hadn't wondered what it would feel like?—but his imagination had been laughably inadequate. This wasn't dirty or perverse or any of the shameful things he'd been taught to expect. This was beautiful, intimate, right in a way that made his heart race along with his breathing.

When release finally claimed him, Patrick cried out David's name with an abandon that would have embarrassed him if he'd been capable of coherent thought. But all he could do was lie there gasping while David moved up to kiss him softly, sharing the taste of his pleasure between them.

"Are... are we boyfriends?" Patrick blurted out, the words escaping before his post-orgasmic brain could filter them.

David paused, propped up on one elbow, looking down at Patrick with an expression that was surprised but not displeased. It was such a Patrick thing to ask—direct, honest, slightly naive—and David felt something warm spread through his chest at the familiarity of it.

The question hung in the air between them, more loaded than Patrick probably realized. David had never been anyone's boyfriend, had never wanted the obligations and expectations that came with the label. But looking down at Patrick—hair wild from sleep and passion, green eyes vulnerable and hopeful, lips still swollen from kissing—David found himself considering the possibility for the first time in his life.

"Sure," David said finally, the word feeling strange but not unwelcome on his tongue. "But let's enjoy the weekend, okay? We can keep talking about the future. Will that work?"

It wasn't exactly what Patrick had hoped to hear—he would have preferred David to sweep him up and shout "Yes!" to the entire city. But it wasn't a no, either, and David's hand was tracing gentle patterns on his chest in a way that suggested affection rather than dismissal.

"That works," Patrick said, smiling up at him.

"Good." David leaned down to kiss him again, soft and lingering. "Because I have plans for us today. Starting with a shower."

Patrick's eyes widened. "Together?"

"Together," David confirmed, grinning at Patrick's expression. "Unless you'd rather take turns being civilized about it."

"No," Patrick said quickly, then blushed at his own eagerness. "I mean... together sounds nice."

David's laugh was warm and fond. "You're going to be the death of me, Packy."

They made their way to the small bathroom hand in hand, and Patrick tried not to think too hard about how natural this felt, how right it seemed to be sharing these intimate moments with David. The shower was barely big enough for one person, let alone two, but they made it work, taking turns under the hot water, washing each other's hair with a domesticity that felt both thrilling and completely normal.

"Ready to see New York?" David asked as they toweled off, and Patrick caught the excitement in his voice. David wanted to share his world with him, wanted to show Patrick what his life had become.

"Ready," Patrick said, and realized he meant it completely.

They dressed quickly and headed out into the bright Friday morning, Patrick's hand finding David's as they walked down the narrow Village streets. The city was just waking up around them, but David moved through it with the confidence of someone who belonged, leading Patrick toward adventures he'd only dreamed about.

And for the first time in four years, Patrick felt like the future was full of possibilities he'd never dared to imagine.

# CHAPTER
## Twenty-One

DAVID HAD NEVER WANTED to impress someone with a city before, but watching Patrick discover New York felt like showing off his firstborn child.

They walked hand in hand down Bleecker Street, Patrick's head turning constantly to take in the narrow storefronts, the fire escapes zigzagging up brick buildings, the sheer density of life packed into every square block. David found himself cataloguing Patrick's reactions—the way his eyes widened at the vintage clothing stores, how he stopped to read every historical marker they passed, the unconscious way he squeezed David's hand whenever something particularly charmed him.

"Hold on," Patrick said suddenly, pulling out a small disposable camera and snapping a quick photo of David in front of a particularly colorful mural. "I picked this up at O'Hare. I want to remember all of this."

"It's so... vertical," Patrick said, craning his neck to see the tops of the buildings surrounding them. "Chicago has tall buildings, but this feels different. Like the whole city is reaching up toward something."

"Wait until you see Midtown," David said, steering them toward Washington Square Park. "This is just the beginning."

The park was coming to life with Friday morning energy— street musicians tuning their instruments, dog walkers navigating the maze of paths, students from NYU scattered across the grass with books and newspapers. David led Patrick to a bench near the fountain and watched him take it all in.

"This is where I come when I need to think," David said. "Or when work gets too intense and I need to remember why I moved here."

Patrick was quiet for a moment, studying the arch that dominated the north end of the park, the way sunlight filtered through the trees onto the faces of passersby. "I can see why. It feels... alive. Like anything could happen."

David felt something warm spread through his chest. This was exactly what he'd hoped Patrick would understand about New York—not just the ambition and energy, but the possibility that lived in every corner, the sense that you could reinvent yourself as many times as you needed to.

"Come on," David said, standing and offering Patrick his hand. "I want to show you the library."

They walked north through the Village, David pointing out his favorite restaurants, the bodega where he bought his morning coffee, the small park where he sometimes sat with takeout dinner when his apartment felt too cramped. Patrick absorbed it all with the kind of focused attention that made David remember why he'd fallen for him in the first place—the way Patrick engaged with everything, finding beauty and meaning in details others might overlook.

The New York Public Library rose before them like a temple, its marble steps crowded with people reading, talking, eating lunch in the spring sunshine. David had walked past this building hundreds of times on his way to work, but he'd never really seen it until he watched Patrick's face light up with recognition and wonder.

"Stephen A. Schwarzman Building," Patrick read from the

inscription above the entrance. "1911. God, David, do you realize what's in there? Original manuscripts, first editions, archives that go back centuries..."

Patrick raised his camera and took a quick shot of the imposing facade, then another of David standing between the famous lion statues. "My folks back home are never going to believe this," he said with a grin.

David felt that familiar flutter of affection at Patrick's enthusiasm. "Want to go in?"

"Can we? I mean, are we allowed to just... walk in?"

"It's a public library, Packy. That's literally the point."

They climbed the steps together, Patrick practically vibrating with excitement, and David realized he was seeing his adopted city through completely new eyes. Inside, the library was even more magnificent—soaring ceilings, reading rooms that looked like cathedrals, thousands of people quietly pursuing knowledge and wonder.

"This is incredible," Patrick whispered, his voice properly hushed for the sacred space around them. "How do you not spend every weekend here?"

David laughed quietly. "I guess I never thought about it. It's just... there, you know? Part of the landscape."

"Just there?" Patrick looked at him with something approaching horror. "David, this is one of the greatest libraries in the world. They have manuscripts here that changed human history. Books that people died trying to preserve."

And there it was again—Patrick's ability to find the extraordinary in what David had dismissed as ordinary. David found himself studying Patrick's face as he gazed around the main reading room, noting the reverence there, the genuine awe. This was what David had been missing in his New York life—someone who could show him magic he'd been walking past every day.

They spent an hour wandering through the stacks, Patrick occasionally pulling books from shelves and reading passages aloud in a whisper, David content to follow and listen. Eventually they made their way back outside, where the afternoon sun had warmed the marble steps enough to sit comfortably.

"Thank you," Patrick said as they settled side by side, watching the flow of people up and down Fifth Avenue.

"For what?"

"For sharing this with me. Your city. Your life." Patrick leaned against David's shoulder, and David felt that familiar rightness, the sense that this was exactly where they both belonged. "I know it probably seems silly to you, getting excited about libraries and markets and..."

"It doesn't seem silly," David interrupted. "It seems like seeing things clearly. I've been living here for three years, and I think I've been sleepwalking through most of it."

They sat in comfortable silence for a while, watching the city move around them. David found himself memorizing details—the way Patrick's hair caught the afternoon light, how relaxed his body felt against David's side, the contented expression on his face as he observed the world passing by.

"What are you thinking?" Patrick asked, catching David's stare.

David considered lying, giving some casual answer, but something about the golden light and Patrick's presence made honesty feel like the only option. "I'm thinking that I don't want this weekend to end."

Patrick was quiet for a moment. "It doesn't have to. I mean, not permanently. We could... we could figure something out. Visits. More weekends."

The hope in Patrick's voice made David's chest tight. He wanted to say yes, wanted to make promises about regular visits and long-distance relationships and ways to bridge the gap between New York and Chicago. But he also knew how life worked, how busy they both were, how easy it was for good intentions to get lost in the day-to-day reality of separate lives.

"We'll see," David said finally, which wasn't a yes but wasn't a no either.

Patrick nodded, seeming to understand. "We'll see."

As the afternoon light began to fade and the city shifted into evening mode around them, David felt something precious settling into his memory. This moment—Patrick beside him on the library steps, their quiet conversation, the way the golden light painted everything in warm tones—this would stay with him long after Patrick returned to Chicago.

"Wait," Patrick said suddenly, reaching for his camera again. "I want to get one of us together here."

He held the camera at arm's length, angling it to capture both of them against the backdrop of the library's columns and the city beyond. "This one's special," he said, and David found himself grinning genuinely, not the practiced expression he usually wore for photos but something real and unguarded.

The camera clicked, and Patrick lowered it with a satisfied expression. "Perfect."

David watched Patrick tuck the camera back into his pocket, something about the gesture making his chest tight. Patrick was collecting memories, creating something tangible to take back to Chicago. Weeks later, David would learn that this photo—the two of them laughing on the library steps in the golden afternoon light —would become Patrick's most prized possession, framed in silver and following him through every apartment, every move, every change in his life. A reminder of the weekend when anything had seemed possible.

He just didn't know yet that he'd be writing about it for years to come, trying to capture the feeling of perfect contentment that seemed to exist only in Patrick's presence.

For now, it was enough to sit together and watch the world go by, pretending that Sunday would never come and this magical weekend could last forever.

# CHAPTER
## Twenty-Two

PATRICK HAD NEVER UNDERSTOOD why people called it a broken heart until his chest literally ached at the thought of leaving David behind.

Sunday morning arrived with the kind of crisp April clarity that made New York look like a postcard, all blue skies and golden light streaming through David's bedroom window. Patrick woke slowly, consciousness returning in layers—the unfamiliar sounds of the city outside, the warmth of David's body pressed against his back, the gentle pressure of David's arm around his waist holding him close.

For a moment, Patrick let himself pretend this was his life. That he woke up every morning in David's arms, that they shared coffee and the newspaper and easy conversation before heading off to their respective jobs. That this intimacy, this rightness, was something thing permanent rather than a beautiful weekend stolen from their separate realities.

"Morning," David murmured against the back of his neck, his voice rough with sleep.

"Morning," Patrick replied, turning in David's arms to face him. In the soft morning light, David looked younger, more vulnerable, his perfect hair mussed from sleep and his face relaxed in a way Patrick suspected few people ever got to see.

They lay there looking at each other, neither wanting to acknowledge that this was their last morning together, that Patrick's flight back to Chicago left at 6 PM.

"What time is it?" Patrick asked, though he wasn't sure he wanted to know.

David reached for the clock on his nightstand, squinting at the display. "Almost ten. We slept in."

"Good," Patrick said, snuggling closer. "I like sleeping with you."

David's arms tightened around him. "I like it too. A lot."

They eventually forced themselves out of bed and into David's tiny kitchen, where David attempted to make breakfast with the limited supplies in his refrigerator. Patrick sat at the small table wearing only his underwear, something that would have mortified him just days ago but now felt natural—part of their new routine of intimacy and trust. He watched David move around the cramped space with practiced efficiency, still marveling at how comfortable he felt being this exposed, this vulnerable with another person.

"Coffee's terrible," David warned, handing Patrick a mug. "I haven't figured out how to make it properly in this thing yet." He gestured at a small coffee maker that looked like it had seen better decades.

"It's perfect," Patrick lied, taking a sip of what tasted like brown water with aspirations. But David's smile was so hopeful that Patrick would have drunk motor oil if it made him happy.

They ate scrambled eggs and toast while discussing the day ahead. David had planned a walking tour of the Village, maybe a stop at a museum if Patrick was interested, lunch at a place he promised would "change your life forever" even though it was just a sandwich shop.

But underneath the casual planning, Patrick could feel the weight of departure pressing down on both of them. Every sugges-tion David made was followed by a quick calculation of time—

how long would this take, would they still have time for that, when did they absolutely have to leave for the airport?

"David," Patrick said suddenly, setting down his coffee mug. "Can we talk about something?"

David's fork paused halfway to his mouth. "Sure. What?"

Patrick took a breath, gathering courage. "Yesterday, when I asked if we were boyfriends, you said 'sure' but then suggested we just enjoy the weekend." He met David's eyes directly. "I need to know what that means."

David set down his own fork, and Patrick could see him choosing his words carefully. "It means... I don't know what it means, exactly. I've never done this before."

"Done what?"

"This. Us. Whatever this is." David gestured vaguely between them. "I don't know how to be someone's boyfriend, Patrick. I've never wanted to try before."

The admission was honest but not particularly reassuring. Patrick felt something cold settle in his stomach. "But you want to try now?"

"I think so. Maybe. I just..." David ran a hand through his hair, frustrated. "I don't want to promise you something I can't deliver. Long-distance relationships are hard. I travel for work, you have your life in Chicago. What if we set up all these expectations and then disappoint each other?"

Patrick stared at him across the small table, feeling the careful distance David was creating with his words. This wasn't the passionate declarations of love from last night. This was David the Wall Street professional, David the realist, David who was already protecting himself from potential disappointment.

"So what are you saying?" Patrick asked quietly.

"I'm saying maybe we should see how it goes. Keep in touch, visit when we can, not put pressure on it to be something it might not be ready to be."

The words hit Patrick like a slap. Keep in touch. Visit when we can. These were the phrases people used when they were backing away from commitment, when they wanted to keep their options open.

"Right," Patrick said, forcing his voice to remain steady. "See how it goes."

David must have heard something in his tone, because his expression immediately shifted to concern. "Patrick, I didn't mean—"

"No, it's fine," Patrick said, standing abruptly from the table. "You're being practical. Smart, even. We barely know each other anymore, really. Four years is a long time."

"That's not what I meant—"

"It's okay, David. Really." Patrick moved toward the bedroom to pack his things, needing space to process the whiplash of emotions. Last night they'd said they loved each other. This morning David was talking about "keeping in touch" like Patrick was a college acquaintance instead of the person he'd just made love with for the first time.

David followed him into the bedroom, clearly distressed. "Patrick, please. I think you're misunderstanding—"

"Am I?" Patrick turned to face him, and David could see the hurt Patrick was trying to hide. "Because it sounds like you're having second thoughts about whatever this is between us."

"I'm not having second thoughts," David said firmly. "I'm having anxiety. There's a difference."

The honesty in his voice made Patrick pause in his packing. "What kind of anxiety?"

David sat heavily on the bed, looking suddenly exhausted. "The kind where I'm terrified of screwing this up. Where I want you so much it scares me, and I don't know how to handle that. Where I've never cared this much about someone's happiness before, and I have no idea what I'm doing."

Patrick set down his duffel bag and sat beside David on the bed. "You think I know what I'm doing? David, this is all new to me too. Everything. But that doesn't mean we have to be careful about it."

"What if I disappoint you?"

"What if you don't?"

They stared at each other, and Patrick could see David wrestling with something internal, some fear he couldn't quite name.

"I love you," Patrick said simply. "That's not going to change because you live in New York and I live in Chicago. It's not going to change because we don't know what we're doing. I loved you four years ago, I love you now, and I'm probably going to love you for the rest of my life whether we figure this out or not."

David's eyes widened at the raw honesty of the statement. "Patrick..."

"So the question isn't whether we're going to be perfect at this," Patrick continued. "The question is whether we're going to try. Whether what we have is worth the effort of figuring it out as we go."

David reached for Patrick's hand, interlacing their fingers in the gesture that had become automatic between them. "It is. You are. I just... I've never had anything real to lose before."

"Neither have I," Patrick said softly. "But maybe that's what makes it worth having."

David lifted their joined hands and pressed a kiss to Patrick's knuckles. "Okay. Let's try. Really try. Visits, phone calls, figuring out how to make this work."

"Boyfriends," Patrick said, not quite a question.

"Boyfriends," David confirmed, and this time his smile reached his eyes.

They spent the rest of the morning in David's neighborhood, walking through farmers markets and bookstores, Patrick snapping photos of everything that caught his eye. David bought flowers from a vendor—daffodils, bright yellow and hopeful—and presented them to Patrick with a formal bow that made them both laugh.

"For my boyfriend," David announced loudly enough that several passersby smiled, and Patrick felt his heart soar at the public declaration.

Lunch was at the promised sandwich shop, where David

insisted Patrick try the pastrami despite Patrick's protests that he didn't usually eat meat for lunch. It was, as promised, life-changing, though Patrick suspected that had more to do with the company than the food.

"I need to tell you something," Patrick said as they shared a piece of cheesecake that was roughly the size of a small car. "I'm really proud of you. Of what you've built here. The job, the apartment, this whole life. I know it wasn't easy after..."

"After Steve," David finished when Patrick trailed off.

"Yeah. And I know I wasn't much help, being so far away."

David reached across the table to take his hand. "You were everything, Patrick. Those phone calls, the emails, knowing someone cared... it saved me. Literally."

The intensity in David's voice made Patrick's throat tight. "I wanted to come to the funeral. I looked at flights, I had the money saved, but I didn't know if... I didn't want to intrude—"

"I wished you had," David said quietly. "I kept looking for you in the crowd, which was stupid because how would you have even known where it was? But I kept hoping somehow you'd be there."

They stared at each other across the small table, and Patrick felt the weight of that missed opportunity settle between them. Another moment when timing and distance had kept them apart, when they'd both wanted the same thing but been too afraid or too uncertain to reach for it.

"We're here now," Patrick said finally.

"We're here now," David agreed.

That afternoon, they visited the Metropolitan Museum of Art, where Patrick spent twenty minutes in front of a single Van Gogh while David watched him with fond amusement. They walked through Central Park, rented a rowboat on the lake despite David's insistence that he had no idea how to row, and ended up spinning in circles while they both laughed helplessly.

As evening approached and departure time drew near, they found themselves walking more slowly, taking longer routes, stopping to look in shop windows they had no interest in visiting. Anything to postpone the inevitable.

"I should probably get you to JFK," David said finally, checking his watch as they stood outside his building.

"Yeah," Patrick agreed, though neither of them moved toward the door.

The drive to the airport was quiet, both of them lost in their own thoughts. Patrick spent the time memorizing details—the way David's hands looked on the steering wheel, the profile of his face in the late afternoon light, the sound of his breathing in the confined space of the car.

At the airport, they walked together as far as security would allow, and Patrick couldn't help but think of that morning at O'Hare four years earlier when their positions had been reversed. The symmetry was painful and perfect and absolutely wrong— another airport goodbye, another separation just when they were finding each other again.

"So," David said, shifting Patrick's bag to his other shoulder. "This was..."

"Yeah," Patrick agreed. "It was."

They looked at each other, and Patrick felt that familiar pull, that magnetic force that seemed to draw them together despite every practical consideration. He stepped closer, not caring who might see, and David met him halfway.

The kiss was soft and lingering, a promise and a goodbye all at once. When they broke apart, both were breathing hard.

"I'll call you tomorrow," David said.

"Okay."

"And we'll figure out when I can come to Chicago. Or when you can come back here."

"Okay."

But even as they made these promises, Patrick could see something in David's eyes that looked like doubt. The same uncertainty that had colored his breakfast conversation, the careful distance of someone already protecting himself from disappointment.

Patrick forced himself to walk away, to show his ID at security, to turn and wave from the other side of the checkpoint. David waved back, but he was already stepping backward, already beginning the process of returning to his New York life without Patrick in it.

As Patrick found his gate and settled in to wait for boarding, he tried to hold onto the magic of the past three days. The way David had looked at him with such tenderness, the perfect intimacy of their mornings together, the rightness of walking through New York hand in hand.

But underneath the warmth of those memories, a small voice whispered warnings he wasn't ready to hear. David's careful words about not putting pressure on whatever this was between them. The way he'd started to retreat even as he was making promises about visits and phone calls.

Patrick pulled out his disposable camera and held it carefully, thinking about all the photos he'd taken over the weekend—David on the library steps, the two of them together outside the sandwich shop, moments he'd captured but wouldn't be able to see until he got the film developed back in Chicago. He had one picture left. On impulse, he held the camera at arm's length and quickly snapped a photo of himself, his face raw with all the emotion of the moment—love, heartbreak, hope, fear all mixed together. He wound the film and returned the camera to his bag, not knowing that years later he would look at that single image occasionally, keeping it hidden from everyone as life went on, a secret record of the exact moment when everything felt possible and impossible at once. David would see it many years later and recognize immediately what it captured.

Whatever happened next, whatever complications distance and time might create, they'd had this perfect weekend. They'd finally said the words that mattered.

Patrick tried to focus on that hope as his flight began boarding. Some connections were strong enough to survive anything.

Weren't they?

# CHAPTER

## Twenty-Three

PATRICK HAD NEVER REALIZED how loud silence could be until David's voice stopped filling it.

The photos came back from Walgreens on a Thursday afternoon, two weeks after his return from New York. Patrick sat in his childhood bedroom with the small envelope, his hands actually shaking as he pulled out the stack of 4x6 prints. There they were—evidence that the weekend had really happened, that those three perfect days weren't just some elaborate fantasy his lonely mind had constructed.

David in front of the colorful Village mural, looking perfectly at home in his city. The farmers market, David chatting with vendors, looking completely at home in his adopted city. The two of them together outside the sandwich shop, David holding those ridiculous daffodils like he was proposing. And then the one that stopped Patrick's breath completely—the library steps photo. The two of them sitting side by side in the golden afternoon light, both laughing at something now forgotten, looking so happy, so natural together, like they belonged in each other's orbit. Patrick studied their faces in the photo, remembering exactly how that moment had felt, David's arm around his waist, both of them grinning at the camera like they had all the time in the world.

He flipped through the rest slowly, his chest tight with the kind of nostalgia usually reserved for much older memories. And then, at the bottom of the stack, the photo he'd almost forgotten taking. Himself at JFK, face raw with every emotion he'd been feeling in that moment—love, fear, hope, heartbreak all written in his green eyes and the uncertain curve of his mouth. He looked young and vulnerable and completely overwhelmed, like someone standing at the edge of a cliff trying to decide whether to jump.

Patrick stared at that photo for a long time, then carefully slipped it between the pages of the book on his nightstand where no one would ever find it. The rest he arranged in a small album, something he could flip through when he needed to remember that David was real, that what they had was real, even when the distance made it feel like a beautiful dream.

But the library steps photo—that one was special. That one deserved better than being hidden away in a drawer.

The first week after his return, they'd talked every night. Long conversations that stretched past midnight, David calling from his apartment after getting home from work, Patrick taking the phone into his parents' basement for privacy. They'd planned David's visit to Chicago—maybe in three weeks, when David's work schedule calmed down. They'd talked about Patrick coming back to New York, about finding ways to see each other more regularly.

But then David's work had exploded. Some crisis with a major client that required sixteen-hour days, weekend travel, constant attention. His calls became shorter, more sporadic. "I'm sorry," he'd say, his voice exhausted even through the static of long distance. "This deal is killing me, but once it's done..."

Patrick understood. Of course he understood. David was building a career, making his mark in one of the most competitive cities in the world. Patrick had his own deadlines at Meridian Press, his own obligations that sometimes kept him late at the office. Life was complicated. Love had to fit around the edges of everything else.

But understanding didn't make the silence any easier to bear.

The phone calls dropped to twice a week, then once a week, then every other week. The emails became shorter, more practical —updates about work, brief questions about family, the kind of communication that maintained connection without requiring emotional investment. Patrick found himself starting messages he never sent, picking up the phone to call David then hanging up before dialing, afraid of seeming needy or desperate.

*I don't want to bother him,* Patrick told himself. *He's busy. Important things are happening in his life. My loneliness isn't his problem.*

The irony wasn't lost on him. They'd both been so afraid of putting pressure on their relationship that they'd stopped feeding it entirely. Like two gardeners so worried about overwatering a plant that they let it die of thirst.

Patrick threw himself into work, staying late at the office, volunteering for projects that required weekend hours. Anything to avoid sitting in his childhood bedroom surrounded by reminders of David, staring at the phone that never rang. Mark Hoffman noticed the change in him—the way Patrick's easy humor had faded, how he'd started declining invitations to grab drinks after work.

"You're punishing yourself for something," Mark observed one evening as they waited for their Metra train home. "Want to talk about it?"

"Nothing to talk about," Patrick said, but his voice lacked conviction.

"Right. And that's why you've been working sixty-hour weeks and looking like someone stole your dog."

Patrick almost smiled at that. If only it were as simple as a missing pet. "It's complicated."

"It's always complicated with the ones that matter," Mark said, echoing his words from weeks earlier. "But maybe complicated is better than empty."

Patrick didn't respond, but Mark's words stayed with him during the long train ride home. Was that what his life had become? Empty?

That night, he carefully placed the library steps photo inside the frame and set it on his nightstand. Now, every morning when he woke up and every night before he went to sleep, he could see David's face laughing in the golden New York light, could remember what it felt like to be that happy together. The rest of the photos went into his nightstand drawer, along with that final, secret selfie he would keep hidden from everyone.

Six months after New York, the phone rang on a Tuesday night at 11:30 PM. Patrick was already in bed, reading a manuscript for work, and he almost didn't answer. But something made him reach for the receiver on the second ring. As he did, his eyes fell on the framed photo on his nightstand—David's face caught in that moment of perfect happiness—and his heart melted as much as his spirit.

"Hello?"

"Patrick? It's David."

The sound of his voice after weeks of silence hit Patrick like a blow. He sat up in bed, his heart immediately racing. "David. Hi. I... how are you?"

"I'm..." David paused, and Patrick could hear city sounds in the background—sirens, car horns, the constant hum of New York life. "I'm not sure, actually. Can we talk?"

Patrick glanced at his clock, calculating. It was 12:30 AM in New York, definitely late for a casual call. "Of course. What's going on?"

"I was just..." Another pause, longer this time. "I was sitting here thinking about that weekend, about how good everything felt when you were here. And now it's been six months, and we've barely talked, and I keep wondering..."

"Wondering what?"

"If this feels right to you. Any of this. The way we've been... not communicating. The way we've both been pretending everything's fine when it's clearly not."

Patrick felt something crack open in his chest. The careful distance he'd been maintaining, the polite emails and surface-level conversations, suddenly felt as exhausting as they actually were.

"No," Patrick said quietly. "It doesn't feel right."

"Thank God," David breathed. "I thought maybe I was going crazy."

They sat in silence for a moment, eight hundred miles apart but somehow closer than they'd been in weeks.

"I miss you," Patrick said finally, the admission feeling like jumping off a cliff. "I miss you so much it hurts, and I've been trying not to call because I didn't want to seem clingy or desperate or—"

"I've been doing the same thing," David interrupted. "Picking up the phone and hanging up. Starting emails I never send. Telling myself you're probably happier without me constantly bothering you."

"David." Patrick's voice was sharp with something approaching anger. "You could never bother me. Never."

"But this is what I was afraid of," David said, his voice cracking slightly. "In New York, when we talked about trying to make this work. I was afraid we'd hurt each other trying to love each other from so far away."

Patrick closed his eyes, remembering David's careful words that Sunday morning, his anxiety about long-distance relationships and unmet expectations. "I understand now. What you meant. I didn't then, but I do now."

"Do you hate me for being right?"

"I don't hate you." Patrick's voice was soft, sad. "I could never hate you. But David... I don't know how to do this. How to love you the way I want to love you when you're not here. How to be your boyfriend when we can't... be together."

The words hung between them, honest and terrible and completely true. They both felt it—the impossibility of maintaining intimacy across such distance, the way their separate lives kept pulling them in different directions, the exhaustion of always missing each other.

"So what do we do?" David asked.

Patrick was quiet for a long time, thinking. What they had was real—the connection, the love, the way they fit together when they were in the same place. But the practical reality of maintaining a relationship between Chicago and New York in 1992, with demanding careers and separate lives, felt overwhelming.

"I don't know," Patrick admitted. "I love you. That hasn't changed, and it's not going to change. But I can't keep feeling like I'm failing at being your boyfriend every day we don't talk. And I can't keep wondering if you're getting tired of trying to love someone you never see."

"I'm not getting tired—"

"Aren't you?" Patrick's voice was gentle but direct. "Be honest, David. When you think about calling me, do you feel excited or obligated?"

David was quiet for so long that Patrick wondered if the connection had been lost. Finally, in a voice barely above a whisper: "Sometimes... sometimes it feels like work. And I hate that. I hate that loving you has started to feel complicated instead of simple."

Patrick felt tears sting his eyes, but also relief. Finally, honesty instead of careful politeness. "Yeah. I know what you mean."

"So what do we do?" David asked again.

Patrick stared at the ceiling of his childhood bedroom, surrounded by reminders of the safe, predictable life he'd built in Chicago. Down the hall, his parents were probably asleep, dreaming ordinary dreams about ordinary futures. Outside his window, Arlington Heights slept peacefully under streetlights, everything familiar and comfortable and completely separate from the complicated beauty of what he'd found with David.

"Maybe..." Patrick started, then stopped, afraid to voice what he was thinking.

"What?"

"Maybe we stop trying so hard. Maybe we just... let it be what it is. We love each other. That's real. But maybe we're not meant to be boyfriends right now. Maybe we're meant to be... something else."

"What else?"

Patrick searched for words to describe the feeling. "People who matter to each other. People who will always matter to each other, no matter what. Even if we can't figure out how to make the distance work."

David was quiet, and Patrick could almost hear him thinking. "You mean like..."

"Like we stop putting pressure on it to be a traditional relationship and just... love each other the way we can. From where we are."

"Would that be enough for you?"

Patrick considered the question honestly. Would it be enough to love David without possessing him, to care about his happiness without needing to be part of his daily life, to accept that some connections transcended geography and circumstance even when they couldn't overcome them?

"I think it has to be," Patrick said. "Because the alternative is losing you completely, and I can't... I won't do that."

"So we're..."

"We're Patrick and David," Patrick said simply. "Whatever that means. However that works."

David laughed, but it sounded sad. "That's not very defined."

"Maybe that's okay. Maybe some things don't need definitions."

They talked for another hour, working through the practical details of their new undefined relationship. Less frequent calls, so they wouldn't feel the pressure of constant contact. Emails when they felt like sharing something important. No expectations about visits, but no closing the door to them either. Permission to live their separate lives without guilt, but with the understanding that what they shared would always be there, waiting in the background like a song you couldn't quite forget.

When they finally said goodbye, Patrick felt something settle in his chest that wasn't quite peace but was closer to acceptance than the anxiety he'd been carrying for weeks.

They loved each other. That was real and unchanging and didn't require daily maintenance to survive. Everything else—the visits, the phone calls, the possibility of a future together—could exist in potential rather than pressure.

As Patrick hung up the phone, his eyes fell on the framed

photo on his nightstand—the two of them on the library steps, caught in that moment of perfect happiness. His heart melted as much as his spirit, remembering how that afternoon had felt, how right everything had seemed when they were together.

Patrick tried not to calculate how long it might be before he saw David again. Some connections were strong enough to survive anything, including the inability to be together.

At least, he hoped they were.

# CHAPTER
## Twenty-Four

PATRICK HAD FORGOTTEN how easily they could pretend everything was normal until David's lips touched his neck and shattered the illusion completely.

The weekend had started well enough. David picked him up at JFK with the same genuine smile, the same easy conversation during the drive back to the Village. They'd fallen into their old rhythm almost immediately—David showing off new restaurants he'd discovered, Patrick taking photos of street art and architecture, both of them carefully avoiding any mention of their last phone conversation or what it meant that Patrick was here again after a year of careful distance.

It felt like playing house with someone you used to love, Patrick thought as they wandered through the farmers market on Saturday afternoon. All the motions of intimacy without any of the substance. David bought flowers again—tulips this time, spring-bright and hopeful—but when he handed them to Patrick, there was something performative about the gesture, as if they were both acting out a script they'd memorized but no longer believed in.

"These are beautiful," Patrick said, accepting the flowers with a smile that felt foreign on his face.

"I thought you'd like them," David replied, but his voice carried the same artificial quality.

They cooked dinner together in David's tiny kitchen, their movements coordinated but cautious, careful not to brush against each other accidentally. When David reached around Patrick for the salt, he made sure to announce his presence first. When Patrick needed to get to the refrigerator, he waited for David to move aside completely before approaching. It was like a dance performed by strangers who'd learned the steps from watching the original performers.

After dinner, they sat on David's couch with carefully maintained space between them, talking about work, about books they'd been reading, about mutual friends from college—safe topics that didn't require them to acknowledge the elephant in the room. Patrick found himself cataloguing the changes in David's apartment, the new furniture, the different arrangement of books, evidence of a life that had continued evolving without him.

"I should probably get ready for bed," Patrick said when the conversation finally flagged, exhaustion and emotional strain making his eyelids heavy.

"Of course," David said, standing quickly. "You know where everything is."

They moved around each other in the small bedroom with the same careful choreography they'd maintained all day. Patrick pulled his pajamas from his duffel bag and began to undress, his back to David, while David rummaged through his dresser for his own sleeping clothes. It felt formal, polite, like roommates who barely knew each other rather than former lovers trying to navigate the wreckage of what they'd once shared.

Patrick had just pulled his shirt over his head when he felt David's presence behind him, warm and familiar and suddenly, devastatingly close. David's hands settled gently on Patrick's bare shoulders, and then his lips found the sensitive spot where Patrick's neck met his shoulder, the same place he'd always kissed, the same gentle pressure that had once made Patrick melt with desire.

For a moment, Patrick's body responded with muscle memory, leaning back into David's warmth, his head tilting to give David better access. But then reality crashed over him like cold water— the year of silence, the careful redefinition of their relationship, the way they'd been tiptoeing around each other all weekend like actors who'd forgotten their lines.

Something broke inside Patrick's chest, sharp and sudden and completely overwhelming.

The sob escaped him before he could stop it, harsh and ragged in the quiet bedroom. His shoulders shook as a year's worth of suppressed longing and frustration and heartbreak came pouring out of him all at once.

"Patrick?" David's hands immediately fell away, his voice sharp with concern. "What's wrong? What did I do?"

Patrick turned around, tears streaming down his face, still shirtless and vulnerable and completely undone. "I can't," he choked out. "I can't do this anymore."

David's face went pale. "Do what? Patrick, I don't understand—"

"This!" Patrick gestured wildly between them, his voice breaking. "This pretending. This weekend where we act like we're still... something... and then I go back to Chicago and we don't talk for months and I spend every day wondering if I imagined the whole thing."

David stared at him, something like recognition dawning in his eyes. "Patrick..."

"If we're going to do this," Patrick continued, his voice gaining strength even as tears continued to fall, "then we really need to do it. Or we need to do nothing at all. I can't keep getting my heart tugged into thinking we're together only to have it all pulled apart again the moment I get on that plane."

David's expression crumpled, and Patrick could see his own pain reflected there, multiplied by David's guilt and helplessness.

"I know. God, Patrick, I know. I've been thinking the same thing all weekend."

They stood there looking at each other across the small space of David's bedroom, both half-dressed and completely exposed, finally acknowledging what they'd been dancing around for two days.

"So what do we do?" Patrick asked, wiping his eyes with the back of his hand.

David moved to sit on the edge of his bed, running his hands through his hair. "I don't know. I've been asking myself that question for months."

Patrick pulled on his discarded shirt and sat beside David, close enough to feel his warmth but not quite touching. "We could... I could move to New York. There are publishing houses here, I could find something—"

"No." David's voice was firm. "You'd hate it here. Really hate it. The pace, the noise, the way everything costs twice what it should. And I'd hate myself for letting you give up your life, your family, everything you love about Chicago."

"Then you could move to Chicago. There are finance jobs there, you know the city—"

"And spend the rest of my life wondering what would have happened if I'd stayed in New York? If I'd kept building what I started here?" David shook his head. "That's not fair to either of us."

Patrick felt fresh tears threaten. "So we're stuck. We love each other, but we can't be together. We can't make it work long-distance, and we can't make the practical changes that would let us be in the same place."

"What about... what if one of us flew to see the other every other weekend? We could make it work if we really committed—"

"With what money?" Patrick's laugh was bitter. "David, I'm a junior editor at a mid-level publishing house. Do you know what I make? And you're working eighty-hour weeks building your career. When would we have time? When would we have energy for anything besides traveling and being exhausted?"

David was quiet for a long moment, and Patrick could see him running through the same calculations, the same impossible math of love versus logistics.

"We could move somewhere else entirely," David said finally. "Start fresh somewhere that belongs to both of us instead of one or the other."

"And give up everything we've both worked for? Our careers, our families, our friends?" Patrick shook his head. "David, if we did that, it would always be in the back of our heads. When things got difficult—and every relationship has difficult times—we'd wonder if we made the right choice. We'd resent each other for the sacrifices, even if we tried not to."

"So what are you saying?" David's voice was small, defeated.

Patrick felt the tears start again, hot and inevitable. "I'm saying I can't win. We can't win. I love you more than I've ever loved anyone, and it doesn't matter. Love isn't enough to overcome geography and timing and all the practical realities that keep us apart."

"Don't say that." David's voice cracked. "Don't say love isn't enough."

"Then tell me how to make it enough," Patrick pleaded, turning to face David fully. "Tell me how to love you without destroying myself in the process. Because I don't know how, David. I've tried for over a year, and I'm so tired of hurting all the time."

David stared at him, and Patrick could see the exact moment when David realized he didn't have an answer. The silence stretched between them, heavy with everything they couldn't fix, couldn't change, couldn't make work no matter how much they wanted to.

"Maybe..." David started, then stopped, looking like the words were being torn from his throat. "Maybe we need to try to move on. Date other people. Try to build lives that don't revolve around missing each other."

The words hit Patrick like a physical blow. He'd known they were coming, had maybe even been thinking the same thing, but hearing David say them out loud made them real in a way that felt devastating.

"You want us to give up," Patrick said quietly.

"I want us to stop torturing ourselves." David's voice broke completely. "I want you to be happy, Patrick. Really happy. Not this half-life where you're always waiting for something that might never happen."

"And you think I can be happy with someone else?"

David was crying now too, silent tears that he didn't bother to wipe away. "I think you deserve the chance to try. We both do."

Patrick looked at David—really looked at him—and saw his own heartbreak reflected there. David didn't want this any more than Patrick did. He was just brave enough to say what they were both thinking, to voice the solution neither of them wanted but both knew made sense.

"This is so fucked," Patrick whispered.

"Yeah," David agreed, his voice thick with tears. "Everything about this is fucked."

They sat in silence for a moment, both crying quietly, both trying to process what they'd just decided without actually deciding it. Then, without discussing it, they moved toward each other at the same time, David's arms coming around Patrick, Patrick's face burying in David's shoulder.

They held each other tightly, desperately, like they were trying to memorize the feeling for all the lonely nights ahead. Patrick could feel David's tears in his hair, could hear the soft sounds of David's grief mixing with his own.

"I love you," Patrick whispered against David's neck. "I'm always going to love you."

"I love you too," David replied, his arms tightening around Patrick. "That's never going to change. That's never going to stop being true."

They stayed like that for a long time, holding each other while their hearts broke in perfect synchronization. Outside David's window, New York continued its relentless pulse, millions of people pursuing their own complicated dreams and desires, oblivious to the quiet tragedy unfolding in a fourth-floor walk-up in the Village.

Eventually, they lay down together on top of the covers, still fully clothed, still clinging to each other like survivors of some beautiful disaster. Neither spoke about tomorrow, about Patrick's flight back to Chicago, about what would happen next. There would be time for those conversations later, for the careful redrawing of boundaries and the slow, painful process of learning to be apart.

For now, they just held each other and tried not to think about how this might be the last time they'd fall asleep in each other's arms.

Some love stories, Patrick realized as consciousness finally claimed him, don't end with weddings or happily ever after. Some end with two people who love each other enough to let go, who care more about each other's happiness than their own desperate need to hold on.

It didn't make it hurt any less. But maybe, someday, it would make it hurt with purpose.

# CHAPTER
## Twenty~Five

DAVID HAD SEEN Patrick nervous before, but he'd never seen him look like he was facing his own execution.

Standing in the marble lobby of Patrick's office building in River North, David tried to make sense of what he was seeing. Patrick emerged from the elevator looking pale and hollow-eyed, moving with the careful deliberation of someone trying not to fall apart in public. When their eyes met, Patrick's attempt at a smile was so forced it made David's chest ache.

"Hey," Patrick said, his voice barely above a whisper.

"Hey yourself," David replied, studying Patrick's face. Something was very, very wrong. Patrick looked like he'd seen a ghost— or maybe like he was becoming one.

They walked the few blocks to the restaurant in near silence, Patrick's hands shaking slightly as he pointed out directions David didn't need. It had been two months shy of a year since their "breakup" in New York, and David had prepared himself for awkwardness, for the careful distance they'd both promised to maintain. He hadn't prepared for this—Patrick looking like his world had ended sometime between their phone call last week and this moment.

The restaurant was one of those trendy River North places with exposed brick and too-loud music, filled with business lunches and first dates. They were seated at a small table near the window, and David watched Patrick stare at his menu without seeming to see it.

"So," David said, attempting normalcy, "how's work been? You mentioned that new project with the—"

"Fine," Patrick interrupted, his voice flat. "It's fine."

David tried again. "And your family? How are your parents?"

"Good. They're good."

There's only so many ways you can ask if someone is okay, David thought, but he didn't know what else to do. Patrick was answering his questions but wasn't really present, his green eyes focused somewhere past David's shoulder like he was seeing something terrible that only he could perceive.

"Patrick," David said gently. "What's going on?"

"Nothing. I'm just tired."

David ordered for both of them when the server came, Patrick barely acknowledging the interaction. As they waited for their food, David carried the conversation alone—updates about his work, funny stories about his neighbors, safe topics that required minimal response. Patrick gave small answers, nodding at appropriate moments, but seemed to be somewhere else entirely.

Finally, David had enough.

"Look," he said, leaning forward and lowering his voice. "I flew all the way out here to see you. Nothing more, nothing complicated, just to see you. Can you at least tell me why you're not really here? What the hell has gotten into you?"

Patrick's face crumpled completely. The tears came suddenly and silently, rolling down his cheeks as his shoulders began to shake. Other diners started to look over, probably wondering if David had just broken up with him. *If only*, David thought desperately. A breakup he could handle. This felt like something much worse.

David's protective instincts kicked in immediately. He switched to the overly empathetic tone he'd perfected for client crises, leaning closer and lowering his voice to barely above a whisper.

"Hey, hey," he said softly, reaching across the table to take Patrick's hand. He'd decided before flying out that he'd keep his distance, that touching Patrick would only make everything more complicated. But seeing Patrick fall apart like this made all those careful boundaries irrelevant. "Talk to me. Whatever it is, we can figure it out."

Patrick tried to speak, but the words came out in fragments, tossed from his mouth like he couldn't bear to hold them any longer. David could only catch pieces—"Mark's party... sweet guy... thought he was safe..."

"Patrick, slow down," David said, squeezing his hand. "I can't understand what you're saying."

Patrick paused, wiped his eyes with his free hand, and looked David directly in the eye for the first time since he'd arrived. What David saw there made his blood run cold.

"The guy I met," Patrick said softly, his voice barely audible over the restaurant noise. "Through Mark at work. At a party Mark threw. The guy Mark vouched for. The one who was sweet and quiet." Patrick's voice caught. "The one I slept with on the third date. The one who wasn't anything like you, and I didn't love him."

David felt something cold settle in his stomach. "What about him?"

"He called me last night." Patrick's voice was getting smaller, more fragile. "He told me he tested HIV positive. He said I should go get tested. We only slept together the one time. We weren't even boyfriends."

The words hit David like a physical blow. The restaurant noise faded to white static as the full implications crashed over him. HIV. AIDS. Death sentence. Patrick could be... Patrick might be...

"You didn't wear a condom?" The words escaped before David could stop them, sharp and accusatory.

Patrick began to cry like a child whose parent had just scolded them, the sound so broken it made David's heart shatter. Through his sobs, Patrick tried to explain, but it came out in bursts: "I wasn't the top... he was aggressive... it didn't take very long... please forgive me..."

David stared at Patrick across the table, emotions warring in his chest. Part of him wanted to comfort and console, to hold Patrick and tell him everything would be okay. Another part wanted to shake him, to yell *What were you thinking? You CAN'T die on me, you son of a bitch!*

But mostly, David was terrified. AIDS had killed friends of friends since he'd moved to New York—young, vital men who'd been fine one day and wasting away the next. David had been careful since their breakup, always wearing condoms during his few hookups, getting tested every couple of months at the clinic on Christopher Street. But Patrick...

Sweet, trusting Patrick who'd been a virgin until that weekend in New York. Patrick who probably didn't know how to negotiate safe sex, who would trust someone Mark vouched for, who would assume the best of people even when he shouldn't.

"Why are you asking for forgiveness?" David asked quietly, his voice thick with emotion. "You're the one who might be facing a..." His voice broke completely, and suddenly David was crying too, his own tears falling as the reality of what they were discussing hit him full force. They both knew what he couldn't bring himself to say.

Patrick's sobs intensified at seeing David break down, the sound raw and desperate in the noisy restaurant.

Patrick's sobs intensified, and David felt his own eyes fill with tears. He couldn't go to another funeral. Not Patrick's. Not the person he loved more than anyone else in the world, even if they couldn't be together.

"I'm so sorry," Patrick whispered. "I'm so sorry, David. I know you told me to date other people, but I never thought... I didn't know how to... I should have been more careful."

David reached across the table and took both of Patrick's hands in his, not caring who was watching. "Patrick, listen to me. This is not your fault. Do you hear me? This is not your fault."

They sat there in the noisy restaurant, Patrick quietly sobbing over his untouched club salad, David equally hurt and ashamed and terrified. He wanted so desperately to make it all better for Patrick, to somehow turn back time and protect him from this, to take the fear away. But all he could do was hold Patrick's hands and try not to think about what life would look like if the test came back positive.

David signaled for the check, paid quickly, and stood up. "Come on," he said, helping Patrick to his feet. "We're leaving."

"Where are we going?" Patrick asked, wiping his eyes.

"Boystown," David said firmly, guiding Patrick toward the exit. "There's bound to be a clinic somewhere that can test you. And we're going to do it now. Right now."

Patrick stopped walking. "David, I can't. I'm not ready—"

"Ready for what? To find out if you're going to live or die?" David's voice was sharper than he intended, but fear was making him aggressive. "Patrick, you can't just pretend this isn't happening. The longer you wait, the worse it's going to be."

Patrick looked at him with such raw terror that David immediately softened his tone. "I'm sorry. I'm scared too. But we need to know. And whatever the result is, we'll deal with it. Together."

"Together?" Patrick's voice was small, hopeful.

David nodded, even though he wasn't sure what that meant anymore. They'd broken up. They'd agreed to move on, to date other people, to build separate lives. But in this moment, none of that mattered. All that mattered was making sure Patrick was okay.

"Together," David confirmed. "Now come on. Let's go find out."

They walked toward the Red Line station, David's arm around Patrick's shoulders, both of them trying not to think about what the next few hours might bring. The Chicago afternoon was bright and warm, completely at odds with the darkness they were carrying.

But as they descended into the subway, reality began to set in. The test would take days, maybe weeks for results. David had to fly back to New York tomorrow for a client meeting he couldn't miss. What would they do? He couldn't imagine the results coming back positive and Patrick being alone when he found out. Would he come back to go with him? How would this work?

"Goddamn," David muttered under his breath, the weight of their situation crushing down on him. "I hate living so fucking far apart."

Somewhere in Boystown, there would be a clinic that could draw Patrick's blood. But then would come the waiting—the agonizing uncertainty of Patrick going through this terror alone while David sat in meetings eight hundred miles away, powerless to help.

David had never hated the distance between them more than he did in this moment.

# CHAPTER
## Twenty-Six

PATRICK HAD NEVER SEEN David so demanding, so uncompromising, so absolutely authoritative about anything in the years he'd known him.

After they'd found the clinic in Boystown, after the blood draw and the paperwork and the technician's matter-of-fact explanation that results would take about two weeks given the current backlog, David had gripped Patrick's shoulders and looked him directly in the eye.

"Listen to me," David had said, his voice carrying a steel Patrick had never heard before. "When they call—no matter what day, no matter what time—you contact me first. Before you go in for the results. Before you do anything. You call me, I get on a plane, and we go together. Under no circumstances do you go alone. Do you understand me?"

Patrick had nodded, somewhat stunned by this side of David he'd never seen. David was normally so sweet, so compassionate, so careful about not being too demanding. But with this, he was unchanging, uncompromising. There was no room for negotiation.

"Patrick. Do you understand me?"

"Yes," Patrick had whispered. "I understand."

But it tugged at Patrick in ways he tried not to examine too closely. It gave him hope. If David cared this much, then perhaps he... No, Patrick stopped himself. He couldn't let himself get too attached to the idea of David and him being together again. Still, a casual friend doesn't just drop everything to fly out simply to get a two-minute test result, does he?

———

The waiting was agony.

Twelve days that stretched like months, each one beginning with the same terrible awareness that today might be the day the phone rang. Patrick developed a routine born of desperation: wake up, check the answering machine (though he'd been in the room all night), shower (because normal people shower), force down coffee and toast (because normal people eat breakfast), drive to work (because normal people have jobs), and spend eight hours pretending to focus on manuscripts while his mind catalogued every article about HIV he'd ever read.

By day three, Patrick had convinced himself he had night sweats. By day five, he was certain the small cut on his hand was taking too long to heal. By day seven, he'd checked his lymph nodes so many times that they actually were swollen from the constant prodding.

He hadn't told his parents anything. How could he? The conversation would require explanations he wasn't prepared to give—why he'd needed the test, who he'd been with, what kind of life he was really living when he said he was "dating around." His mother still held out hope that his "phase" would pass, that he'd meet the right woman and settle down. Learning that her son might be dying of a disease she associated with drug addicts and deviants would destroy something in her that Patrick wasn't sure could be repaired.

Work became both salvation and torture. During busy periods, Patrick could lose himself in the mechanical process of editing—fixing grammar, restructuring paragraphs, catching inconsistencies. But in quiet moments, his mind would drift to the clinic, to test tubes and lab technicians and the numbers that would determine whether he had a future or a death sentence.

Mark had noticed the changes, of course. Patrick's running times had gotten slower, his concentration at work had become sporadic, and he'd declined every social invitation for nearly two weeks. But when Mark asked if everything was okay, Patrick just said he was feeling tired, fighting off a cold, nothing serious.

The nights were the worst. Patrick would lie in his childhood bedroom, staring at the ceiling and trying not to think about what AIDS looked like in its final stages. He'd seen the news reports, the gaunt faces, the purple lesions, the way strong men wasted away to nothing while their families watched helplessly. He'd read the statistics—the average time from infection to death, the experimental treatments that weren't working, the way the disease turned your own immune system against you.

On night nine, Patrick had gotten up at 2 AM and written letters. One to his parents, trying to explain why he'd kept this secret, asking them to forgive him for the choices that had led to this moment. One to Sean, encouraging him to be braver than his uncle had been, to live honestly and safely. One to David, full of apologies and gratitude and the admission that he'd never stopped loving him, not for a single day.

He'd sealed the letters in separate envelopes and hidden them in his desk drawer, insurance against the possibility that he'd be too shocked or too devastated to speak coherently after getting the results.

David had called every other day, checking in with carefully casual questions about how Patrick was feeling, whether he'd heard anything yet, if he needed anything. Patrick could hear the worry underneath David's controlled tone, could sense that David was managing his own fear by trying to manage Patrick's. It was both comforting and heartbreaking—proof that David still cared, but also evidence of the burden Patrick had placed on him by allowing David to be part of this crisis.

"I keep thinking about statistics," Patrick had confessed during one of these calls, staring out his bedroom window at the familiar suburban street where he'd grown up. "About odds and transmission rates and whether a single encounter with someone who might not even have been positive yet is enough to..."

"Stop," David had said firmly. "Patrick, you can't think your way out of this. The numbers don't matter anymore. What happened, happened. All we can do now is wait for the results and deal with whatever they tell us."

"But what if—"

"No what-ifs. We wait, we get the answer, and we go from there." David's voice had softened. "Whatever it is, we'll figure it out. I promise."

It was 12 days almost to the hour when his answering machine picked up the call. Patrick had been at work, staying late again to avoid going home to his childhood bedroom where the silence felt too loud and his thoughts got too dark. When he came home and saw the blinking red light, his heart stopped.

"This message is for Patrick O'Brien. This is Carlo from the Belmont Health Clinic. Your test results are in. Please call to schedule an appointment to receive them. Our office hours are Monday through Friday, 9 AM to 6 PM. Thank you."

Patrick stood in his parents' kitchen, staring at the answering machine, and felt the world tilt around him. Thank God his parents weren't home—his father was still at work, his mother at her book club. He couldn't imagine what either of them would have thought hearing that message.

With shaking hands, Patrick dialed David's number in New York.

"David Chen."

"It's Patrick. They called."

The line went quiet for a moment. Then: "When?"

"Just now. I just got home and there was a message. They want me to call and schedule an appointment."

"Don't call yet. I need to check flights. What time is it there?"

Patrick glanced at the kitchen clock. "Almost seven."

"Okay. I'll call you back in twenty minutes. Don't do anything until I call you back."

"David—"

"Twenty minutes, Patrick. I mean it."

The line went dead, and Patrick was left standing in his parents' kitchen, holding the receiver and feeling like he might throw up. Twenty minutes felt like twenty hours.

When David called back, his voice was efficient, controlled. "There's a flight tomorrow at 11 AM that gets in at 12:30 your time. Can you get off work early?"

"I... yes. I can say I have a doctor's appointment."

"Good. Call the clinic now and schedule the appointment for 3 PM tomorrow. That'll give me time to get there and for us to... prepare."

Patrick called the clinic back, but the earliest appointment they had available was 4:30 PM. David said that would be fine—it would give them even more time to prepare themselves for whatever they were about to hear.

"David, you don't have to—"

"Yes, I do." His voice softened slightly. "We're doing this together, remember?"

————

David's plane was delayed by forty minutes, turning Patrick's already frayed nerves into something approaching panic. He sat in the arrival area at O'Hare, watching the monitor flash "DELAYED" next to David's flight number and imagining having to face the results alone after all. What if David missed the appointment? What if the clinic couldn't reschedule? What if Patrick had to hear the worst possible news without David there to help him process it?

When David finally emerged from the gate, looking harried and worried, Patrick felt such relief that he nearly collapsed. David spotted him immediately and crossed the terminal in quick strides, pulling Patrick into a hug that was fierce and desperate and completely inappropriate for two people who were supposedly just friends.

"I'm sorry," David said into Patrick's ear. "There were storms and... Are you okay?"

Patrick wanted to say yes, wanted to be strong and composed and ready to handle whatever came next. Instead, he found himself clinging to David like a life preserver, breathing in the familiar scent of his cologne and letting himself believe, for just a moment, that everything would be okay as long as David was there.

They took a cab from the airport to the clinic, both of them too nervous to make conversation. David kept checking his watch, calculating and recalculating whether they'd make it on time. Patrick stared out the window at the familiar Chicago streets and tried not to think about whether this might be one of the last times he'd see them.

"Patrick," David said as they sat in traffic on Lake Shore Drive. "Whatever happens in there, I want you to know something."

Patrick turned to look at him, noting the tension in David's jaw, the way his hands were clenched in his lap.

"I want you to know that these past two weeks have been some of the longest of my life. Not because I was worried about getting back together or what this might mean for us, but because I couldn't stand the thought of you going through this alone. You matter to me, Patrick. More than I probably should admit, more than is probably smart given our situation. But you matter to me, and I need you to be okay."

Patrick felt tears sting his eyes. "David..."

"Let me finish. Whatever the results are, whatever happens next, I'm not going anywhere. We'll figure out how to be friends, how to support each other, how to make this work even with eight hundred miles between us. Because losing you to distance is one thing, but losing you to this..." David's voice broke slightly. "I can't lose you to this."

David sat in the waiting area of the Belmont Health Clinic alongside a couple of other people, his leg bouncing with nervous energy. Patrick sat beside him, pale and quiet, occasionally glancing at the clock on the wall. 4:45 PM. They'd been waiting for fifteen minutes that felt like hours.

During those fifteen minutes, David had catalogued every detail of the clinic waiting room—the motivational posters about safe sex practices, the bowl of condoms on the reception desk, the other patients who looked just as nervous as Patrick. He'd counted the acoustic tiles on the ceiling (forty-eight), noted the number of chairs (twelve), and read the same pamphlet about HIV prevention three times without absorbing a single word.

Beside him, Patrick seemed to be holding his breath, as if exhaling might somehow make the results worse. David wanted to take his hand, wanted to offer some physical comfort, but the waiting room felt too public, too exposed. Instead, he settled for sitting close enough that their shoulders touched, a small anchor of contact in the storm of anticipation.

"Patrick O'Brien?" Carlo appeared in the doorway, a kind-faced man in his forties wearing a white coat and a gentle expression that suggested he'd done this many times before.

They followed him into a sterile office with fluorescent lighting and motivational posters about safe sex practices. Carlo sat behind his desk and opened a manila folder. David found himself studying Carlo's face for clues—was his expression sympathetic? Professional? Did he look like someone about to deliver devastating news, or just another routine appointment?

"I'm going to be direct with you, Patrick, because I find that's usually best. Your HIV antibody test came back negative."

The word hit Patrick like a physical blow. Negative. Negative meant good. Negative meant he was okay. Negative meant he was going to live.

Patrick broke down completely, sobs of relief and terror and gratitude pouring out of him all at once. Beside him, David made a sound that was half laugh, half choke, his own relief so overwhelming he had to grip the arms of his chair to keep from collapsing.

Neither of them had understood how much weight they'd been

carrying until that moment, how the fear had been sitting on their chests for twelve days, making it hard to breathe, hard to think, hard to imagine any future beyond this appointment. Now the house of cards seemed to crash down all at once, two weeks of suppressed emotion flooding out in the sterile safety of Carlo's office.

David's first instinct was to reach for Patrick, to pull him close and hold him while they both processed the magnitude of their relief. But something held him back—an awareness that this moment belonged to Patrick, that the fear and the relief were primarily his to experience. Instead, David found himself crying quietly, overwhelmed by gratitude and the sudden understanding of how close he'd come to losing someone who still meant everything to him.

Carlo watched them with the patience of someone who'd seen this reaction many times before. At least these young men were crying with relief. Too many others remained quiet when they heard the word "positive," unable to accept the reality of what that meant. He'd much prefer the sobs of relief to the deadly quiet that accompanied a death sentence.

"Take your time," Carlo said gently, pushing a box of tissues across his desk. "This is a lot to process."

When they'd finally composed themselves enough to listen, Carlo went through the standard speech about continued safe practices, about the window period, about getting tested again in six months just to be absolutely certain. Patrick nodded at all the right moments, but David could see he was barely listening. The word "negative" was echoing in his head, drowning out everything else.

"Do you have any questions?" Carlo asked, looking between them.

David found his voice first. "The window period—what exactly does that mean?"

"It means there's a small possibility that if Patrick was infected very recently, the antibodies might not have developed enough to show up on the test yet. That's why we recommend retesting in six months. But given the timeline Patrick described, and the fact that his potential exposure was several weeks ago, I'm confident these results are accurate."

Patrick spoke for the first time since hearing the results, his voice still shaky. "So I'm really okay? I'm really not going to die?"

Carlo's expression softened. "Based on this test, you don't have HIV. You're going to be fine, Patrick. But I want you to remember how this felt—the fear, the uncertainty, the relief. Let it motivate you to be more careful in the future. Safe sex isn't just about protecting yourself; it's about protecting the people you care about from having to go through what you both just experienced."

They walked out of the clinic into the late afternoon Chicago sunshine, both of them moving slowly, as if they were learning how to use their bodies again. Patrick was alive. He was going to be okay. The terror that had consumed them both for nearly two weeks was over.

As they stood on the sidewalk outside the clinic, the full weight of what they'd just been through began to settle over them. For twelve days, they'd both been living with the possibility that Patrick might be facing a death sentence. For twelve days, David had been imagining a future where he watched Patrick waste away, where their last conversations would be colored by regret and lost opportunities.

Now, suddenly, they had to readjust to the idea of a future that stretched ahead of them, uncertain but not doomed. Patrick would continue his life in Chicago, David would return to New York, and they'd both have to figure out what this experience meant for them.

David wanted so much to tell Patrick "let's make this work," to use this reprieve as a reason to try again, to argue that life was too short and too uncertain to waste time being apart. But looking at Patrick's exhausted face, seeing the way he was still trembling slightly from the emotional release, David decided it was best just to be present. They'd both had enough drama for one day, for one lifetime, with all of this.

Instead, he just put his arm around Patrick's shoulders as they walked toward Clybourn station to catch the Metra train, and for now, that was enough.

But as they rode the train back to Patrick's parents' house, David found himself thinking about the way Patrick had clung to him at the airport, about the relief in Patrick's voice when he'd called to say the results were in, about the twelve days they'd both spent terrified of losing something they'd convinced themselves they could live without.

Maybe, David thought as he watched Patrick's reflection in the train window, maybe some things were worth fighting for after all. Maybe some connections were strong enough to survive distance and uncertainty and even the fear of losing everything.

Maybe this scare had taught them both something about what really mattered.

The train pulled into Patrick's stop, and they walked in comfortable silence through the familiar suburban streets where Patrick had grown up. Neither of them spoke about what came next—David's flight back to New York tomorrow, the return to their separate lives, the question of whether this experience had changed anything fundamental between them.

But something had shifted, some wall had cracked open during those twelve days of shared fear and the overwhelming relief that followed. As they reached Patrick's parents' house, David found himself reluctant to let this moment end, reluctant to return to the careful distance they'd maintained for so long.

"Patrick," David said as they stood on the front porch. "Can I ask you something?"

Patrick turned to look at him, his green eyes still bright with unshed tears but calmer than they'd been in weeks.

"Are you happy?" David asked. "I mean, really happy. With your life, with the choices you've made, with the way things are between us?"

Patrick was quiet for a long moment, studying David's face in the porch light. "Are you asking if I'm happy we broke up?"

"I'm asking if you're happy with where we are now. Because I'm not. I haven't been for a long time." David took a deep breath, knowing he was about to cross a line they'd both been carefully avoiding. "These past two weeks, thinking I might lose you... it made me realize that I've been lying to myself about being okay with this distance, with this careful friendship we've constructed."

"David..."

"I'm not saying we should get back together. I'm not saying I have answers or solutions or that I know how to make this work. I'm just saying that I'm not happy with the way things are, and I don't think you are either."

Patrick leaned against the porch railing, suddenly looking exhausted by the weight of everything they'd been through. "What are you suggesting?"

"I don't know. Maybe we could try talking about it. Really talking, not just these careful conversations where we both pretend we're fine with being apart." David moved closer, close enough to see the freckles across Patrick's nose, the familiar pattern that he'd memorized years ago. "Maybe we could admit that we're both miserable and see if there's something we can do about it."

Patrick was quiet for so long that David began to worry he'd pushed too far, too fast. But then Patrick smiled—a real smile, the first one David had seen from him in weeks.

"You know what's funny?" Patrick said. "During the worst moments of the past two weeks, when I was lying awake at night thinking about dying, the thing that made me saddest wasn't leaving my family or my job or any of the things I thought I'd regret. It was the idea of dying without ever really trying to make things work with you."

David felt his heart stop. "Patrick..."

"I wrote you a letter," Patrick continued, his voice soft but steady. "On one of the bad nights when I was sure the results would be positive. I told you things I should have said years ago, things I should have said before we broke up. And sitting there writing it, I realized I'd been a coward. Not just about the HIV test, but about us. About what I wanted and what I was willing to fight for."

They stood there on the porch, the weight of Patrick's words settling between them like a bridge neither of them was quite ready to cross. But it was there now, this admission that they'd both been living with regret, both been questioning the choices that had led them to this careful, distant friendship.

"So what do we do?" David asked.

Patrick smiled again, and this time it reached his eyes. "I don't know. But maybe we could start by admitting that we want to figure it out."

Inside the house, they could hear Patrick's parents moving around, the familiar sounds of a family settling in for the evening. Tomorrow, David would fly back to New York and they'd both return to their separate lives. But something had fundamentally changed during those twelve days of shared fear and the overwhelming relief that followed.

For the first time in years, they both had hope that maybe, just maybe, they could find their way back to each other.

# PART
*Three*

# CHAPTER
## *Twenty-Seven*

PATRICK HAD NEVER THOUGHT MUCH about the rhythm of commuter trains until Kevin Baker started sitting in the same car.

It was Tuesday evening, sometime in the fall of 1998, when Patrick first noticed the man boarding at the new Ogilvie Transportation Center and settling into a seat three rows ahead. There was something about the way he moved—purposeful but unhurried, like someone who'd found his pace in life and wasn't interested in rushing toward anything he couldn't control.

Patrick was thirty-four now, and the Metra train had become as much a part of his daily routine as coffee in the morning or brushing his teeth before bed. He'd been making this commute between downtown Chicago and Arlington Heights for almost a decade, watching the city give way to suburbs through windows that had become as familiar as mirrors. A few years ago, he'd finally saved enough to buy a modest starter home—nothing fancy, but his own place in a quiet neighborhood adjacent to his parents. Instead of taking the familiar right turn toward his childhood home, he now took a left into his own driveway, his own front door, his own life carefully constructed away from but not too far from family.

Most days, he read manuscripts or reviewed galley proofs, using the forty-five minutes to decompress from whatever chaos had consumed him at Meridian Press. His colleague Mark Hoffman occasionally took the same train, but they rarely sat together—work friendships were one thing, but the commute home was Patrick's time to transition from his professional self back to whatever he was becoming in his carefully ordered personal life.

But something about this particular passenger caught his attention. Maybe it was the way he held his book—not like he was killing time, but like he was genuinely absorbed in whatever story had captured him. Maybe it was the fact that he seemed to be reading actual literature instead of the business magazines and newspapers that dominated most commuter reading material.

"Murakami?" Patrick found himself asking one evening in late October, when he'd moved to the seat across the aisle and caught a glimpse of the cover.

The man looked up, and Patrick was struck by his smile— warm and genuine, the kind that suggested he was actually pleased to have been interrupted. "Hard-Boiled Wonderland and the End of the World. Have you read it?"

"I have," Patrick said, settling more comfortably into his seat. "It's brilliant. Completely bizarre, but brilliant."

"Kevin Baker," the man said, extending his hand across the narrow aisle.

"Patrick O'Brien."

And just like that, Patrick had a train friend.

Kevin worked in a different department at a consulting firm downtown, something involving logistics and supply chain management that sounded impressive and complicated when he tried to explain it. He was younger than Patrick—just turning thirty that weekend, he mentioned with a grin—with an easy laugh and the kind of intellectual curiosity that made conversations stretch longer than either of them intended. He'd grown up in Wisconsin, graduated from UW-Madison, and had been living in Chicago ever since, drawn by the city's energy but still carrying that particular Midwestern practicality that Patrick recognized in himself.

When Patrick mentioned his house, Kevin's eyebrows shot up. "You own? At thirty-four? Man, I can't even imagine having that kind of money saved up. I'm still trying to figure out how people afford anything in this city."

The conversation naturally drifted toward the practical realities of their lives—rent versus mortgage, the challenges of dating in Chicago, the careful navigation required around colleagues and family when it came to personal relationships. There was a delicate dance they both recognized, the way conversations could approach certain topics without quite naming them, testing the waters before deciding how much truth was safe to share.

"So," Kevin said finally, during one of their evening train rides in November, "are you seeing anyone? Dating?" He paused, then added with the kind of casual precision that suggested he'd thought about how to phrase this: "Anyone... special?"

Patrick caught the slight emphasis, the way Kevin's eyes stayed steady on his face, and understood they were having a different conversation than the one most people would hear. "No. Not for a while, actually." He met Kevin's gaze directly. "What about you?"

"Same. It's... complicated, you know? Meeting people. Finding the right people." Kevin's smile was knowing. "Especially when you're not always sure if you're reading the signals right."

Patrick felt something relax in his chest that he hadn't realized he'd been holding tight. "Yeah. I know exactly what you mean."

With that careful acknowledgment, their friendship deepened. Not just because they were both gay—though that shared under-standing was important—but because they could finally drop the exhausting performance of heterosexual assumption that colored so many interactions. They both understood the second face they put on around the larger straight world, the constant mental editing required to navigate professional spaces, family dinners, casual conversations with acquaintances who assumed everyone was just like them.

Their train conversations became a routine. Kevin would save the seat across from Patrick, or Patrick would look for Kevin's distinctive leather messenger bag and settle nearby. They talked about books, about work, about the city and the way it changed depending on which direction you were traveling. Kevin had opinions about everything—restaurants Patrick should try, movies he shouldn't waste his time on, neighborhoods that were worth exploring on weekends.

"You know," Kevin said one evening in November, "there's a whole world beyond River North and Arlington Heights. When's the last time you actually explored Chicago?"

Patrick considered the question. "I go to the Art Institute fairly regularly."

"That doesn't count. That's work-adjacent." Kevin grinned. "I'm talking about wandering around just to see what you find. Getting lost on purpose."

"I don't really get lost on purpose," Patrick admitted.

"Of course you don't. You're the most deliberately organized person I've ever met." Kevin gestured toward Patrick's briefcase, where manuscripts were sorted by deadline and marked with color-coded tabs. "But sometimes the best discoveries happen when you're not looking for anything specific."

It was a philosophy that felt foreign to Patrick, who'd spent most of his adult life carefully managing expectations and avoiding unnecessary complications. But there was something appealing about Kevin's easy confidence, his assumption that good things would happen if you just remained open to them.

"What did you do this weekend?" Kevin asked the following Monday, as their train pulled away from the station.

"Laundry. Grocery shopping. Visited my parents." Patrick realized how boring that sounded even as he said it. "Read a manuscript that was actually quite good, which was a pleasant surprise."

"Exciting stuff," Kevin said, but his tone was gentle rather than mocking.

"What about you?"

"Went to a gallery opening in Wicker Park. Tried a new Ethiopian restaurant with some friends. Ran along the lakefront Sunday morning." Kevin stretched in his seat. "Nothing earth-shattering, but it felt like living instead of just existing, you know?"

Patrick did know, though he wasn't sure he'd ever articulated the distinction quite that way. There was something about Kevin's approach to life that made Patrick aware of how carefully he'd constructed his own routines, how much energy he spent avoiding surprises or disruptions.

By December, they'd graduated from train conversations to occasional drinks after work. Kevin knew a bar in River North that served excellent burgers and had booth seating where they could actually hear each other talk. Patrick found himself looking forward to these evenings in a way that surprised him—not just because Kevin was good company, but because he felt like himself in a way he hadn't in years.

"Can I ask you something?" Kevin said one evening in February, after they'd settled into their usual booth and ordered their usual drinks. Their friendship had evolved over the months since that careful conversation about being gay, moving beyond the relief of not having to pretend around each other into something deeper—genuine affection, shared interests, the kind of easy companionship Patrick hadn't experienced in years.

"Sure."

"Are you dating anyone? I mean, really dating. Not just..." Kevin gestured vaguely, and Patrick understood he meant not just the casual encounters or half-hearted first dates that sometimes happened in their world.

The question caught Patrick off guard, not because it was inappropriate—they'd moved well past those boundaries months ago—but because he realized he hadn't thought about dating, really dating, in longer than he cared to admit. "No. Not right now."

"When's the last time you were in a relationship? Like, a real relationship?"

Patrick took a sip of his beer, buying time to think. How did you explain that you'd spent most of your twenties measuring every potential connection against someone you couldn't have? That you'd gone on dates with perfectly nice men who left you feeling emptier than you'd felt when you were alone?

"It's been a while," he said finally.

"Why?"

"It's complicated."

Kevin studied his face with the kind of perception that made Patrick nervous. "It's always complicated with the ones that matter. But Patrick, you can't spend your whole life waiting for uncomplicated."

"I'm not waiting for anything," Patrick said, but even as he said it, he knew it wasn't entirely true.

Kevin didn't push, but Patrick could see him filing the information away, adding it to whatever mental picture he was constructing of Patrick's carefully controlled life. It should have felt intrusive, but instead it felt like someone was finally paying attention to the parts of himself Patrick had gotten used to keeping hidden.

"You know what you need?" Kevin said, finishing his beer.

"I'm afraid to ask."

"You need to come running with me. Tuesday and Thursday evenings. Nothing crazy, just a few miles along the lake."

Patrick stared at him. "I don't run."

"Of course you don't. But you could. It's good for clearing your head, and it'll give you something to do besides read manuscripts and visit your parents."

"I like reading manuscripts."

"I'm sure you do. But when's the last time you did something that made your heart race? In a good way?"

The question hit Patrick harder than Kevin probably intended. When was the last time? He couldn't remember. Somewhere along the way, he'd stopped taking risks, stopped putting himself in situations where he might feel too much or want things he couldn't have.

"I don't have running clothes," Patrick said weakly.

"We'll fix that." Kevin's grin was triumphant. "There's a sporting goods store right by the train station. We can stop tomorrow on the way home."

And that was how Patrick O'Brien, who'd spent his entire adult life avoiding unnecessary physical discomfort, found himself standing in a store full of athletic equipment, letting Kevin Baker convince him that running might be exactly what his carefully ordered life was missing.

"Trust me," Kevin said, as Patrick reluctantly tried on his first pair of running shoes. "This is going to be good for you."

Patrick looked at himself in the small mirror, noting how foreign he looked in athletic gear, how young and uncertain he seemed when stripped of his usual professional armor. For a moment, he felt like that nervous boy Kelly had dressed up for Medusa's all those years ago—someone pretending to be braver than he actually was, hoping the costume might transform him into the person he wanted to be.

The memory made him pause, wondering what had happened to Kelly. They'd kept in touch after college for a few years— Christmas cards, occasional phone calls, updates about jobs and moves and the general chaos of figuring out adult life. But then she'd moved somewhere—Portland, maybe? Or was it Seattle?— and gradually their contact had drifted into nothing. The way friendships sometimes did when geography and time conspired against the best intentions. He wondered if she was married now, if she still had that wicked laugh, if she ever thought about that night she'd dragged a terrified redhead to a gay club and acciden- tally changed his life forever.

"Okay," Patrick said, surprising himself. "Let's try it."

Kevin's smile was radiant. "That's the spirit. You're going to love it."

Patrick wasn't sure about that, but as they walked toward the train station with Patrick's new running gear in a bag slung over his shoulder, he felt something he hadn't experienced in years: anticipation. Not anxiety about what might go wrong, but genuine curiosity about what might go right.

It was a feeling that reminded him of someone he used to be, someone who'd once been brave enough to let himself be transformed by unexpected possibilities. Someone who'd once believed that the best parts of life happened when you stopped trying to control everything and let yourself fall into something beautiful and unknown.

For the first time in a long time, Patrick wondered if that person might still exist somewhere underneath all the careful layers he'd built around himself. And maybe, just maybe, Kevin Baker was exactly the kind of friend who could help him find out.

# CHAPTER
## Twenty-Eight

DAVID HAD NEVER THOUGHT success would feel so much like sleepwalking until he found himself standing on the steps of the New York Public Library at midnight, wondering how he'd gotten there.

It was November 1998, and he'd been walking aimlessly through Midtown for over an hour, his mind still buzzing from the client dinner that had stretched until nearly eleven. Another deal closed, another commission earned, another step up the carefully constructed ladder he'd been climbing since he'd first arrived in the city six years ago. The restaurant had been the kind of place where entrees cost more than most people spent on groceries in a week, and David had smiled and laughed and played his part perfectly—the charming young associate who could navigate any social situation, who understood exactly what clients wanted to hear.

But somewhere between the appetizer course and the hand-shakes in the lobby, David had felt that familiar sensation of watching himself from a distance, as if he were an actor who'd been playing the same role for so long he'd forgotten there had ever been a script. He was becoming his father—that same calculated charm, the ability to say exactly what people wanted to hear, the careful construction of success as a substitute for genuine connection. Everything his father had taught him, explicitly and by example: how to navigate rooms full of powerful people, how to make others feel important while revealing nothing real about yourself, how to build a fortress of achievement around whatever vulnerabilities might lie beneath.

It was a facade his father had perfected over decades—polished, professional, untouchable. And lately, David could see himself disappearing behind the same kind of careful performance, becoming the sort of man who closed deals and attended the right parties and said all the appropriate things while his actual self retreated further and further from view.

The library steps were empty except for a homeless man sleeping under a pile of newspapers near the base of one of the lion statues. David sat down halfway up the marble stairs, his expensive suit probably worth more than most people earned in a month, and tried to remember the last time he'd felt genuinely excited about anything.

Work was going well—better than well, actually. His portfolio had grown substantially over the past year, and there was talk of promoting him to senior associate ahead of schedule. He'd found his niche in international markets, particularly Asian investments, where his background and language skills gave him an edge over his predominantly white colleagues. The money was good, the apartment in the Village was finally starting to feel like home, and he'd even started dating someone.

Prescott Allen Winthorp Cabot II—Scott to his friends—was everything David should have wanted in a partner. Tall, classically handsome in that old-money way that spoke of generations of careful breeding, with a trust fund that meant he could afford to work at a nonprofit focused on historic preservation rather than chasing Wall Street bonuses. They'd met at a client function, where Scott had been representing a foundation interested in investing in emerging markets, and David had been immediately struck by his easy confidence and genuine interest in David's work.

Scott was the kind of man David's parents would approve of—well-educated, well-connected, the sort of person who could navigate charity galas and country club dinners with equal ease. They'd been seeing each other for three months now, nothing too serious but pleasant enough. Scott had introduced David to his circle of friends, mostly other trust fund kids who worked in art or publishing or causes that allowed them to feel good about themselves without sacrificing their comfortable lifestyles.

It was all very civilized, very adult, very much the kind of relationship David had always assumed he'd eventually have. So why did he feel like he was going through the motions?

David pulled out his phone and checked the time—12:15 AM. Scott would be at his family's place in Connecticut for the weekend, attending some cousin's engagement party that David had begged off from, claiming work obligations. Which wasn't entirely untrue—there were always work obligations in David's life. But the truth was, he'd wanted a weekend alone, a break from the careful performance of being Scott's boyfriend.

The walk from the restaurant to the library had been unconscious, his feet carrying him through the familiar grid of Manhattan streets while his mind wandered. It wasn't until he'd climbed these specific steps that David realized where he was, and why.

Patrick.

The memory hit him without warning—Patrick's face lighting up as they'd walked through the Met, the way he'd spent twenty minutes in front of a single Van Gogh while David watched him with fond amusement. That had been... God, when had that been? Eight years ago? Nine? The weekend that had felt like a beginning until it became an ending, when everything had been possible and nothing had worked out the way they'd planned.

David rarely let himself think about Patrick anymore. What was the point? They'd tried twice to make something work, and twice they'd failed. Different cities, different lives, different priorities. The HIV scare had brought them together briefly, but even that crisis had ultimately reinforced how impossible their situation was. Patrick was building a life in Chicago, and David was building one in New York, and sometimes love wasn't enough to bridge an 800-mile gap.

But sitting here on these steps, David couldn't help but remember how Patrick had looked at this place—not just at the building, but at what it represented. The possibility of discovery, the excitement of learning something new, the reverence for knowledge and beauty that David had found both charming and completely foreign to his own practical approach to life.

When was the last time David had felt that kind of wonder about anything? When had he stopped looking at the world as a place full of potential discoveries and started seeing it as a series of transactions to be completed?

A group of young people stumbled past the library, clearly drunk and laughing about something that probably wouldn't be funny in the morning. They reminded David of himself in college, though he'd never been quite that carefree. Even then, he'd been focused on building toward something, planning his next move, thinking strategically about how to get from where he was to where he wanted to be.

The problem was, he'd achieved most of what he'd wanted. The career, the money, the apartment, the sophisticated boyfriend with the ridiculous name. So why did it all feel so empty?

David's phone buzzed with a text from Scott: "Party was deadly boring. Missed you. See you Sunday night?"

David stared at the message for a long moment before typing back: "Sure. Hope you survived the cousins."

Scott's response came immediately: "Barely. They spent an hour discussing the proper way to fold napkins for the wedding. I may need therapy."

Despite himself, David smiled. Scott was funny, and kind, and genuinely interested in making the world a better place. There was nothing wrong with him, nothing that explained the distance David felt between them. Maybe that was the problem—it was all so reasonable, so sensible, so devoid of the kind of messy passion that David had once thought was essential to love.

David stood up, brushing dust from his suit pants, and started walking back toward the Village. Tomorrow he'd go for a run in the park, maybe grab brunch somewhere, spend Sunday afternoon reviewing market reports for Monday's meetings. It was a good life, a successful life, the kind of life he'd dreamed about when he first arrived in New York with a suitcase and a head full of ambition.

But as he walked through the empty streets, David found himself thinking about Patrick again. Wondering what he was doing, whether he was happy, whether he ever thought about those two perfect weeks when anything had seemed possible. David had heard through mutual college friends that Patrick was still in Chicago, still working in publishing, still single as far as anyone knew.

Still carrying that framed photo on his nightstand, maybe. Still thinking about the boy who'd gotten away.

David shook his head, forcing himself back to the present. Patrick was part of his past, a beautiful memory that belonged to a different version of himself. Now he was thirty-four, successful, building something real with someone appropriate. It was time to stop looking backward and focus on the life he was actually living.

But when he got home to his carefully curated apartment, David found himself pulling out a notebook he'd been meaning to use for work notes. Instead of quarterly projections or client strategies, he found himself writing about tonight—the dinner, the walk, the unexpected pull of memory that had led him to those library steps.

He wrote about the way the city looked at midnight, about the disconnect between success and satisfaction, about the strange ache of missing someone you'd trained yourself not to think about. It was the first time he'd written anything personal since college, and he was surprised by how good it felt to put words to feelings he'd been carrying for years.

When he finally looked up from the notebook, it was nearly two in the morning. David closed the journal and placed it on his nightstand, next to the photo of him and Scott from Scott's birthday party last month. They looked happy in the picture, David thought. Like they belonged together.

Tomorrow he'd call Scott, make plans for dinner, continue building the relationship he'd committed to. But tonight, for just a few hours, David had allowed himself to remember what it felt like to want something so much it hurt.

Some feelings, he realized, never really went away. They just learned to hide in the spaces between what you had and what you'd dreamed you might have.

And sometimes, on nights when the city felt too big and too small all at once, those feelings found their way to the surface, demanding to be acknowledged before they retreated back into the careful silence of a well-constructed life.

# CHAPTER
## Twenty-Nine

PATRICK HAD NEVER BEEN good at reading signals, but even he couldn't miss the way Kevin's eyes lingered as he handed him the towel.

The November evening had turned brutally cold during their training run, the kind of Chicago weather that made your lungs burn and your muscles seize up despite all the layers. They'd pushed through their longest distance yet—four miles in preparation for Patrick's first 5K race in December—and both were soaked with sweat despite the freezing temperature.

"Jesus, that was brutal," Kevin said as they climbed the stairs to his Lincoln Park condo, both of them breathing hard and shivering in their damp running gear. "I can't feel my fingers."

Patrick laughed, pulling off his gloves and flexing his own numb hands. "I think my tights are actually frozen to my legs. How is that even possible?"

It had become routine over the past few months—finishing their runs at Kevin's place, Patrick grabbing a quick shower before heading home to Arlington Heights. Kevin's condo was closer to the lakefront path they preferred, and he always had plenty of hot water and clean towels. It was practical, friendly, completely normal.

"Go ahead and jump in," Kevin said, heading toward his kitchen. "I'll grab us some water. Take your time—I need to cool down anyway."

Patrick peeled off his layers in Kevin's bedroom, grateful for the warmth as feeling gradually returned to his extremities. The running tights came off with some difficulty—Kevin had been right about them practically freezing to his skin—and Patrick headed toward the bathroom wrapped in one of Kevin's robes.

The hot water was pure salvation, washing away the sweat and cold and muscle fatigue. Patrick stood under the spray longer than usual, letting the heat work its way into his bones while steam filled the small bathroom. He was shampooing his hair when he heard Kevin's voice through the shower door.

"—so I was thinking we could probably bump up to five miles next week if you're feeling good about the four," Kevin was saying, his voice clear and casual. "The race is only three point one, so if we can handle five, you'll cruise through it."

Patrick rinsed the shampoo from his hair, confused by how clear Kevin's voice sounded. "That sounds good," he called back. "Though I'm still not convinced I won't collapse at mile two."

"Are you kidding? You're a natural at this. I've seen people training for months who don't have your endurance."

Patrick reached for the conditioner, still processing Kevin's voice. It sounded like he was right outside the shower, not in the bedroom where Patrick had assumed he was changing. "Kevin? Are you—"

The bathroom door opened wider, and Patrick heard Kevin moving around near the sink. Through the frosted shower door, Patrick could see Kevin's silhouette leaning against the counter, clearly having stripped out of his running gear.

"Sorry," Kevin called out, continuing their conversation as if nothing unusual was happening. "I needed to grab some ibuprofen. That last hill killed my calves."

Patrick blinked, water running into his eyes. This was... unexpected. Not inappropriate exactly—they were both men, both adults, both athletes who'd grown comfortable with the casual nudity that came with locker rooms and changing after runs. But something felt different about Kevin being in the bathroom while Patrick showered, something more intimate than their usual post-run routine.

Patrick turned to face the back wall of the shower, giving Kevin privacy while he did whatever he needed to do at the sink. But Kevin kept talking, his voice relaxed and friendly, as if sharing bathroom space during showers was something they did all the time.

"I was thinking," Kevin continued, and Patrick could hear him moving around, opening and closing what sounded like a medicine cabinet, "maybe we should think about signing up for the Turkey Trot at Thanksgiving too. It's only a 5K, so it would be good practice for December."

"Um, sure," Patrick said, focusing on rinsing the conditioner from his hair. "That sounds like a good idea."

He could see Kevin's silhouette still near the sink, not moving toward the door, just... staying. Talking. Patrick felt a flutter of something—not exactly discomfort, but awareness. Kevin was naked in the same small space, close enough that Patrick could hear every word clearly over the running water.

"Plus," Kevin added, his voice carrying a smile Patrick could hear even if he couldn't see his face, "it would give us an excuse to carb-load the night before. I make an incredible pasta carbonara."

Patrick turned off the water and reached for his towel on the hook outside the shower door, but his hand met empty air. He looked around, confused—he was sure he'd hung it right there.

"Looking for this?"

Kevin's voice was closer now, right beside the shower door. Patrick looked through the frosted glass and saw Kevin holding the towel, standing close enough that Patrick could make out more than just his silhouette. Kevin was definitely naked, definitely in no hurry to leave the bathroom, and definitely looking directly at Patrick through the shower door.

"Thanks," Patrick said, his voice slightly strangled. He opened the shower door just enough to accept the towel, trying to keep his eyes on Kevin's face. But Kevin made no effort to avert his gaze, his eyes clearly appreciating what he could see as Patrick wrapped the towel around his waist.

"No problem," Kevin said, his voice warm and just slightly lower than usual. "Take your time."

Patrick stepped out of the shower, acutely aware of Kevin's presence in the small space. Kevin was still talking—something about their training schedule for next week—but Patrick was no longer listening to the words. He was too busy trying to process the way Kevin was looking at him, the casual way Kevin displayed his own athletic body without any self-consciousness, the growing realization that this wasn't accidental or innocent.

Kevin was checking him out. Obviously, deliberately, appreciatively checking him out.

Patrick felt heat that had nothing to do with the shower climb his neck. This was flirtation. This was Kevin making his interest known in the most unmistakable way possible, and Patrick—who'd spent most of his adult life completely oblivious to romantic signals—couldn't miss it.

"I'll just..." Patrick gestured vaguely toward the door, suddenly feeling like he needed space to think.

"Of course," Kevin said, moving toward the shower with the easy confidence of someone completely comfortable in his own skin. "I'll be quick."

Patrick escaped to Kevin's bedroom, his mind racing. Kevin was attracted to him. Kevin had been attracted to him, probably for weeks or months, and Patrick had been completely clueless. All those friendly dinners, all the encouragement during their runs, all the casual touches and lingering glances that Patrick had interpreted as friendship—it had been courtship.

And Kevin was... Patrick allowed himself to really think about it for the first time. Kevin was handsome, athletic, kind, intelligent. Exactly the type of person Patrick should be interested in.

Someone available, someone present, someone who clearly found Patrick attractive and worth pursuing.

So why did the realization make Patrick feel guilty instead of flattered?

Patrick pulled on his underwear and was reaching for his jeans when Kevin's voice called from the bathroom. "Patrick? Would you maybe want to stay for dinner tonight? I could whip up something quick, and we could watch a movie or something."

The invitation hung in the air, casual on the surface but loaded with implication. Patrick knew—they both knew—that this wasn't just about dinner. This was Kevin making his move, offering Patrick the opportunity to take their friendship in a different direction.

Patrick stared at his reflection in Kevin's dresser mirror, seeing his own uncertainty written clearly on his face. Kevin was sweet, available, interested. They had chemistry, shared interests, genuine affection for each other. This should be easy. This should be exactly what Patrick needed—a chance to move forward, to stop living in the past, to build something real with someone who was actually present in his life.

But even as Patrick tried to convince himself, he felt a familiar ache in his chest. The same ache that had been his companion for over a decade, the one that reminded him every day that his heart was still eight hundred miles away with someone who probably didn't think about him anymore.

"Actually," Patrick called back, his voice carefully casual, "I should probably head home. Early morning tomorrow."

There was a pause from the bathroom, and Patrick could hear the disappointment even through the running water. "Rain check?" Kevin asked, his voice still friendly but with an edge of hurt he couldn't quite hide.

"Yeah," Patrick said, pulling on his shirt with unnecessary force. "Rain check."

Kevin emerged from the shower a few minutes later, a towel wrapped around his waist, his hair damp and his expression carefully neutral. He moved around the bedroom collecting his clothes, and Patrick couldn't help but notice the way water droplets caught the light on Kevin's shoulders, the easy strength in his movements.

Patrick should want this. Kevin was beautiful, kind, available. Everything Patrick had convinced himself he was looking for.

"Kevin," Patrick said as Kevin pulled on his underwear, "I want you to know that I... I mean, you're..." He stopped, frustrated by his inability to find the right words.

Kevin looked up, his expression hopeful and vulnerable. "Yeah?"

"You're amazing," Patrick said finally. "Really. And I'm flattered, and I... I care about you. A lot."

"I hear a 'but' coming."

Patrick ran a hand through his still-damp hair, suddenly feeling exhausted. "I'm sorry. I should have realized... I'm not very good at reading signals."

Kevin finished dressing and sat on the edge of his bed, studying Patrick's face. "Can I ask you something?"

"Sure."

"Is there someone else?"

The question was gentle but direct, and Patrick felt something crack open in his chest. "Yes and no."

"What does that mean?"

Patrick sat heavily in Kevin's desk chair, his shoulders sagging with the weight of the truth he'd been carrying for so long. "There was someone. In college. We tried to make it work a couple times, but..." He gestured helplessly. "Geography. Bad timing. Life."

"And you're still in love with him."

It wasn't a question, but Patrick nodded anyway. "I know how that sounds. Pathetic, right? Wasting my life pining for someone who's probably moved on, probably forgotten I exist."

Kevin was quiet for a moment, his expression thoughtful rather than hurt. "What's his name?"

"David."

"And where is he now?"

"New York. Wall Street. Building the kind of life that makes sense on paper." Patrick's voice was barely above a whisper. "I haven't talked to him in over a year. For all I know, he's married to some gorgeous investment banker and they have a perfect apartment overlooking Central Park."

"But you haven't tried to find out."

"What would be the point? Nothing's changed. I'm still here, he's still there, and we're both..." Patrick trailed off, realizing he didn't actually know what David was doing, who he was with, whether he ever thought about Patrick at all.

Kevin stood up and moved to sit on the arm of the chair where Patrick was sitting, close enough that Patrick could smell his soap and see the concern in his eyes. "Patrick, can I tell you something?"

"Sure."

"I've been attracted to you since the second week we started running together. Not just physically—though you're gorgeous and completely oblivious to it—but because you're kind and funny and passionate about things that matter." Kevin paused, his voice growing softer. "But even more than that, I've been fascinated by how completely unavailable you are. Not because you're playing hard to get, but because your heart is already taken by someone who isn't even here."

Patrick felt tears sting his eyes. "I'm sorry. I should have been clearer, should have told you—"

"No," Kevin interrupted gently. "You shouldn't have had to. Your availability isn't something you owe anyone, and the fact that you're loyal to someone you love—even when it's complicated— isn't a character flaw. It's actually pretty beautiful."

They sat in comfortable silence for a moment, the weight of Patrick's confession settling between them. Finally, Kevin spoke again.

"But Patrick? If you're going to spend the rest of your life loving this guy from a distance, don't you think you should at least find out if there's still something there to love?"

The words hit Patrick like a physical blow. "What do you mean?"

"I mean call him. Write to him. Show up at his door. Do something other than just... waiting for the universe to magically fix everything." Kevin's voice was gentle but insistent. "Because from where I'm sitting, it looks like you're using David as an excuse not to live your life. And that's not fair to either of you."

Patrick stared at Kevin, feeling like he'd been stripped bare in a way that had nothing to do with the shower they'd shared. "What if he doesn't want to hear from me?"

"Then at least you'll know. And you can stop wondering and start figuring out what comes next." Kevin stood up, moving toward his dresser. "But what if he does want to hear from you? What if he's been waiting for you to make the first move just like you've been waiting for him?"

Patrick felt something shift inside his chest, a possibility he'd been too scared to consider for years. What if David did think about him? What if the silence between them wasn't indifference but the same kind of fear that had kept Patrick paralyzed?

"I don't know how," Patrick admitted.

Kevin leaned forward, his expression growing serious. "Start small. Email. Phone call. Carrier pigeon. Whatever feels manageable." He paused. "But Patrick? Do something. Because life's too short to spend it loving someone in silence, and you're too good a person to waste your heart on what-ifs."

Patrick looked up to find Kevin watching him with an expression that was sad but not resentful. "I really am sorry," Patrick said.

"Don't be sorry for being honest," Kevin replied. "And don't be sorry for loving someone this much. Just... promise me you'll do something about it."

As Patrick drove home through the dark Chicago streets, Kevin's words echoed in his mind. *You're using David as an excuse not to live your life.* It was a hard truth, but Patrick couldn't deny it. For over a decade, he'd used his love for David as a shield against other possibilities, a reason to keep his heart safely locked away where it couldn't be broken again.

But maybe Kevin was right. Maybe it was time to find out if the love he'd been carrying all these years was real or just a beautiful memory he'd been too afraid to let go of.

Maybe it was time to stop waiting for someday and find out what was possible right now.

# CHAPTER
## Thirty

PATRICK HAD NEVER UNDERSTOOD why people talked about "runner's high" until his third week of training with Kevin, when something shifted and his body finally stopped fighting the rhythm his feet were trying to find.

They met Tuesday and Thursday evenings at North Avenue Beach, Kevin arriving with the easy confidence of someone who'd been doing this for years, Patrick still feeling like an imposter in his new running gear. The first few sessions had been brutal—Patrick gasping for air after half a mile while Kevin jogged in place beside him, offering encouragement and water breaks with the patience of a saint.

"You're overthinking it," Kevin had said during their second run, watching Patrick's rigid form and labored breathing. "Running isn't about perfection. It's about showing up."

"Easy for you to say," Patrick had wheezed, hands on his knees as he tried to catch his breath. "You're not dying after ten minutes."

Kevin had laughed, but not unkindly. "Give it time. Your body's just remembering how to move."

Now, three weeks later, Patrick was beginning to understand what Kevin meant. His legs had found their stride, his breathing had settled into something approaching natural, and for brief moments—usually around mile two—Patrick felt something he could only describe as freedom. The constant chatter in his mind would quiet, replaced by the simple rhythm of feet on pavement, breath in lungs, the steady progression of one step after another.

"There it is," Kevin said, grinning at Patrick as they finished their fourth mile along the lakefront path. "I can see it in your face. You're getting it."

Patrick wiped sweat from his forehead, surprised to realize he wasn't completely exhausted. "Getting what?"

"The addiction. The reason people become obsessed with this." Kevin stretched against a light post, his face flushed but relaxed. "It's not about the exercise, really. It's about the headspace."

They walked back toward their cars, cooling down in the evening air that carried the scent of lake water and the sounds of the city winding down for the night. Patrick had started looking forward to these walks almost as much as the running itself—the easy conversation, the sense of accomplishment, the way Kevin managed to draw him out without making it feel like inter-rogation.

"Can I ask you something?" Kevin said one evening, after they'd settled into their usual booth and ordered their usual drinks. Their friendship had evolved over the months since that careful conversation about being gay, moving beyond the relief of not having to pretend around each other into something deeper—genuine affection, shared interests, the kind of easy companion-ship Patrick hadn't experienced in years.

"Sure."

"How are you doing with David?" Kevin asked simply.

Patrick took a sip of his beer, feeling the familiar tightness in his chest that always accompanied thoughts of David. Ever since their conversation at Kevin's place months ago—after that awkward but enlightening evening when Kevin had made his feel-ings clear and Patrick had finally articulated why he couldn't reci-procate—David had been even more present in Patrick's mind.

Kevin had been patient, never pushing, but Patrick could sense his gentle concern.

"I keep thinking about what you said," Patrick admitted. "About how I'm using him as an excuse not to live my life."

Kevin leaned forward, his expression gentle but direct. "And?"

"And I think you're right. But I don't know how to... I don't know how to stop." Patrick fidgeted with his napkin, not meeting Kevin's eyes. "It's been so long, Kevin. What if I reach out and he doesn't want to hear from me? What if he's happy and I'm just... a complication from his past?"

"Then at least you'll know," Kevin said, echoing his words from that night at his condo. "But Patrick, what if it's the opposite? What if he's been waiting for you to make the first move just like you've been waiting for him?"

Patrick stared at his beer, thinking about the last time he'd heard David's voice, the careful distance they'd maintained in their sporadic communications. "When we talked about whether we were dating anyone, and I told you it was complicated—I meant it. David and I, we've tried twice to make something work. College, then again in our mid-twenties. Both times it fell apart because of geography, because we couldn't figure out how to build a life together when we lived eight hundred miles apart."

"But that was then," Kevin pointed out. "You're both older now, more established. Maybe the circumstances have changed."

"Or maybe we're both too set in our ways now. Maybe the window closed years ago and I've just been too stubborn to accept it."

Kevin studied Patrick's face with the kind of perception that made Patrick nervous. "You know what I think?"

"What?"

"I think you're scared that if you find out David has moved on, you'll have to actually move on too. And that terrifies you because loving David—even from a distance—has become part of who you are."

The words hit Patrick like a physical blow because they were so completely, devastatingly accurate. "Jesus, Kevin."

"I'm not trying to be cruel. I'm trying to be honest." Kevin's voice was gentle but insistent. "You're thirty-six years old, Patrick. You have a good life, a career you love, friends who care about you. But you're living like you're in some kind of holding pattern, waiting for permission to be happy."

Patrick felt tears threaten, the weight of a decade's worth of unspoken longing suddenly feeling unbearable. "What if I call him and he's married? What if he has this perfect life and I'm just... a reminder of something he'd rather forget?"

"Then you'll know," Kevin said simply. "And you can stop wondering and start figuring out what comes next. But Patrick? What if he's not married? What if he's been measuring every relationship against you the same way you've been measuring them against him?"

They sat in silence for a moment, the weight of Kevin's words settling between them. Patrick thought about David's voice, about the way he'd looked in those photos they'd taken years ago, about all the conversations they'd never had and all the chances they'd let slip away.

"I'm scared," Patrick said finally, his voice barely above a whisper.

"Of course you are. This matters too much not to be scary." Kevin reached across the table to squeeze Patrick's hand briefly. "But you know what scares me more than you getting hurt? You spending the rest of your life wondering what might have been."

Patrick looked up to find Kevin watching him with an expression of such genuine care that it made his throat tight. This was what friendship looked like, he realized—someone who loved you enough to push you toward your own happiness, even when it meant losing something for themselves.

"You really think I should contact him?"

"I think you should stop punishing yourself for loving someone this much," Kevin said. "And I think David deserves to know that you never stopped caring about him." He paused, his expression becoming slightly rueful. "I'll admit, I'm biased here. If it turns out David has moved on and doesn't want you... well, I'd like a chance to try winning your heart properly. But that's not why I'm pushing you to find out. I'm pushing you because watching someone I care about live in limbo is killing me."

As they finished their dinner and prepared to leave, Patrick felt something shift inside him that he couldn't quite name. Not resolution, exactly, but possibility. For the first time in years, the idea of reaching out to David felt less like reopening an old wound and more like... hope.

Maybe Kevin was right. Maybe it was time to find out if the love he'd been carrying all these years was real or just a beautiful memory he'd been too afraid to let go of.

Maybe it was time to stop waiting for someday and find out what was possible right now.

# CHAPTER
## Thirty-One

DAVID HAD NEVER REALIZED how performative love could be until he found himself applauding Scott's cousin's engagement announcement with the exact level of enthusiasm expected of a serious boyfriend.

They sat in the conservatory of the Winthorp family estate in Greenwich, Connecticut, surrounded by three generations of old money and older manners. Crystal champagne flutes caught the afternoon light streaming through floor-to-ceiling windows, and David smiled at all the right moments while Scott's aunt explained the intricate genealogy that made this union particularly suitable. The bride-to-be was a Cabot, naturally, and the groom's great-grandfather had been in shipping with Scott's great-grandfather, which apparently made this engagement as inevitable as the changing seasons.

"Isn't it wonderful?" Scott murmured in David's ear, his hand resting possessively on David's knee. "Emma's been waiting for Charles to propose for three years. I was beginning to think he'd lost his nerve entirely."

David made the appropriate sounds of agreement while calculating how much longer he'd have to maintain this careful facade of belonging. Scott's family had been nothing but welcoming—his mother had taken an immediate liking to David, praising his "exotic good looks" and "entrepreneurial spirit" in ways that managed to be both complimentary and subtly othering. They saw him as Scott's interesting phase, David suspected, the kind of brief rebellion that proved their son was worldly before he settled down with someone more appropriate.

If only they knew how little rebellion David actually represented. He was exactly what Scott's parents should want—successful, well-educated, financially independent, with no interest in their family money beyond the social access it provided. He could glide through formal dinners and weekend house parties with the same effortless competence he brought to client meetings, never saying anything controversial enough to cause discomfort or interesting enough to be remembered.

"David's in international markets," Scott was explaining to his uncle Harrison, a man whose greatest achievement seemed to be maintaining the family's textile investments through three decades of industrial decline. "He's been absolutely brilliant with some emerging Asian opportunities."

"How fascinating," Harrison replied with the tone of someone who found very little fascinating at all. "And where did you say you were from originally?"

"California," David answered smoothly, the same response he'd given a dozen times since arriving. Nobody ever asked which part of California, or about his family, or anything that might require him to venture beyond the careful surface he'd constructed.

That was the thing about Scott's world—they were perfectly content with surfaces, as long as those surfaces were appropriately polished. David's ethnicity was exotic enough to be interesting but not so foreign as to be threatening. His career was impressive enough to prove his worth but not so demanding as to interfere with social obligations. His background was vague enough to avoid awkward questions about class or family money.

It was all very civilized, very manageable, very empty.

Later that evening, as they drove back to the city in Scott's

Mercedes, David found himself studying Scott's profile in the dashboard light. Everything about him was precisely what David should want—intelligent, thoughtful, secure in himself and his place in the world. Scott never questioned whether he belonged anywhere, never second-guessed his choices, never seemed to struggle with the gap between what he had and what he might want.

"You were wonderful today," Scott said, reaching over to squeeze David's hand. "Mother absolutely adores you. She was telling Aunt Millicent that you're the most charming young man I've ever brought home."

"Have there been many?" David asked, curious despite himself.

Scott's laugh was slightly embarrassed. "A few. But never anyone serious. Never anyone I wanted them to meet, you know?" He glanced at David with an expression that was hopeful and vulnerable. "I think they're starting to understand that this is different. That you're different."

The weight of Scott's expectations settled over David like a heavy coat. This was what he'd wanted, wasn't it? A relationship with someone appropriate, someone who could navigate his professional world and his social aspirations with equal grace. Someone whose family wouldn't blink at his success, whose friends wouldn't question his presence at the right restaurants and the right parties.

So why did he feel like he was suffocating?

"That's good," David said, because something was expected, and Scott's smile in response was so genuinely pleased that David felt guilty for the lie.

Back at David's apartment, they fell into their usual routine—Scott showered while David checked his messages, then they made tea and settled on the couch to watch the late news. It was comfortable, domestic, exactly the kind of relationship David had always imagined he'd want. Scott fit easily into David's space, never rearranging things or making demands, content to exist parallel to David's life without disrupting it.

"I should probably head home," Scott said around eleven, but his tone suggested he was hoping to be convinced otherwise.

"You could stay," David offered, though the words felt automatic rather than desire-driven.

"Are you sure? I know you have that early meeting tomorrow."

"It's fine. Stay."

They went through the motions of preparing for bed—Scott borrowing a toothbrush, David setting an extra alarm, both of them careful not to take up too much space in David's meticulously organized bathroom. In bed, Scott curled against David's side with the easy affection of someone who assumed he was wanted, and David stared at the ceiling while Scott's breathing gradually deepened into sleep.

This was what contentment was supposed to feel like, David told himself. Stability, companionship, someone warm beside you in the dark. But lying there with Scott's arm across his chest, David felt more alone than he had in years.

When he was certain Scott was asleep, David carefully extracted himself and moved to the small desk by the window. The notebook he'd started using a few weeks ago sat beside his work papers, and David found himself opening it without consciously deciding to write.

*March 15, 1999*

*Scott's family announced Emma's engagement today. Three generations of Connecticut society celebrating the union of two bloodlines that have been intertwining since the Mayflower. Scott was so happy, so proud to be part of it all, so eager for me to understand why this mattered.*

*And I do understand. I understand that this is what his world values —continuity, appropriateness, the careful preservation of everything that has always been. I understand that I fit into this picture as Scott's exotic but acceptable choice, proof that he's modern and open-minded without being actually rebellious.*

*What I don't understand is why it all feels so hollow.*

David paused, pen hovering over the page. In the darkness beyond his window, the city hummed with its relentless energy, millions of people pursuing their own complicated dreams and desires. Somewhere out there, people were falling in love in ways that weren't careful or appropriate or sensible. Somewhere, people were taking risks that might destroy them or transform them or both.

*I keep thinking about that weekend at the library with Patrick. The way he looked at art, at books, at everything, like he was seeing magic in ordinary things. The way he made me feel like I was seeing magic too, just by being with him.*

*Scott looks at everything with appreciation, but never wonder. He sees value where he's been taught to see value, beauty where it's appropriate to see beauty. He would never spend twenty minutes in front of a single painting unless it was painted by someone whose name belonged in conversation.*

*I don't know what that says about me, that I miss someone who made me feel reckless when I have someone who makes me feel safe.*

David closed the notebook and returned to bed, sliding carefully back under the covers. Scott stirred slightly but didn't wake, his breathing resuming its steady rhythm. David lay there in the dark, listening to the sound of another person sleeping beside him, and tried to remember the last time he'd felt anything approaching passion.

Not desire—he could summon that when necessary, and Scott was undeniably attractive. But passion in the broader sense, the kind that made you want to stay up all night talking, that made ordinary moments feel electric with potential, that made you believe the future might hold surprises worth having.

*Maybe this is what growing up means,* David thought as sleep finally claimed him. *Maybe passion is what you trade for stability, wonder for security, magic for something real and lasting.*

But even as he told himself this, David couldn't shake the feeling that he was settling for something that looked like what he wanted while being completely different from what he needed.

In his dreams that night, he walked through empty museums while someone with red hair stayed always one room ahead, just out of reach, leading him toward something he could never quite catch up to.

When he woke, Scott was already gone, having left a note about an early meeting and a promise to call later. David made coffee and read the financial section while getting ready for work, the same routine he'd followed for years. But as he knotted his tie and checked his reflection in the mirror, David caught sight of the notebook on his desk and felt something stir in his chest—a small rebellion against the careful life he was building, a reminder that somewhere inside the successful investment banker lived someone who had once been brave enough to fall in love with wonder itself.

It wasn't much, but it was a start.

# CHAPTER
## Thirty-Two

DAVID HAD NEVER UNDERSTOOD self-sabotage until he found himself walking away from everything safe and reasonable toward something that could destroy him completely.

The text from Scott had come at 6:30 PM, just as David was finishing up a client report that should have been completed hours earlier. *Dinner at Daniel with the Ashfords at 8. Can you make it? They're dying to meet you properly.*

Daniel. 65th and Park. The kind of place where Scott's trust fund friends gathered to discuss their latest charitable endeavors over hundred-dollar entrees, where David would smile politely and deflect personal questions while Scott beamed with the pride of someone showing off a particularly impressive acquisition.

David stared at the text for a full minute before typing back: *Swamped with work. Rain check?*

It wasn't entirely a lie. He was behind on several projects, and the thought of spending three hours making small talk with people who saw him as Scott's exotic but appropriate choice made his skin crawl. But the truth was simpler and more damning: he couldn't face another evening of pretending to be grateful for inclusion in a world that would never truly accept him as anything more than a well-dressed outsider.

Scott's response came immediately: *Of course! Work comes first. Miss you.*

The casual understanding in Scott's reply only made David feel worse. Scott really was a good person—kind, thoughtful, completely undeserving of David's growing resentment. The problem wasn't Scott's friends or his family or his privileged background. The problem was that David felt like he was suffocating in the life he'd thought he wanted, drowning in comfort and security and all the things that should have made him happy.

By 8:45 PM, David was walking through the doors of a gym on the Lower East Side that he visited occasionally on weekend afternoons. It wasn't convenient to his apartment or his office—he had to take two trains to get there—but it served a purpose that his regular gym couldn't. The clientele was younger, more diverse, more openly appreciative of what David had to offer. On Saturday afternoons, it was cruisy but relatively tame, filled with men who worked out seriously but weren't opposed to making eye contact across the weight room.

Thursday night at 9 PM was a different animal entirely.

The gym was dimly lit, half the overhead fluorescents turned off to create pools of shadow between the equipment. The usual crowd of serious athletes had been replaced by a different demographic—younger men with lean builds and hungry eyes, older men who moved through the space with predatory confidence. David recognized the energy immediately, the electric tension of a place where working out was secondary to other activities.

*What the fuck am I doing here?* David thought as he changed into his workout clothes, but he didn't leave. Instead, he climbed onto a treadmill and started running, letting the rhythmic pounding of his feet drown out the voice in his head that was asking increasingly uncomfortable questions about his choices.

Three miles passed in a blur of sweat and self-recrimination. Around him, the gym's real purpose became increasingly obvious —conversations that lasted longer than necessary, touches that lingered, glances that promised more than friendship. David kept his eyes on the display screen in front of him, watching his heart rate climb while his mind wandered to Scott and their comfortable, passionless relationship, to his parents and their careful acceptance of his "lifestyle," to the life he'd built that looked perfect from the outside and felt empty from within.

And inevitably, to Patrick.

*Goddamnit.* David increased his pace, as if he could outrun the memory of green eyes and red hair and the way Patrick had looked at him like he was worth loving completely. It had been over a year since their last real conversation, longer since they'd seen each other, but Patrick's absence was a constant ache that David had learned to carry like a low-grade fever.

Why couldn't they make it work? The question had haunted David for years, cycling through his mind during client meetings and dinner parties and all the moments when he should have been focused on his actual life instead of the one he'd lost. They'd tried twice—really tried—and both times they'd failed because of geography, because of timing, because they'd been too scared or too practical or too fucking careful to fight for what they had.

*We didn't try hard enough,* David realized as he slowed the treadmill to a walk. *We gave up because it was hard, not because it was impossible.*

The thought hit him like a physical blow, stopping him mid-stride. They'd had love—real, transformative, once-in-a-lifetime love—and they'd let it slip away because neither of them had been brave enough to sacrifice everything else for it. And now David was trapped in a relationship with someone who would never ask him the hard questions, who would never demand that he be more than the polished version of himself he presented to the world.

Scott was safe. Scott was easy. Scott would never break David's heart because David would never give it to him completely.

And that realization made David want to destroy something.

He stalked back to the locker room, his mood darker than when he'd arrived. The space was nearly empty, just a few men changing clothes and one guy who'd been checking David out since he'd walked in—early twenties, lean build, the kind of pretty boy who probably made his living being decorative for older men with money and poor impulse control.

David stripped out of his workout clothes with unnecessary force, his movements sharp and aggressive. In the shower, he let the hot water pound against his shoulders while his mind continued its relentless cycle of frustration and self-doubt. He was thirty-four years old, successful by every metric that mattered, and he felt like he was sleepwalking through someone else's life.

The pretty boy appeared at the shower head two spaces down, making a production of soaping himself while stealing glances at David. Under normal circumstances, David would have ignored the obvious invitation. He'd learned years ago that anonymous encounters left him feeling emptier than he'd started, that sex without connection was just elaborate masturbation.

But tonight wasn't normal circumstances. Tonight, David was angry—at Scott for being too comfortable, at his parents for their conditional acceptance, at himself for building a life that felt like an expensive prison. And most of all, at Patrick for haunting him from eight hundred miles away, for being the standard against which every other relationship would always fall short.

The boy turned toward him, positioning himself so David could see everything he was offering. In the dim light of the shower room, with its dark slate walls and dramatic shadows, he looked like a fantasy made flesh—young, eager, available for whatever David needed to take the edge off his frustration.

David moved before his rational mind could stop him, closing the distance between them and grabbing the boy's waist. He gasped and let David turn him toward the wall, pressing him against the slate while hot water cascaded over both of them. For a moment, David lost himself in the pure physicality of it—the heat and steam and willing body beneath his hands.

But then reality crashed over him like cold water.

*This is exactly the bullshit that almost cost Patrick his life.*

The memory hit David with devastating clarity—Patrick's terrified voice on the phone, the HIV scare that had brought them together for one brief, shining moment before tearing them apart again. The casual encounter that had nearly destroyed the person David loved most in the world.

David pulled back like he'd been burned, his hands falling away from the boy's body. "I can't," he said, stepping backward under his own shower head.

"What?" The boy turned around, confusion and disappointment written across his pretty features. "What's wrong? Did I do something?"

"No, it's not... this isn't..." David couldn't finish the sentence, couldn't explain that he'd almost made the same stupid, reckless choice that had once threatened to steal Patrick from the world. "I'm sorry. I have to go."

He turned off the water and walked away without another word, leaving the boy standing confused and naked under the spray. In the locker room, David dressed with shaking hands, his movements jerky and uncontrolled. His reflection in the mirror looked haggard, hollow-eyed, like someone coming down from a high that had turned toxic.

*What the hell am I doing with my life?*

The question followed him out of the gym and onto the street, where the March air felt sharp enough to cut. David walked aimlessly through the Lower East Side, his gym bag slung over his shoulder, trying to process what had just happened. He'd come within seconds of throwing away everything he'd built—his relationship with Scott, his carefully constructed reputation, his health—for what? A few minutes of meaningless pleasure with a stranger whose name he didn't even know?

*Why the fuck can't I just figure it out?*

Tears stung David's eyes as he finally hailed a cab back to his apartment. Through the window, he watched the city blur past— all those lights representing other people's lives, other people's choices, other people who'd probably managed to figure out how to be happy without destroying themselves in the process.

When he got home, Scott had left a voicemail: "Hope work

went well, sweetheart. The Ashfords sent their regards—maybe next time? Love you."

David listened to the message three times, noting the genuine affection in Scott's voice, the complete absence of suspicion or hurt feelings. Scott trusted him completely, loved him as much as he was capable of loving anyone, and deserved so much better than what David was giving him.

David deleted the message and poured himself three fingers of scotch, then sat in his living room staring at nothing while the alcohol burned away the last of his adrenaline. On the side table, barely visible in the lamplight, sat the framed photo of him and Patrick from their college days—two young faces grinning at the camera like they held some wonderful secret.

*I'm thirty-four years old,* David thought, *and I'm still measuring every choice against someone I can't have.*

It was pathetic and self-destructive and completely unsustainable. But as David stared at Patrick's face in the photograph, he couldn't shake the feeling that tonight's near-disaster was a wake-up call he'd been avoiding for years.

Something had to change. He couldn't keep living in this liminal space between the life he'd built and the one he'd walked away from. He couldn't keep using Scott as a substitute for what he really wanted, and he couldn't keep sabotaging himself because he was too scared to fight for what mattered.

But what that meant in practical terms—whether it meant finally letting go of Patrick or finally fighting for him—David had no idea.

All he knew was that he couldn't keep going like this. Something had to give before he destroyed everything he'd built in pursuit of something he'd convinced himself he couldn't have.

The question was whether he'd have the courage to make the right choice when the moment came.

# CHAPTER
## Thirty-Three

PATRICK HAD ALWAYS THOUGHT his mother's Friday evening interrogations were about grocery lists and weekend plans until the day she cornered him in the kitchen and asked why he looked like he was sleepwalking through his own life.

It was a crisp Friday evening in March 1999, and Patrick sat at the familiar kitchen table where he'd done homework for twelve years, helping his mother plan the menu for his nephew's upcoming birthday party. His father was still at the office—some client crisis that would keep him late—and the house felt smaller somehow, more intimate, the way it always did when it was just Patrick and his mother alone.

"Tommy wants a Batman cake," his mother was saying, consulting the notepad where she kept track of such important details. "And your sister specifically said no nuts because of allergies, though I'm not sure if that's new or if I just forgot." She paused, glancing up at Patrick with the kind of look that suggested this conversation was about to take an unexpected turn. "Patrick, can I ask you something?"

"Sure," Patrick said, though something in her tone made him wary.

Margaret O'Brien set down her pen and studied her youngest son with the kind of focused attention that had always made Patrick feel both loved and slightly transparent. At sixty-two, she still had the sharp green eyes that Patrick had inherited, though hers held a lifetime of watching children grow up and learning to read the spaces between what they said and what they meant.

"Are you happy?" she asked simply.

The question caught Patrick completely off guard. "What do you mean?"

"I mean exactly what I said. Are you happy? Because from where I'm sitting, you look like you've been wandering through life for the past few years like you're lost." She leaned forward slightly, her voice gentle but determined. "You come here every Friday, you help with errands, you show up for every family gathering, but you look... I don't know. Like you're going through the motions."

Patrick felt something uncomfortable shift in his chest. "I'm fine, Mom. Work is good, I bought the house, I'm—"

"You're thirty-five years old and you've never brought anyone home for dinner."

The words hung in the air between them, honest and direct in the way that only mothers could manage. Patrick stared at his hands, suddenly feeling like he was twelve again and his mother had caught him in some elaborate lie.

"I know you're gay, Patrick," she continued when he didn't respond. "Your father and I have known since you were in high school. We're okay with it. More than okay—we just want you to be happy. But you never talk about dating, you never mention anyone special, and when we ask you just change the subject."

Patrick looked up to find his mother watching him with an expression of patient concern. This was the conversation he'd been avoiding for years, the one that would require him to explain why his love life was such a carefully guarded territory.

"It's not that simple," Patrick said finally.

"What's not simple about it? You're a good man, Patrick. You're kind and smart and funny when you let yourself be. Why wouldn't you be dating?"

"I am dating. Sometimes. It just... it's complicated."

His mother raised an eyebrow. "Complicated how?"

Patrick took a deep breath, realizing that after thirty-five years, his mother deserved more than evasions and half-truths. "There was someone. In college. It was serious, but it didn't work out. Geography, timing, just... life." He paused, hearing how practiced those words sounded, how many times he'd offered that same sanitized explanation. "God, I've said that so many times I almost believe it myself."

"What was his name?"

The directness of the question made Patrick smile despite himself. Of course his mother would want details. "David. David Chen. We met at the University of Chicago."

"And you loved him."

It wasn't a question, but Patrick nodded anyway. "Yeah. I did. I do."

"Present tense?"

Patrick felt heat climb his neck. "It's been over for years, Mom. We tried to make it work a couple times, but he lives in New York, I'm here, and we just... we couldn't figure out how to bridge the gap."

"So you gave up."

"We were realistic. Sometimes love isn't enough to overcome practical problems."

Margaret O'Brien studied her son with the kind of expression that suggested she was seeing him clearly for the first time in years. "And that's why you won't let yourself get serious about anyone else. Because you're still comparing them to David."

Patrick stared at her, amazed by how quickly she'd grasped what he'd been struggling to understand about himself for years. "How did you—"

"Patrick, I'm your mother. I've been watching you measure every decision against some invisible standard since you graduated college. I just never knew what that standard was." She reached across the table to take his hand. "The question is, what are you going to do about it?"

"What do you mean?"

"I mean, are you going to spend the rest of your life waiting for something that might never happen, or are you going to figure out how to be happy with the life you're actually living?"

The question hit Patrick like a physical blow. It was the same thing Kevin had been gently suggesting, the same realization that had been lurking at the edges of his consciousness for months.

"I don't know how," Patrick admitted. "I don't know how to stop loving him, and I don't know how to love someone else the same way."

"Maybe you don't have to love someone else the same way. Maybe you have to learn to love someone differently." His mother squeezed his hand. "Or maybe you need to find out once and for all if there's still something there with David."

"Mom, it's been years. He's probably moved on, found someone else—"

"Have you? Really moved on?"

Patrick was quiet for a long moment, thinking about all the men he'd dated casually, all the relationships that had ended before they really began, all the nights he'd spent staring at that framed photo on his nightstand.

"No," he said finally. "I haven't."

"Then maybe it's time to stop pretending you have."

They sat in comfortable silence for a moment, the weight of a decade's worth of unspoken truths settling between them. Patrick felt something loosen in his chest that he hadn't even realized was wound tight—the relief of finally being honest with someone who loved him enough to ask the hard questions.

"I'm scared," Patrick said quietly. "What if I reach out and he doesn't want to hear from me? What if he's happy and I'm just... a complication from his past?"

"Then at least you'll know. And you can stop wondering and start figuring out what comes next." His mother stood up and moved to the stove, where she'd been preparing dinner. "But

Patrick? I think you're braver than you give yourself credit for. You bought a house, you're building a career, you're taking care of yourself and showing up for family. Those aren't the actions of someone who's given up on life."

"They're not exactly the actions of someone who's taking risks either."

"No," she agreed, stirring something that smelled like the pot roast she'd been making since Patrick was a child. "But maybe it's time to start."

The sound of the front door opening interrupted them, followed by Patrick's father's voice calling out his usual greeting. Patrick and his mother exchanged a look of shared understanding —this conversation was between them, at least for now.

"We're in the kitchen," his mother called back, then turned to Patrick with a smile. "Think about what I said, okay? Life's too short to spend it waiting for permission to be happy."

As his father appeared in the doorway, loosening his tie and complaining about traffic, Patrick felt something shift inside him. For the first time in years, the future felt less like something that was happening to him and more like something he might have some control over.

Maybe his mother was right. Maybe it was time to stop waiting and start deciding what kind of life he actually wanted to live.

The question was whether he was brave enough to find out what that might look like.

———

Two weeks later, Patrick found himself back at his parents' kitchen table, but this time his mother's expression carried a different kind of concern.

"I need to ask you something," she said, setting down her coffee cup with the deliberate care she used when approaching delicate subjects. "About Sean."

Patrick's stomach clenched slightly. His nephew had always been one of his favorite people—sixteen years younger than

Patrick, with the same red hair and green eyes but a confidence Patrick had never possessed at that age. "What about Sean? Is he okay?"

"He's fine, physically. But Patrick..." His mother paused, choosing her words carefully. "He told his parents something last weekend. About himself. About his... preferences."

Patrick felt understanding dawn. "He came out."

"Yes." His mother's voice carried relief that Patrick had said the words she couldn't quite manage. "And while your sister and Mike are trying to be supportive, they're also terrified. They don't know anything about... today's culture, as they put it. They keep asking me what to do, and I told them they should talk to you."

Patrick almost smiled at the careful way his mother was navigating this conversation. "And what exactly did you tell them I could do?"

"Show him the ropes," his mother said with such earnest determination that Patrick did laugh out loud. "You know what it's like, what he's going through. He needs someone who understands."

"Mom, that's not really how it works. Being gay isn't like joining a club with a handbook." But even as Patrick said it, he was thinking about his own coming out process, how isolated and confused he'd felt, how much he would have valued having someone to talk to who understood. "But I'll call him."

His mother's relief was immediate and profound. "Thank you. I think... I think he could use his uncle right now."

———

Patrick called Sean that evening, and they arranged to meet for lunch the next day at a burger place near Northwestern, where Sean was finishing his undergraduate degree in music education. Patrick arrived first and was studying the menu when Sean walked in—taller than Patrick remembered, his red hair longer and slightly disheveled in that way that suggested either artistic temperament or not enough sleep.

"Uncle Patrick!" Sean's grin was immediate and genuine as he slid into the booth across from Patrick. "Thanks for calling. And thanks for not making this weird."

"Why would I make it weird?"

"I don't know. Everyone else has been acting like I told them I have some rare disease. Mom keeps asking if I'm 'sure' and if I've 'tried dating girls,' and Dad just nods a lot and changes the subject." Sean picked up a menu, though his attention was clearly on the conversation rather than food choices. "Grandma said you'd understand."

Patrick studied his nephew's face, noting the slight defensiveness beneath the casual confidence. "How are you doing? Really?"

Sean considered the question seriously. "Honestly? I'm fine. It was weird finally saying it out loud, and I'd known I was gay since I could remember, but I felt like I couldn't hide it much longer. Didn't want to, especially since Marcus and I are getting serious."

Patrick felt a smile tug at his lips. "Who's Marcus?"

The question made Sean's cheeks color slightly, but his expression softened in a way that told Patrick everything he needed to know. "He's my boyfriend."

"Ooooh," Patrick said, camping it up slightly for his nephew's benefit and enjoying the way it made Sean laugh. "I want to know everything!"

Over burgers and french fries, Sean told Patrick about Marcus —a mixed German and Vietnamese graduate student in art history, just a year older than Sean, with a dry sense of humor and an encyclopedic knowledge of obscure painters. They'd met at a coffee shop near campus, where Marcus had been working on his thesis research and Sean had been struggling with a composition assignment.

"He just started talking to me about the music I was writing," Sean said, his whole face lighting up as he spoke. "Not hitting on me, just genuinely interested in what I was working on. And he had all these insights about how visual art and music intersect that I'd never thought about before."

Patrick watched his nephew talk about Marcus with the kind of unconscious joy that came from being completely smitten, and felt something warm settle in his chest. Sean was experiencing the same kind of discovery Patrick remembered from his own early relationships—the wonder of finding someone who saw the world in a complementary way, who made you feel more like yourself rather than less.

"So," Patrick said, stealing a french fry from Sean's plate, "I have to give you the obligatory talk now."

"Uncle Patrick," Sean protested, his face going red.

"Are you two having sex?"

"Oh my God." Sean buried his face in his hands, but Patrick could see he was smiling. "Yes. Okay? Yes, we're having sex. And yes, we're being safe. And yes, we both got tested. Can we please never talk about this again?"

Patrick laughed, but his expression grew more serious. "Actually, there's something I want to tell you. About being safe, and why it matters."

Sean looked up, catching the change in Patrick's tone.

"A few years ago, I had a scare. HIV scare." Patrick watched Sean's eyes widen with alarm. "I'm fine," he added quickly. "The test came back negative. But Sean, for two weeks I thought I might be facing a death sentence because... I met this guy and that night... well, let's just say we didn't use a condom."

Sean's face had gone pale. "Uncle Patrick..."

"I'm telling you this not to scare you, but because I want you to understand something. Even someone like me, who should have known better, who was careful most of the time, almost slipped up. It only takes once." Patrick reached across the table to squeeze Sean's hand. "You're being smart, getting tested, using protection. Keep doing that. No one is worth risking your life for, no matter how much you love them."

Sean nodded solemnly, and Patrick could see the weight of the conversation settling on him. They sat in comfortable silence for a moment, the easy banter of earlier replaced by something deeper.

"Thank you," Sean said finally. "For telling me that. For treating me like an adult."

"You are an adult. And Sean? I'm proud of you. For coming out, for being honest with the family, for finding someone who makes you happy. That takes courage."

Sean's smile was radiant. "I want you to meet him. Marcus. Maybe we could all have dinner sometime?"

"I'd love that," Patrick said, and meant it completely.

As they left the restaurant, Sean threw his arm around Patrick's shoulders in a gesture that was both casual and deeply affection-ate. "Thanks, Uncle Patrick. For understanding. For not making it weird."

"Thanks for trusting me with it," Patrick replied. "And Sean? If you ever need to talk about anything—relationships, family stuff, whatever—you know you can call me, right?"

"Yeah," Sean said, his voice soft with gratitude. "I know."

He knew now.

# CHAPTER
## Thirty-Four

"SO," Scott said over his Dover sole, cutting into the fish with surgical precision, "who's Patrick?"

David's fork stopped halfway to his mouth, the carefully prepared bite of salmon suddenly feeling like sawdust on his tongue. "What?"

Scott's smile held the slightly guilty pleasure of someone who'd eaten the last cookie and was confessing to the crime. "Patrick. You've been writing about him quite a lot lately. I couldn't help myself—you leave that journal right there on your nightstand, and you've been so... distant lately."

David set down his fork, his mind racing. They were at Le Bernardin, the kind of restaurant where conversations were conducted in hushed tones and where the other diners—mostly couples celebrating anniversaries or closing business deals—wouldn't notice if the world ended at the next table. Scott had suggested dinner here to celebrate David's latest promotion, another rung up the ladder that was supposed to make him feel accomplished but instead left him feeling more empty than ever.

"You read my journal," David said quietly. It wasn't a question.

"I snooped," Scott admitted with that same sheepish expression, part apology, part defiance. "You'd been writing so much, staying up late with that notebook. I was curious." His tone carried the casual presumption of someone who assumed his transgression would be forgiven because his motives were rooted in affection rather than malice. "Sorry, but not sorry."

David stared at Scott across the pristine white tablecloth, noting the way the candlelight caught the self-satisfied gleam in his eyes. Scott wasn't angry or hurt or even particularly concerned. If anything, he seemed amused, as if he'd uncovered evidence of a harmless quirk rather than David's most private thoughts.

"And what did you find?" David asked, his voice carefully controlled.

"Old college romance, right? The one who got away?" Scott took another bite of his fish, chewing thoughtfully. "Completely normal, really. Everyone has someone they remember fondly. I'm not the jealous type, you know that. I just thought it was sweet that you still think about him sometimes."

Sweet. David felt something cold settle in his stomach as he watched Scott continue eating, completely oblivious to the magnitude of what he'd just dismissed. Patrick wasn't a fond memory or a nostalgic footnote. Patrick was the reason David had started writing in the first place, the reason he lay awake at night staring at the ceiling, the reason every relationship since college had felt like settling for something smaller than what he knew was possible.

"Scott," David said carefully, "this isn't going to work."

Scott's fork paused midway to his mouth, his expression shifting from amused to puzzled. "What isn't going to work? David, it was just a peek at a journal. I didn't mean anything by it—"

"Us," David interrupted, his voice gaining strength as the certainty crystallized inside him. "This. What we're doing. It's not going to work."

"What are you talking about?" Scott set down his fork, leaning forward with the kind of earnest attention he usually reserved for discussing grant applications. "David, you're overreacting. So I read a few pages of your private thoughts—yes, I shouldn't have, but it's not exactly grounds for—"

"It's not about the journal," David said, though even as he said it, he knew that wasn't entirely true. Scott's casual invasion of his privacy, his dismissive reduction of Patrick to "an old college romance," his complete inability to understand what he'd stumbled upon—it all crystallized everything that was wrong between them.

"Then what is it about?" Scott's voice carried the first hint of panic, as if he was finally beginning to understand that this conversation wasn't going the way he'd expected.

David looked at Scott—really looked at him—taking in the handsome, concerned face, the perfectly pressed shirt, the careful way he held himself even in crisis. Scott was everything David should want, everything his parents would approve of, everything that made sense on paper. And David felt absolutely nothing.

"I don't love you," David said simply. "I've been trying to convince myself that I could, that what we have is enough, but it's not. And you don't love me either—you love the idea of me, the way I fit into your world, the way your family approves of your exotic but appropriate choice."

Scott's face went through a series of expressions—confusion, hurt, something that might have been relief. "David, that's not— my family adores you. Mother was just saying yesterday—"

"Your mother likes that I'm successful and well-mannered and that I don't embarrass you at dinner parties," David said, surprising himself with how calm he felt. "But she doesn't know me, and neither do you. You've never asked me about my family beyond where I went to college. You've never wondered why I don't talk about growing up, or what I want beyond what I already have, or why I sometimes stare at nothing and look sad."

"I..." Scott started, then stopped, clearly realizing he had no defense.

"And I've never asked you those things either," David continued. "Because I don't want to know. I've been going through the motions of a relationship because it's what I'm supposed to want, what makes sense, what everyone expects. But I don't want to spend Sunday afternoons at your parents' house talking about proper napkin folding for the rest of my life."

Scott stared at him, his mouth slightly open. Around them, the restaurant continued its elegant pantomime—servers gliding between tables, other couples murmuring over wine, the soft clink of silverware against china. No one was paying attention to their quiet dissolution.

"So that's it?" Scott asked finally. "You're ending this because of some journal entries about a guy from college?"

"I'm ending this because I'm thirty-four years old and I've never been in love with you," David said. "And you deserve better than someone who's just pretending."

He stood up, reaching for his wallet, but Scott waved him away with a gesture that was more automatic than generous. David nodded once, a polite acknowledgment of Scott's courtesy, and walked away from the table, through the pristine dining room, past the maître d's concerned expression, and out into the cool Manhattan evening.

The walk from the restaurant to Central Park was a blur of city streets and traffic lights, David's feet carrying him north without conscious direction. He found himself at the carousel, closed for the night but still visible through the chain-link fence. In the darkness, the painted horses looked ghostly, frozen mid-gallop, their bright colors muted by streetlight and shadow.

David gripped the fence, staring at the silent carousel and thinking about all the life happening around him that he'd been walking past. Children who rode these horses on weekend afternoons, squealing with delight at the simple magic of movement and music. Couples who sat on park benches and talked about their dreams instead of their investment portfolios. People who fell in love messily, impractically, completely.

People like Patrick, who could spend twenty minutes in front of a single painting because it moved him, who saw wonder in ordinary things, who made David feel like the world was full of possibilities he'd never considered.

David turned away from the carousel and ran. Actually ran through the park, his expensive dress shoes slipping on the path, his tie flapping behind him like a flag of surrender. He ran past late-night joggers and dog walkers, past couples stealing kisses under streetlights, past all the life he'd been too careful to participate in.

By the time he reached his apartment, David was breathless and sweating, his heart pounding from more than just physical exertion. He fumbled with his keys, finally managed to unlock his door, and went straight to the phone.

He dialed Patrick's number from memory, the digits as familiar as his own name despite the years that had passed since he'd last used them. The phone rang once, twice, three times, and David realized he had no idea what he was going to say.

What did you say to someone you'd loved for over a decade? Someone you'd walked away from because it seemed impossible, because geography and timing and practical considerations had made it too hard to try?

What did you say when you finally understood that nothing else would ever be enough?

The phone rang a fourth time, and David held his breath, waiting to hear the voice that had been living in his dreams and his journal entries, hoping it wasn't too late to find out if some connections really were strong enough to survive anything.

Even the stupid decisions of two people who'd been too scared to fight for what mattered most.

# CHAPTER

## Thirty~Five

PATRICK WAS STILL SITTING at his parents' kitchen table, processing his conversation with his mother.

His father had retreated to the living room with the evening paper, and his mother was cleaning up the dinner dishes. The familiar sounds of Friday night at the O'Brien house—the gentle domestic rhythm that had remained unchanged for decades—created a cocoon of safety around Patrick as he tried to absorb everything his mother had said.

*Maybe it's time to stop pretending you have moved on.*

The phone's shrill ring cut through the quiet, and Patrick glanced at the clock on the kitchen wall. 8:30 PM. Late for a social call, early for an emergency. His mother looked up from the stove, her hands still covered in flour from the bread she was preparing for tomorrow's family dinner.

"Could you get that, sweetheart?" she asked. "My hands are..." holding up her breaded hands, finishing the sentence.

Patrick pushed back from the table and reached for the wall-mounted phone, the same avocado green model that had hung in this spot since he was in high school. "O'Brien residence."

"Patrick?"

The voice hit him like a physical blow. He gripped the phone receiver so tightly his knuckles went white, his other hand reaching for the kitchen counter to steady himself. Eight hundred miles away, David's voice sounded exactly the same—and completely different. Breathless, urgent, raw with emotion in a way Patrick had never heard before.

"David." Patrick's voice came out as barely a whisper. His mother looked up sharply from the dishes, her maternal radar immediately detecting the shift in her son's energy.

"I..." David started, then stopped. Patrick could hear city sounds in the background—distant sirens, the hum of traffic, the ambient noise of New York that never quite went silent. "I know it's been forever since we talked. I know this is probably weird, calling out of nowhere like this."

"It's not weird," Patrick said quickly, then immediately stumbled over his words. "I mean, it's unexpected, but not weird. You're actually lucky you caught me here—I don't usually answer my parents' phone anymore since I moved out."

"Moved out?" David's voice carried genuine surprise. "Wait, what do you mean?"

"I, uh..." Patrick felt heat climb his neck. "I bought a house. A few years ago. It's been so long since we've really talked, I guess I never mentioned it."

"Oh my God, Patrick, that's incredible! Congratulations!" David's excitement was immediate and genuine. "Where is it?"

"Down the block," Patrick said, then immediately started laughing at how that sounded.

David's laughter joined his across the miles. "Of course it is. Patrick O'Brien, breaking free from his childhood home by moving a whole block away."

"Hey, what's that supposed to mean?" Patrick protested, but he was still laughing.

"Nothing, nothing! It's just... so perfectly you. Close enough to help with family stuff but far enough to have your own space."

They were both laughing now, and Patrick felt something loosen in his chest that he hadn't realized was wound tight. It felt so good to laugh with David again, to fall into that easy rhythm they'd always shared. But as their laughter faded, the awkwardness crept back in, along with the weight of the question Patrick was afraid to ask.

"So," Patrick said finally, his voice quieter now. "What... I mean, why are you calling? It's been..."

"Forever," David finished. "I know."

His mother was watching him now with barely concealed interest, her hands still in the sudsy dishwater but her attention completely focused on Patrick's half of the conversation. Patrick caught her eye and mouthed "private," then gestured toward the hallway. She nodded understanding and deliberately turned back to her dishes, giving him the illusion of privacy while probably listening to every word.

"How are you?" David asked, and Patrick could hear something fragile in the question, as if the answer really mattered.

"I'm..." Patrick paused, thinking about everything that had happened in the past few hours. His conversation with Kevin about dating like someone who was already taken. His mother's gentle interrogation about why he looked lost. The growing realization that maybe it was time to stop waiting for permission to want what he wanted. "I'm okay. Different, maybe. But okay."

"Different how?"

Patrick found himself smiling despite the turmoil in his chest. This was so like David—cutting straight to the heart of things, wanting to understand rather than just make polite conversation. "I've been... I don't know. Thinking about things. About life. About what I want instead of what I think I should want."

"Yeah," David said quietly. "Yeah, I know what you mean."

They fell into silence for a moment, and Patrick could feel the weight of everything unsaid pressing down on the phone line between them. Years of careful distance, of birthday cards and Christmas emails, of lives lived parallel but separate. But underneath all of that, the same magnetic pull that had drawn them together in that crowded nightclub so many years ago.

"David," Patrick said finally, "are you okay? You sound..."

"I'm standing in my apartment in my dress clothes, having just literally run home from dinner because I needed to call you," David said in a rush. "I broke up with someone tonight. Someone I was supposed to be happy with, someone who made sense on paper, someone my family would approve of. And I realized I couldn't keep pretending anymore."

Patrick's heart started beating faster. "Pretending what?"

"That I could build a life that didn't include you in it somehow." David's voice cracked slightly. "That I could find someone else who would make me feel the way you made me feel. That I could stop measuring every relationship against those two weeks we had in college."

Patrick closed his eyes, feeling tears threaten. In the kitchen behind him, he could hear his mother quietly moving around, giving him space while probably absorbing every word of this conversation she'd been waiting years for him to have.

"I've been doing the same thing," Patrick whispered. "Exactly the same thing."

"Really?"

"Really. I was just talking to my mother about it tonight. About how I've been..." Patrick struggled for the words, his voice beginning to crack. "How I've been going through the motions of dating but never really letting anyone get close because they weren't you."

The words came out choked with emotion, and suddenly Patrick was crying—not just tears, but the kind of deep, silent sobs that come from years of suppressed longing finally finding release. Behind him, he heard his mother's instinctive step forward, her maternal need to comfort him, but then she caught herself and turned back to the sink, washing the same pan for the fourth time, her own heart breaking for her son as she gave him the space he needed for this moment.

David made a sound that was half laugh, half sob. "We're idiots."

"Complete idiots," Patrick agreed, and found himself laughing despite the tears that were now flowing freely down his cheeks.

"Patrick," David said, his voice suddenly urgent. "I don't know what this means. I don't know how to fix the geography or the timing or all the practical shit that's kept us apart. But I needed you to know that I never stopped... that I still..."

"I love you too," Patrick said quietly, finishing the sentence David couldn't quite complete. "I've never stopped loving you. Not for a single day."

The silence that followed was different—not empty or awkward, but full of recognition and relief and the terrifying excitement of finally saying the words they'd been carrying for over a decade.

"So what do we do now?" David asked finally.

Patrick glanced toward the kitchen, where his mother was still puttering around with studied casualness, and thought about her words from earlier in the evening. *Maybe it's time to stop pretending you have moved on.*

"I don't know," Patrick said honestly. "But I think we figure it out together this time. Really together."

"Yeah," David said, and Patrick could hear the smile in his voice. "Yeah, I'd like that."

They talked for another hour, about everything and nothing, about their jobs and their families and the strange paths that had led them both to this moment of finally being brave enough to admit what they'd never stopped wanting. When they finally said goodbye, it was with promises to talk again soon, to figure out when they could see each other, to stop letting fear and practicality keep them from fighting for what mattered most.

Patrick hung up the phone and stood in his parents' hallway for a long moment, feeling like the entire world had shifted on its axis. After more than an hour of conversation, the house had settled into its familiar evening rhythm—dishes put away, lights dimmed in the kitchen, the quiet murmur of his parents' voices from the living room.

When he finally made his way toward the sound of their

voices, Patrick found them in their usual spots—his father in his recliner with the remote, his mother on the couch with her reading glasses and a magazine. But she looked up the moment Patrick appeared in the doorway, and he could see in her eyes that she'd been waiting, barely containing her curiosity.

"Well?" she said simply, setting down her magazine.

His father looked between them, clearly sensing he was missing something important. "Well what?"

Patrick's mother reached over and put her hand on her husband's arm, preventing him from getting up to head to bed as he usually did around this time. "Patrick had a phone call tonight, dear. From someone very important to him."

"Oh?" His father's eyebrows rose, looking between his wife and son with growing curiosity.

Patrick felt his face flush, realizing he was about to have the conversation his mother had been gently pushing him toward for years. But looking at both of his parents—his mother's encouraging smile and his father's patient, loving expression—Patrick felt only relief. No more secrets. No more careful editing of his life.

"His name is David, Dad," Patrick said, settling into the chair across from them. "We met in college. And Mom's right—everything's complicated. But good. Really good."

His mother beamed, and even his father, despite his confusion about the details, could see the happiness radiating from his son. As Patrick began to explain—about David, about their history, about the call that might change everything—he realized this was what his mother had been waiting for. Not just for him to find love, but for him to stop hiding from it.

When Patrick finished his story, his mother gave him a warm, enveloping hug that smelled of dish soap and the perfume she'd worn since he was little. When she finally released him, they both looked over at his father, who was sitting quietly in his recliner, clearly processing everything he'd just heard—the decade-long love story that could never seem to work itself out.

His father leaned forward in his recliner and gestured for

Patrick to sit back down. His mother quietly pulled up the ottoman, positioning it close to her husband's chair.

"Let me tell you something, son," his father said, settling back with the deliberate manner of someone preparing to share something important. "About how I met your mother."

Patrick's mother blushed, but she was smiling, clearly knowing where this story was headed.

"We could never seem to be at the right place at the right time," his father continued. "Different colleges, different schedules, different ideas about what we wanted our lives to look like. I almost gave up, feeling that maybe if I was trying so hard to swim upstream, that must be God's way of telling me I needed to go another direction."

Patrick found himself leaning forward, completely absorbed, as if he were five years old and his father were telling him a bedtime story. But this was serious, life-changing stuff.

"But something happened," his father said, pausing for effect.

"And what was that?" Patrick asked, as if he didn't know the outcome, even though his mother was sitting right there.

"I realized that it was my fear of accepting I needed to meet her halfway. Accept that I was uncomfortable changing, accepting new things, places..." His father's eyes found Patrick's. "Dreams."

That last word particularly hit his son.

"I was trying so hard to work her life schedule and mine to overlap, to 'work,' as if my dreams for my future were never changing, sacrosanct. But she had hers as well. And it seemed we could never make it work. It was almost... never, now."

Patrick finally understood. His eyes filling with tears told his parents he did.

His father got up and squeezed his son's shoulder as Patrick simply looked up from the chair through watery eyes at the man who had been everything to him growing up, and still was.

"You can always have your life the way you want, follow your dreams, son. But remember, you both will make new dreams together."

And he walked to bed.

Patrick sat there for a long moment, his father's words echoing in his mind. For the first time since that terrible morning at O'Hare, he allowed himself to believe that maybe, just maybe, some love stories were strong enough to survive anything—even geography, and timing, and two people who'd spent too long being scared to meet each other halfway and dream new dreams together.

# CHAPTER
## Thirty-Six

DAVID HAD BEEN STARING at the phone for twenty minutes, Patrick's number written on a piece of paper beside it, when the knock came at his door.

It was Saturday afternoon, less than twenty-four hours since their phone conversation, and David felt like he was coming apart at the seams. The call had ended on such a hopeful note—both of them finally admitting they'd never stopped loving each other, making promises to figure out how to be together. But now David couldn't wait to talk more, to make plans, to hear Patrick's voice again, and his impatience was growing with each unanswered call. He'd barely slept, his mind racing with everything they'd said to each other, everything they'd finally admitted after more than a decade of careful distance. When he'd finally drifted off around dawn, he'd dreamed of Patrick's voice, of green eyes and red hair and the way it had felt to laugh together across the miles.

He'd tried calling Patrick's house three times that morning, letting the phone ring and ring until the answering machine picked up, but there was never an answer. Each time, David had hung up without leaving a message, unsure what to say, afraid that in the harsh light of day Patrick might have second thoughts about their late-night confessions.

Now he was considering calling Patrick's parents' house, even though the thought of explaining himself to Patrick's mother made his stomach clench with anxiety. What would he say? *Hi, Mrs. O'Brien, I'm the guy your son has been in love with for fifteen years, could you tell him I called?*

The knock at his door was firm but polite, the kind of knock that suggested whoever was on the other side wasn't going away anytime soon. David glanced at the clock—2:30 PM—and wondered who could be visiting on a Saturday afternoon. His few friends in the city usually called first, and his upstairs neighbor Mrs. Chen typically just banged on the floor when his music was too loud.

David opened the door and felt his heart stop completely.

Patrick stood in the narrow hallway of his building, looking nervous and determined and absolutely beautiful. He was wearing jeans and a simple blue sweater, his red hair slightly mussed from travel, and he was holding a small duffel bag in one hand and what appeared to be a piece of paper with David's address in the other.

"Hi," Patrick said, his voice soft and uncertain. "I hope this is okay."

"Patrick." David's voice came out as barely a whisper. "What are you... how did you...?"

"I got on a plane," Patrick said, as if this were the most natural thing in the world. "Well, several planes, actually. There was a layover in Detroit that was completely unnecessary, but it was the only flight I could get on short notice." He was talking faster now, nervous energy spilling out of him. "I barely had time to throw some clothes together. I know this is crazy, but after last night I couldn't just sit there anymore. I kept thinking about what my dad said, about meeting halfway, and I realized I've been waiting for you to come to me, or for the perfect moment, or for some sign that it was okay to want this, and I just..." He stopped, taking a shaky breath. "I decided to stop waiting."

David stared at him, unable to process what he was seeing. Patrick was here. Actually here, standing in his hallway, having flown across the country on a whim because of their phone conversation. The Patrick he knew was careful, methodical, someone who planned every decision down to the smallest detail. This spontaneous, reckless gesture felt completely unlike him and absolutely perfect at the same time.

"You flew to New York," David said slowly, still trying to make sense of it.

"I flew to New York," Patrick confirmed. "To see you. To tell you in person that I meant everything I said last night, and to find out if you meant it too."

David felt something break open in his chest, something that had been locked away for so long he'd forgotten it existed. Patrick had come to him. After all these years of missed connections and careful distance, Patrick had gotten on a plane and crossed the country because he was tired of waiting.

"I meant it," David said, his voice rough with emotion. "Every word."

Patrick's smile was radiant, transforming his nervous expression into something luminous. "Good. Because I also came to tell you that I'm tired of being careful. I'm tired of protecting myself from wanting things that might not work out. And I'm tired of loving you from eight hundred miles away."

David stepped back from the doorway, gesturing for Patrick to come in. "Get in here before my neighbors start gossiping."

Patrick laughed and stepped into David's apartment, setting down his bag and looking around with familiar eyes. The space was largely the same as he remembered from his previous visits—clean, organized, expensive in that understated way that spoke of David's success. But as his gaze swept the room, something caught his attention that he'd never seen before.

On the side table, in a simple silver frame, sat a photograph of the two of them. The sight of the frame itself made Patrick's breath catch—it looked so similar to the one he'd bought years ago at that thrift shop by the train station, the one that held their library steps photo on his nightstand back home. His most prized possession, and here was David with something almost identical. It struck him as more than coincidence, as if the gods themselves were demanding they be together.

It took Patrick a moment to place the photo—they looked so young, both grinning at the camera with the kind of unguarded happiness that came from being completely absorbed in each other.

"Where did you get this?" Patrick asked, moving closer to examine the photo.

David closed the door and leaned against it, his cheeks coloring slightly. "I've always had it."

Patrick picked up the frame, studying their faces more closely. "This is from... oh my God. Remember the day we went shopping? We got in that photo booth at the mall?"

"Old Orchard," David confirmed quietly.

"I completely forgot about that." Patrick's voice was soft with wonder. "And... you kept it? All these years?"

David moved into the room, running a hand through his hair. "I never put it out before. For all sorts of reasons. Sometimes it hurt too much to look at. Sometimes it made the loneliness worse. And when I was with Scott..." He shrugged. "It didn't seem fair to him."

"But you kept it close," Patrick said, understanding.

"I kept it close," David admitted. "I could never throw it away. It was... it was proof that we were real. That what we had actually happened."

Patrick set the frame back down carefully, his fingers tracing the edge of the silver. "I can't believe you still have this."

"Patrick, I can't believe you're here. I was just trying to work up the courage to call you again."

"Really?"

"Really. I've been staring at that phone for an hour, wondering if last night actually happened or if I dreamed the whole thing."

They stood there looking at each other across David's living room, both of them seeming to realize at the same moment that they were actually in the same space for the first time in years. The air between them felt charged, full of possibility and nervousness and the weight of everything they'd said to each other the night before.

"So," Patrick said finally, his voice soft. "What do we do now?"

David moved closer, closing the distance between them until he was standing directly in front of Patrick. "Now we stop being scared," he said, reaching up to cup Patrick's face in his hands. "Now we stop making excuses. Now we figure out how to build something together instead of apart."

Patrick leaned into David's touch, his eyes fluttering closed for a moment before opening to meet David's gaze. "I'd like that. I'd like that a lot."

"Good," David said, his thumb tracing across Patrick's cheekbone. "Because I love you, Patrick O'Brien. I've loved you for fifteen years, and I'm done pretending otherwise."

"I love you too," Patrick whispered. "And I'm done waiting for someday."

When David kissed him, it felt like coming home and setting off on an adventure all at once. Like all the years of separation and missed connections had been leading to this moment, when they were finally brave enough to stop protecting themselves from the thing they wanted most.

Outside David's window, New York continued its relentless pace, millions of people pursuing their own complicated dreams and desires. But inside his apartment, time seemed to slow down, creating space for two people who had finally learned that love wasn't about perfect timing or ideal circumstances.

Sometimes it was about getting on a plane when you were scared. Sometimes it was about opening your door to find exactly what you'd been looking for standing in your hallway, holding a piece of paper with your address and a heart full of hope.

Sometimes it was about finally being brave enough to meet each other halfway.

# PART
*Four*

# CHAPTER

## Thirty-Seven

PATRICK HAD NEVER REALIZED how many assumptions people made about your life until he tried to explain why he was dismantling it piece by piece to move eight hundred miles away for love.

The conversation with Mark happened on a Tuesday evening in April, three weeks after Patrick's impulsive flight to New York. They were in their usual booth at the River North restaurant, but everything felt different now—Patrick was glowing with the kind of happiness that made him seem like he was lit from within, while Mark studied him with the careful concern of someone watching a friend make what might be a catastrophic mistake.

"So," Mark said, cutting into his burger with surgical precision, "you're really doing this. You're really moving to New York."

"I'm really doing this," Patrick confirmed, unable to keep the smile out of his voice.

Mark set down his knife and fork, leaning forward slightly. Patrick had been dreading this conversation—not because he doubted his decision, but because he knew Mark would ask all the questions he'd already asked himself during the sleepless nights since returning from David's apartment.

"Patrick, I have to ask," Mark said gently. "Are you sure this is a good idea? I mean, just picking up and moving to New York? You've spent years building a reputation here, making connections. Are you prepared to start completely over?"

Patrick had expected this question. "I've been thinking about freelancing for a while anyway. You know how frustrated I've been with the direction Meridian's been heading. And New York is the heart of publishing—there are opportunities there that don't exist here."

"But breaking into New York publishing..." Mark shook his head. "It's a fortress, Patrick. Everyone knows everyone, and if you're not part of the inner circle, you're nobody. You'll be competing with people who went to Ivy League schools, who have family connections, who've been networking since they were in diapers."

Patrick felt a flicker of the anxiety he'd been pushing down, but David's confidence in him buoyed his response. "I have a good reputation. My work speaks for itself. And David knows people— he's been there for years, he understands how the city works."

Mark's expression grew more serious. "That's another thing. David. Don't get me wrong, he seems like a great guy from what you've told me. But Patrick... is he really worth giving up every- thing you've worked for? Your career, your family being close to your entire support system?"

The question hit Patrick harder than he'd expected, not because he doubted the answer, but because it forced him to articulate something he'd been feeling rather than thinking. "Mark, I've spent fifteen years missing him. Fifteen years wondering what might have been, measuring every relationship against two weeks we had in college. When I was with him in New York..." Patrick paused, searching for words that could capture the feeling. "It wasn't just that I remembered why I loved him. It was like I remembered who I was supposed to be."

Mark studied Patrick's face, noting the absolute certainty there. "And you think that's enough? To build a life on?"

"I think it's everything," Patrick said simply. "I think some people spend their whole lives looking for what David and I have, and most of them never find it. I found it at twenty-two, lost it because I was too scared to fight for it, and somehow got lucky enough to find it again. I'm not going to lose it a second time because I'm too comfortable to take a risk."

Mark was quiet for a long moment, then smiled—sad but genuine. "You know what? I believe you. I can see it in your face, Patrick. You look... I don't know. Like you've been holding your breath for years and can finally exhale."

"That's exactly what it feels like."

"Then I guess I can't argue with that." Mark raised his beer in a mock toast. "To new adventures and brave choices. I'll miss having you around to keep me sane, but I'm happy for you. Really happy."

As they finished their meal, both men understood without saying it that this was probably their last dinner together as regular friends. Mark was a work colleague who'd become a good friend through proximity and shared routine, but he wasn't the kind of friend who would survive eight hundred miles and completely different lives. They would exchange Christmas cards for a few years, maybe an occasional email, but the easy intimacy of their Tuesday and Thursday runs, their after-work dinners, their comfortable friendship would end when Patrick got on that plane to New York.

It was Kevin who surprised Patrick with his reaction.

They met for coffee on Saturday morning at their usual spot in Lincoln Park, the café where they'd had so many conversations about life and love and the courage required to pursue both. Patrick had been nervous about this conversation in a different way—Kevin's feelings for him had always been an undercurrent in their friendship, carefully managed but never entirely absent.

"You look different," Kevin said as soon as Patrick sat down, studying his face with the kind of attention that came from caring about someone deeply. "Happier. More... settled, somehow."

Patrick felt heat climb his neck. "I have something to tell you."

"You called David," Kevin said immediately, his face breaking into a grin. "Oh my God, you actually did it. You called him."

"I did more than call him." Patrick found himself smiling despite his nervousness. "I flew to New York. Last month. I showed up at his apartment unannounced and told him I was tired of waiting for someday."

Kevin's grin widened. "And?"

"And I'm moving to New York. In two months. We're... we're going to try to build something together. Really try this time."

Patrick had expected disappointment, maybe even hurt. What he got instead was pure joy—Kevin's face lighting up like Patrick had just told him he'd won the lottery.

"Patrick, that's incredible!" Kevin reached across the table to grab Patrick's hands. "I'm so proud of you. I know how scared you were to reach out, how much courage this took."

"You're not... upset?" Patrick asked carefully.

Kevin's expression grew more serious, but no less warm. "About you moving? About you choosing him?" He shook his head. "Patrick, I've been in love with you for three years. And you know what I've learned in those three years? That loving someone means wanting them to be happy, even when their happiness doesn't include you."

Patrick felt tears sting his eyes. "Kevin—"

"Let me finish." Kevin squeezed Patrick's hands. "You've been walking around like a ghost since I've known you, going through the motions but never really living. These past few weeks, you look alive again. Actually alive. How could I be upset about that?"

"I don't want to lose your friendship."

"You won't," Kevin said firmly. "It'll be different, obviously. Long distance, letters instead of dinners, visits instead of daily conversations. But Patrick, real friendship survives geography. And I want to be part of your life, whatever that life looks like."

Over the next two months, Kevin proved true to his word. He helped Patrick sort through his belongings, deciding what to take to New York and what to leave behind. He threw Patrick a goodbye party with their running group, complete with a cake decorated with a tiny airplane and "New York or Bust!" written in blue frosting. The night before Patrick's flight, Kevin appeared at his apartment with Chinese takeout and a bottle of wine.

"Last meal as a Chicagoan," Kevin announced, settling on Patrick's living room floor amid the boxes and suitcases that represented eight years of building a life he was now carefully dismantling.

They ate lo mein and talked about everything except the fact that Patrick was leaving, until finally Kevin set down his chopsticks and looked directly at Patrick.

"I need to say something," Kevin said. "About us, about what we had."

Patrick's stomach clenched. "Kevin, you don't have to—"

"Yes, I do." Kevin's voice was gentle but insistent. "I need you to know that loving you, even when you couldn't love me back, was still worth it. You taught me what I actually want in a relationship, what real connection feels like. And someday, when I find someone who can love me the way David loves you, I'll be ready for it because of what I learned from caring about you."

Patrick felt tears threaten. "You're going to find someone incredible. Someone who sees how amazing you are."

"Maybe. But even if I don't, I'll never regret the time we spent together. The runs, the dinners, the conversations about life and love and all the messy complications of being human. You're a good friend, Patrick O'Brien. Don't forget that when you're being all sophisticated and New York-ish."

They spent Patrick's last night in Chicago sitting on his empty living room floor, sharing memories and making promises to stay in touch that they both intended to keep.

———

The transition to New York was smoother than Patrick had dared hope, largely because David had spent weeks preparing. He'd arranged for Patrick to sublease a small office space from a literary agent friend, had introduced him to editors at three different publishing houses, had even found him his first freelance project—editing a memoir for a small press that specialized in LGBTQ+ literature.

"You don't have to take care of everything for me," Patrick said one evening in May, as they sat in David's apartment—their apartment now—surrounded by Patrick's books and the comfortable chaos of two lives being combined.

"I'm not taking care of everything," David replied, looking up from the box of Patrick's vinyl records he'd been organizing. "I'm investing in our future. I want you to succeed here, not just survive."

The first year was challenging in ways Patrick hadn't anticipated. New York publishing was indeed a fortress, full of people who'd been networking since prep school and who regarded newcomers with polite suspicion. But Patrick's work was undeniably good, and David's introductions opened doors that might have remained closed. Slowly, project by project, Patrick built a reputation as a careful, thoughtful editor who could improve a manuscript without losing the author's voice.

Kevin kept his promise about staying in touch. Letters arrived every few weeks—not emails yet, since Kevin was slow to embrace technology—filled with updates about his job, his running times, his dating life, and always questions about how Patrick was adjusting to city life. For Patrick's birthday that first year, Kevin sent a package containing a Chicago guidebook with a note: "For when you want to remember why you left."

The visits started in Patrick's second year in New York. Kevin would come for long weekends, staying in Patrick and David's guest room, marveling at their apartment and the life they'd built together. David, who'd been initially uncertain about hosting Patrick's friend who'd once been in love with him, quickly grew to genuinely like Kevin. There was no awkwardness, no residual tension—just three friends exploring the city, trying new restaurants, going to shows.

"He's good for you," David said after Kevin's first visit. "I can see why you two became such close friends."

"No weirdness about the... you know. His feelings for me?"

David smiled. "Patrick, the man drove three hours to bring you soup when you had the flu last winter, spent the entire weekend making sure you were okay, then went home without expecting anything in return. That's not someone carrying a torch. That's just a really good friend."

It was during Kevin's third visit, in Patrick's fourth year in New York, that Kevin brought someone with him.

"Patrick, David, I'd like you to meet Michael," Kevin said, his arm around a tall, dark-haired man with kind eyes and an easy smile. "My boyfriend."

The evening that followed was one of the most joyful Patrick could remember. The four of them went to a Broadway show, then to dinner at a restaurant David had discovered in the Village. Michael turned out to be a teacher from Milwaukee with a dry sense of humor that complemented Kevin's more earnest nature perfectly. Watching Kevin's face light up when Michael laughed at his jokes, seeing the easy affection between them, Patrick felt something settle in his chest that he hadn't realized was still unsettled.

"They're perfect together," Patrick said later that night, as he and David got ready for bed.

"They are. And Kevin looks so happy. Really, genuinely happy." David paused, studying Patrick's reflection in the bathroom mirror. "How does it feel? Seeing him with someone else?"

Patrick considered the question seriously. "Like everything worked out exactly the way it was supposed to. Kevin was right—he learned what he wanted from our friendship, and now he's found someone who can give it to him." He turned to face David directly. "And I learned that you can love someone as a friend without being in love with them. That's a pretty valuable lesson."

David smiled, pulling Patrick closer. "Speaking of valuable lessons, what did you learn about us? About this crazy thing we did, moving in together, building a life from scratch?"

Patrick thought about the past four years—the challenges of establishing himself professionally, the joy of discovering New York through David's eyes, the quiet satisfaction of domestic routines shared with someone who truly knew him. The fights they'd had and worked through, the lazy Sunday mornings, the way David still reached for his hand automatically when they walked down the street.

"I learned that we were right," Patrick said simply. "About everything. About love being worth the risk, about some connections being strong enough to survive anything. About the difference between settling for good enough and fighting for exactly what you want."

"Any regrets? About leaving Chicago, starting over, giving up the safe life you'd built?"

Patrick shook his head. "The only thing I regret is that it took us fifteen years to get here."

David kissed him then, soft and familiar and full of the promise of all the years ahead. Outside their window, New York hummed with its endless energy, but inside their apartment—their home—everything was exactly as it should be.

Kevin would continue to visit every year or two, sometimes with Michael, sometimes alone when work or life made it difficult for them both to travel. He and Patrick would maintain their friendship through letters that became emails, phone calls on birthdays and holidays, the kind of steady, reliable connection that proved distance really could be overcome when both people cared enough to make the effort.

And when the time came, eight years after Patrick's move to New York, when frightening symptoms began appearing and difficult conversations had to be had, Kevin would be one of the first people Patrick called. Not because he needed anything from Kevin, but because some friendships are strong enough to carry both joy and sorrow, and Kevin had earned his place in the story of Patrick's life by being exactly the kind of friend who showed up when it mattered most.

But all of that was still in the future. For now, there was just the satisfaction of choices made and risks taken, of love chosen over safety, of two people who'd finally learned that some things were worth fighting for, no matter how long the fight took.

# CHAPTER
## *Thirty-Eight*

DAVID HAD NEVER UNDERSTOOD the phrase "domestic bliss" until he found himself standing in their Upper East Side kitchen at 6:30 AM, watching Patrick make coffee with the same methodical precision he brought to everything else, humming something that might have been Vivaldi under his breath.

Eight years. Eight years since Patrick had shown up at his Village apartment with that well-traveled duffel bag and a heart full of courage, and David still felt a small thrill of disbelief every morning when he woke up to find Patrick beside him. Not visiting, not staying for a weekend, but actually living here, building a life here, choosing this—choosing them—over and over again.

"You're staring," Patrick said without turning around, his voice warm with amusement. At forty-seven, Patrick had settled into himself in ways that made David's chest tight with affection. The nervous energy of his twenties and thirties had mellowed into something steadier, more grounded. His red hair was threaded with silver now, and he wore reading glasses that he constantly misplaced, but his eyes still held that same wonder that had first captivated David across a crowded nightclub twenty-five years ago.

"I like the view," David replied, moving to wrap his arms around Patrick's waist from behind. Patrick leaned back against him automatically, their bodies fitting together with the easy intimacy of long practice.

"Flatterer," Patrick murmured, but David could hear the smile in his voice. "Coffee's almost ready."

Through the tall windows of their townhouse, the city was beginning its daily awakening—early commuters hurrying toward the subway, doormen emerging to begin their shifts, the gradual lightening of the sky that promised another perfect September day in Manhattan. David had bought the townhouse three years ago, after they'd decided that David's Village apartment was too small for the life they wanted to build together. Four stories of nineteenth-century elegance on East 78th Street, with enough space for Patrick's books, David's art collection, and the quiet routines that had become the foundation of their happiness.

"Sean called last night while you were at the gym," Patrick said, pouring coffee into two mugs—David's plain white, Patrick's the oversized blue one with "World's Best Uncle" that Sean had given him as a joke. "He and Marcus are thinking about redoing the kitchen."

David smiled at the mention of Patrick's nephew and his boyfriend, who'd been living in Patrick's Chicago house for the past five years. What had started as a temporary arrangement—Sean finishing his master's degree at Northwestern, needing a place to stay—had evolved into something more permanent when Marcus had gotten a job at the Art Institute and they'd both fallen in love with the quiet neighborhood where Patrick had grown up.

"Are they asking permission or forgiveness?" David asked, accepting his coffee and settling onto one of the kitchen stools.

"Permission, thankfully. Sean's learned not to surprise me with home improvement projects after the deck incident." Patrick's grin was fond. "They want to knock out the wall between the kitchen and dining room, make it more open concept."

"What do you think?"

Patrick considered this while adding cream to his coffee, the same thoughtful expression he wore when editing manuscripts. After moving to New York, Patrick had transitioned from Meridian Press to freelance editorial work, building a client base that included several prestigious literary agencies and small presses. The work suited him—he could set his own schedule, choose projects that genuinely interested him, and still maintain the flexibility to travel back to Chicago whenever family needed him.

"I think it's their home now," Patrick said finally. "Has been for years, really. As long as they're happy there, they should make it work for them."

David studied Patrick's face, noting the easy acceptance in his voice. There had been a time when Patrick couldn't imagine living anywhere but Chicago, when the idea of leaving his family and familiar routines had seemed impossible. But the transition to New York had been gentler than either of them had expected, helped by Patrick's growing confidence in his work and the discovery that he actually enjoyed the energy and diversity of the city.

"Any regrets?" David asked, the question coming out softer than he'd intended.

Patrick looked up from his coffee, eyebrows raised. "About what?"

"Leaving Chicago. Letting them have the house. Starting over here."

Patrick was quiet for a moment, his green eyes serious behind his reading glasses. It was a conversation they'd had variations of over the years, usually during times of transition or stress, both of them needing reassurance that the sacrifices they'd made for each other had been worth it.

"You know what I regret?" Patrick said finally. "I regret that we waited so long to try. That we spent all those years convinced it was impossible when really we were just scared." He reached across the small space between them to take David's hand. "But leaving Chicago? Moving here? Building this life with you? Never. Not for a single day."

David felt that familiar flutter of gratitude and amazement that this was his life, that Patrick had chosen to build something with him despite all the practical obstacles that had once seemed insurmountable. The move hadn't been seamless—Patrick had grieved leaving his parents, had struggled with missing family gatherings and the rhythms of Midwestern life. But he'd also discovered parts of himself that David suspected had been waiting for the right opportunity to emerge.

Patrick who knew the best Korean restaurant in their neighborhood and had learned to navigate the subway system with the confidence of a native. Patrick who'd joined a book club at the local library and had become friends with their neighbors. Patrick who'd finally, at forty-four, learned to live for himself instead of just for the expectations and needs of others.

"Besides," Patrick added with a grin, "where else am I going to find someone willing to tolerate my organizational systems and my complete inability to remember where I put my keys?"

"Speaking of which," David said, sliding Patrick's keys across the counter. "Kitchen table, under yesterday's mail."

"See? This is why we work." Patrick pocketed the keys and leaned over to kiss David's forehead. "You know all my patterns."

It was true, David reflected as Patrick moved around the kitchen, cleaning up their breakfast dishes with characteristic efficiency. After eight years of living together, they'd developed the kind of seamless domestic choreography that made their friends either envious or slightly nauseated, depending on their own relationship status. David knew that Patrick liked to read for exactly thirty minutes before falling asleep, that he always made grocery lists on the backs of envelopes, that he got irrationally cranky when the books on his bedside table weren't arranged in the order he planned to read them.

And Patrick knew that David still woke up sometimes in the middle of the night, reaching across the bed to make sure Patrick was really there. That David had framed photos of them throughout the house not because he was sentimental, but because he needed the visual reminder that this was real, that they'd actually managed to build something lasting. That David still sometimes looked at Patrick and felt the same magnetic pull he'd experienced that first night at Medusa's, as if he were falling in love all over again.

"What's your day looking like?" David asked, checking the time on his phone. He had a client breakfast at eight, followed by back-to-back meetings that would keep him downtown until early evening.

"Meeting Laura for lunch to discuss the Henderson project," Patrick said, gathering his messenger bag. "Then I need to get to the library—there's some research I want to double-check for the Morrison biography before I submit the final edit."

Laura Chen—no relation to David—was Patrick's closest friend in the city, a fellow editor who'd become something like the sister Patrick had never had. She'd taken Patrick under her wing during his early days in New York publishing, introducing him to the right people and helping him navigate the social and professional networks that kept the industry functioning.

"Don't forget dinner tonight," David said, following Patrick toward the front hallway where they kept their jackets and Patrick's ever-present messenger bag.

"Right. Your parents." Patrick's expression was carefully neutral, the same look he wore whenever David's parents were mentioned.

David's relationship with his parents had evolved significantly over the years, particularly after his father's mild heart attack three years ago had forced some long-overdue conversations about priorities and expectations. The health scare had also prompted their move from California to a comfortable apartment on the Upper West Side—officially so they could be closer to better medical facilities, but David suspected his mother's growing desire to be more involved in his life had been equally influential. The elder Chens had gradually come to accept that David's life in New York, his partnership with Patrick, and his decision to focus on personal happiness over dynastic obligations weren't temporary phases to be endured.

But "acceptance" was different from "enthusiasm," and Patrick still felt like he was being evaluated whenever they had dinner with David's parents, as if he were a job candidate whose qualifications were perpetually under review.

"They like you," David said, straightening Patrick's collar in a gesture that was both practical and affectionate. "My mother specifically asked if you were coming tonight when I spoke to her yesterday."

"She asked if I was coming, or if you were bringing me?"

"Patrick."

"I know, I know. I'm being paranoid." Patrick sighed, accepting the jacket David held out for him. "It's just... sometimes I feel like I'm still the kid from Chicago who doesn't quite understand the rules of their world."

David cupped Patrick's face in his hands, looking directly into his green eyes. "You know what world you belong in? Our world. The one we built together. Everything else is just... dinner conversation."

Patrick's smile was grateful and slightly rueful. "When did you become the wise one in this relationship?"

"I learned from the best," David said, kissing him softly. "Now go finish that biography. I'll see you tonight."

David grabbed his briefcase and headed toward the door, while Patrick climbed the stairs toward his office. At the landing, Patrick called down, "Good luck with the breakfast meeting."

"Thanks," David called back, pausing at the front door to look up at Patrick on the stairs. Even after eight years, these small moments of domestic routine still felt precious to him—the casual endearments, the way they moved around each other in their shared space, the simple fact of saying goodbye and knowing they'd see each other again that evening.

This was the life they'd built. Not perfect, not without its small frustrations and ongoing negotiations, but real and solid and theirs. After decades of yearning and separation and failed attempts to be together, they'd finally figured out how to exist in the same space, how to make room for each other's dreams and quirks and neuroses.

As David locked the door and headed toward his own day, he allowed himself a moment of pure gratitude for the improbable gift of ordinary happiness. They'd fought geography and timing and their own fears to get here, and some mornings—like this one —David could hardly believe they'd won.

If someone had told him twenty-five years ago that he'd eventually wake up every morning to Patrick making coffee in their kitchen, humming Vivaldi while reading glasses perched on his nose, David would have thought they were describing an impossible dream.

Now it was just Tuesday.

# CHAPTER
## Thirty~Nine

DEATH HAD NEVER ASKED permission before arriving, but Patrick had always assumed it would at least knock first.

The call came at 6:17 AM on a Thursday in October, jarring them both from sleep. David reached for the phone automatically, his Wall Street instincts making him assume it was some crisis in the Asian markets. But the voice on the other end was Sean's, shaky and young and completely undone.

"Uncle Patrick? You need to come home. Grandpa... he's gone."

Patrick sat up in bed, his mind struggling to process the words. His father had been fine just three days ago when they'd talked on the phone—complaining about the Cubs' season, asking when Patrick and David might visit for Christmas, making plans to finally see the renovated kitchen Sean and Marcus had been working on.

"What happened?" Patrick asked, his voice barely a whisper.

"Heart attack. Mom found him this morning when he didn't come down for coffee." Sean's voice cracked. "He was just... gone. The paramedics said it was probably instant."

Patrick felt the world tilt sideways. Beside him, David was already moving, reaching for clothes, understanding without being told that they needed to pack, to get to O'Hare, to somehow transform this impossible news into a reality they could navigate.

The next week passed in a blur of arrangements and rituals Patrick had never imagined he'd need to orchestrate. His mother, seventy-three and suddenly fragile in a way that made Patrick's chest ache, moved through the funeral preparations with the kind of determined grace that came from sixty years of managing crises. His siblings flew in from their scattered lives—his sister from Phoenix, his older brothers from their respective corners of suburban Chicago—and suddenly the house Patrick had grown up in was full of people who looked like him but felt like strangers.

David was extraordinary through it all. He navigated the complex dynamics of Patrick's extended family with diplomatic precision, making himself useful without being intrusive, offering quiet support that never demanded attention or gratitude. Patrick watched him charm his elderly aunts with stories about New York, help his nephews carry flower arrangements, sit patiently through the viewing while Patrick's mother gripped his hand and whispered memories of her husband that she needed someone to witness.

"I don't know how to do this without him," his mother said on the morning of the funeral, sitting in the kitchen where Patrick had eaten breakfast for eighteen years. She looked small and lost in her black dress, her hands wrapped around a cup of coffee that had gone cold hours ago.

"You don't have to figure it all out today," Patrick said, settling beside her at the familiar table. "We'll take it one day at a time."

"But the house, Patrick. This big empty house. And your father handled all the finances, the insurance..." She gestured helplessly at the stack of papers that had been accumulating on the counter—documents that would need to be reviewed, accounts that would need to be transferred, a lifetime of careful planning that had suddenly become Patrick's responsibility to untangle.

David appeared in the doorway with fresh coffee and the kind of quiet competence that had made him successful in business. "Mrs. O'Brien, I've worked with estate planning before. If you'd

like, I could help Patrick review the paperwork, make sure everything gets handled properly."

Patrick felt a wave of gratitude so intense it made his throat
tight. This was what partnership looked like, he realized—not just
sharing the good moments, but showing up for the impossible
ones too.

The funeral itself was a careful balance of grief and celebration,
the kind of Catholic service Patrick's father would have wanted.
The church was packed with people whose lives had been touched
by Kevin O'Brien's quiet kindness—neighbors, colleagues, the
guys from his bowling league, families whose lawns he'd mowed
when they were sick or whose driveways he'd plowed after snow-
storms. Patrick gave a eulogy that focused on his father's gentle
wisdom and terrible jokes, managing to make the congregation
laugh even as tears rolled down his cheeks.

Afterward, at the house, Patrick found himself standing in his
father's garage, surrounded by the tools and projects that had
defined so much of Kevin's retirement. Half-finished birdhouses,
carefully organized screws and nails, the workbench where he'd
spent countless hours fixing things for neighbors who couldn't
afford repair bills.

"He was a good man," David said quietly, appearing beside
Patrick in the doorway.

"The best," Patrick agreed. "I keep thinking he's going to come
around the corner asking if we want sandwiches or telling us
about some bird he saw in the backyard." He paused, looking at
David with eyes that were red-rimmed but grateful. "Thank you.
For being here, for helping with everything. I know this isn't how
you wanted to spend your week."

David turned to face him fully. "Patrick, there's nowhere else I
would want to be. This is your family, which makes it my family
too. We're in this together, remember?"

They flew back to New York the following Sunday, both of
them emotionally drained but relieved to return to their own
routines. Patrick threw himself into work with unusual intensity,
editing manuscripts late into the night as if staying busy could

somehow fill the space his father's absence had carved out. David gave him room to grieve while maintaining the small rituals that kept their life together stable—morning coffee, evening check-ins, the quiet presence that reminded Patrick he wasn't alone.

It was exactly eight weeks later when David's phone rang at 2 AM.

Patrick woke to the sound of David's sharp intake of breath, the kind of sound that meant bad news traveling across time zones. David was speaking in Mandarin, his voice tense and urgent in ways Patrick had rarely heard. When David finally hung up, he sat on the edge of the bed with his head in his hands.

"My father," David said without looking up. "Massive stroke. He's... they don't think he's going to wake up."

Patrick felt something cold settle in his stomach. Not again. Not so soon. But death, as he was learning, didn't respect timing or fairness or the human need for recovery between tragedies.

This time, it was Patrick's turn to be strong. He called the hospital while David sat in stunned silence, helped coordinate with David's mother who was already at his father's bedside. The stroke had been massive and sudden—David's father had collapsed in their Upper West Side apartment while getting ready for bed, and by the time the paramedics arrived, the damage was already done.

They took a taxi to Mount Sinai, where David's mother sat in the ICU waiting room looking smaller and more fragile than Patrick had ever seen her. She stood when she saw David, and for the first time since Patrick had known her, she seemed to forget her careful composure, clinging to her son with the desperate grip of someone watching her world collapse.

"The doctors say there's no brain activity," she whispered against David's shoulder. "They're keeping him on machines, but..." She couldn't finish the sentence.

Patrick stayed in the background, offering quiet support while David and his mother made the impossible decisions that followed. Unlike the sudden shock of Patrick's father's heart attack, this was a slow goodbye, three days of sitting beside a hospital bed, holding hands that couldn't squeeze back, saying words to someone who couldn't hear them.

"I never told him I was happy," David said during one of their long vigils. "All those dinners since they moved here, all those conversations about my career and my choices, and I never just told him that I was happy. That despite everything he worried about, I'd found what I was looking for."

"He knew," Patrick said, squeezing David's hand. "Parents always know, even when we don't say it out loud."

David's father died on a Tuesday evening, surrounded by family, the machines finally turned off after they'd all had a chance to say goodbye. The funeral was held at a Buddhist temple in Chinatown, conducted in a mixture of Mandarin and English that left Patrick feeling like an observer at the edges of David's heritage. But he stayed close, offering the same quiet support David had given him, helping David's mother navigate the receiving line and managing the logistics that grief made impossible to handle alone.

Mrs. Chen, elegant even in her devastation, gripped Patrick's hands during the reception. "Thank you for taking care of my son," she said in accented English. "Richard worried about David being alone in New York. I will tell him David has family now."

It wasn't until they were back in their own home, surrounded by their own things, that the full weight of what they'd been through finally hit them. Two fathers gone in two months. Two families looking to them for guidance and support. Two estates to manage, two sets of grief to navigate, two futures that had suddenly become their responsibility to help shape.

"How are we supposed to do this?" Patrick asked one evening in December, surrounded by stacks of legal documents and insurance forms that covered their dining room table like evidence of lives that had ended too soon.

David looked up from the probate paperwork he'd been reviewing, his eyes tired but determined. "One day at a time," he said, echoing Patrick's words to his mother months earlier. "We figure it out together."

But the stress was taking its toll on both of them in ways they couldn't have anticipated. Patrick found himself forgetting small things—appointments, where he'd put his reading glasses, whether he'd already told David something—lapses he attributed to grief and exhaustion. David, consumed with managing his father's more complex financial affairs and helping his mother adjust to widowhood, didn't notice the small slips, the moments when Patrick seemed momentarily confused or repeated himself.

They were too busy grieving, too focused on supporting their families, too overwhelmed by the sudden weight of responsibility to recognize that something else might be changing. Death had arrived without warning twice in two months, reshaping their world in ways they were still learning to understand.

Neither of them suspected it might not be finished with them yet.

# CHAPTER
## *Forty*

DAVID HAD ALWAYS BEEN the kind of person who noticed patterns before he understood what they meant, but he'd never wished so desperately to be wrong about what he was seeing.

It started with the keys. Patrick had always been absent-minded about keys—it was one of their running jokes, the way David could find them under mail or between couch cushions while Patrick searched frantically. But by spring, six months after David's father's funeral, Patrick was losing his keys almost daily. Not misplacing them in the usual spots, but putting them in completely illogical places: the refrigerator, inside a book, once memorably in the bathroom medicine cabinet.

"Stress," Patrick said with a rueful laugh when David found them in the kitchen junk drawer for the third time that week. "I'm still not sleeping well. My brain feels like it's made of cotton half the time."

David wanted to believe it was stress. God, how he wanted to believe it. They'd been through hell over the past year—two deaths, two estates to settle, the emotional exhaustion of supporting their grieving mothers while managing their own grief.

Anyone would be scattered, forgetful, operating below their usual sharpness.

But then there were other things.

Patrick forgot Laura's birthday in May, something he'd never done in the eight years they'd been friends. When David gently reminded him the night before, Patrick looked genuinely shocked, as if the information was completely new. He rushed out to buy a gift, flustered and apologetic, but David could see something confused and slightly frightened in his eyes.

In June, Patrick got lost coming home from the library. The library he'd been visiting twice a week for five years, in a neighborhood he knew as well as his childhood home. He called David from a coffee shop six blocks away, his voice shaky with embarrassment and something that might have been panic.

"I'm being ridiculous," Patrick said when David arrived to walk him home. "I was thinking about the manuscript I'm editing, not paying attention to where I was going. Just got turned around."

But David noticed how Patrick gripped his arm as they walked, how he seemed to be memorizing their route with unusual concentration. That night, Patrick was quieter than usual over dinner, picking at his food and staring at nothing with an expression David couldn't read.

The worst incident came in July. David returned from a three-day business trip to find their kitchen in chaos—flour everywhere, mixing bowls scattered across the counter, the oven still warm. Patrick was sitting at the kitchen table looking dazed and frustrated, surrounded by what appeared to be the remnants of several failed baking attempts.

"I wanted to surprise you," Patrick said, his voice small and defeated. "I was going to make that chocolate cake you love, the one from your mother's recipe. But I kept... I couldn't remember the measurements. And then I couldn't find where I put the recipe, and I started over but I forgot I'd already put the flour in..." He gestured helplessly at the mess. "I've made that cake a dozen times, David. Why couldn't I remember how to make it?"

David sat down beside Patrick, reaching for his hands. They

were shaking slightly, and Patrick's eyes held a confusion that made David's chest tight with something approaching fear.

"It's okay," David said softly. "We'll clean this up together. And maybe... maybe we should think about seeing someone. Just to check in, make sure the stress isn't affecting your health."

"You think something's wrong with me." It wasn't a question, and Patrick's voice was so quiet David almost missed it.

"I think we've been through a lot this year, and I want to make sure you're okay. That we're both okay." David squeezed Patrick's hands. "There's no shame in asking for help."

Patrick was quiet for a long moment, staring at their joined hands. When he finally looked up, David saw something in his eyes that broke his heart—not just confusion, but the dawning awareness that something was indeed wrong, something that couldn't be explained away by grief or stress or being distracted.

"I've been scared," Patrick whispered. "Not just about forgetting things, but about... about losing myself. About becoming someone you don't recognize."

David felt tears sting his eyes. "Patrick, no matter what happens, no matter what we find out, you're not going to lose me. We're going to figure this out together, okay?"

But even as he said the words, David felt a cold fear settling in his chest. Because he'd started noticing other things too—the way Patrick sometimes paused mid-sentence, searching for words that had always come easily. How he'd started writing everything down in multiple notebooks, as if he didn't trust his memory to hold onto important information. The way he sometimes looked at David with a flicker of uncertainty, as if he was trying to place him in context.

And then there were the moments when Patrick seemed completely himself—editing with his usual precision, laughing at David's jokes, engaging in the same thoughtful conversations they'd always shared. Those moments made David want to believe that everything was fine, that his fears were unfounded, that love could somehow protect them from the unthinkable.

But the pattern was there, undeniable and growing clearer with each incident. Something was happening to Patrick, something that went deeper than stress or grief or the normal forgetfulness that came with age. Something that was quietly, steadily stealing pieces of the man David loved.

That night, after they'd cleaned the kitchen together, David lay awake listening to Patrick sleep beside him. In the darkness, he allowed himself to acknowledge what he'd been trying not to think about—that the geography and timing and external obstacles they'd spent decades overcoming might have been the easy part.

This new challenge felt different. Bigger. Like something that couldn't be solved with plane tickets or job changes or the stubborn determination that had finally brought them together.

But as Patrick shifted closer in his sleep, his hand finding David's across the space between them, David made a silent promise. Whatever this was, whatever they were facing, they would face it together. He'd waited too long to find Patrick to lose him now—not to distance, not to circumstance, and not to whatever was quietly reshaping his mind.

Even if he had no idea how to fight an enemy he couldn't see, couldn't reason with, couldn't charm or negotiate or buy his way out of.

All he could do was love Patrick through it, and hope that would be enough.

# CHAPTER
## Forty-One

PATRICK HAD BEEN STARING at his laptop screen for twenty minutes, the AltaVista search results offering nothing but frustration. Kelly Campbell. The search returned dozens of results—academic papers, business listings, people who were clearly too old or too young or lived in places Kelly had never mentioned. He'd already tried Lycos with similar results.

"What are you looking for?" David asked gently, settling beside Patrick on their living room sofa with two cups of coffee.

"Kelly," Patrick said, his voice thick with emotion. "I keep thinking about her. About that night she dragged me to Medusa's. If it wasn't for her..." He gestured helplessly at the screen. "All I have is her name and that she moved west somewhere. The alumni directory just says 'Portland, OR' as her last known address from 1986."

David set down the coffee and looked at the laptop screen, noting the careful way Patrick was clicking through search results, studying each entry with desperate concentration. This was one of the hardest parts of the diagnosis—Patrick's growing awareness that time was limited, that connections he'd taken for granted might be lost forever.

"Tell me about her again," David said, though he remembered Kelly perfectly well from that first night at Melrose diner—the fierce friend who'd grilled him like a protective older sister, making sure he was worthy of Patrick's trust.

Patrick's face softened as he closed the laptop. "She was fearless. Completely, utterly fearless. She had this laugh that could fill a room, and she never let anyone—including me—get away with hiding from life." He paused, smiling at some memory. "She used to say I was too careful, that I'd organize my way out of every adventure if she didn't stop me."

"I remember her being pretty fierce that night at the diner," David said with a smile. "She made it very clear that if I hurt you, she'd make me regret it."

"She was. And I lost touch with her like an idiot. Christmas cards for a few years after college, then... nothing. All I know is she moved west for a job." Patrick's voice carried the particular frustration that came with memory gaps—not the disease yet, just the normal erosion of time and distance. "I want to find her, David. I want to tell her about us, about how that night changed everything. I want to thank her."

David studied Patrick's face, noting the urgency there, the need to close loops while he still could. "Let's try a different search engine. Yahoo! sometimes finds things the others miss."

Patrick navigated to Yahoo! and typed in "Kelly Campbell Portland" with little hope. The first page of results was the usual mix of irrelevant entries, but one caught his eye: "Kelly's Page!" with a GeoCities URL.

"Worth a try," Patrick muttered, clicking on the link to geocities.com/SunsetStrip/Cafe/4392.

The page that loaded made both men burst into laughter despite Patrick's anxiety. Against a background of animated rainbows and spinning stars, "Welcome to Kelly's Page!" blazed across the top in glittery Comic Sans font. Multiple animated GIFs dotted the page—dancing babies, a cartoon cat chasing its tail, and rotating "UNDER CONSTRUCTION" signs. At the bottom, a visitor counter proudly announced: "You are visitor #32!"

"Oh my God," Patrick wheezed, tears streaming down his face from laughing. "This is either Kelly or someone with exactly her sense of humor."

The page was clearly a relic from the late '90s, with dead links to "My Photos" and "Cool Links" that probably hadn't worked in years. But there, in bright purple text, was an email address:

kellycampbell23@hotmail.com

"It could be a completely different Kelly Campbell," David warned, though he was still chuckling at the dancing babies.

"Only one way to find out," Patrick said, opening his email.

He stared at the blank message for a long moment, then began typing:

```
From: pobi1@yahoo.com
To: kellycampbell23@hotmail.com

Subject: Message from your past (if
you're the right Kelly)

Dear Kelly,

I know this is a long shot, but I'm
looking for Kelly Campbell who went
to University of Chicago and
graduated in 1986. If this is you,
you probably remember dragging a
terrified redhead named Patrick
O'Brien to a gay club called
Medusa's one February night and
changing his entire life.

If this isn't you, I apologize for
the random email and hope you have
a wonderful day.

If this IS you, I have a lot to
catch up on and a very big thank
you to give.

Hope you're well, Patrick O'Brien
```

. . .

He hit send before he could second-guess himself, then closed the laptop with a sigh.

"Now what?" David asked.

"Now we wait. And probably never hear anything back because that email address is probably as dead as those dancing babies."

Three weeks passed. Patrick had completely forgotten about the GeoCities site, his attention consumed by adjusting to his diagnosis and the early symptoms that seemed to worsen whenever he was stressed. He was editing a manuscript when his email chimed with a new message from her.

From: kellycampbell23@hotmail.com
To: pobi1@yahoo.com

Subject: RE: Message from your past
(OH MY GOD YES)

PATRICK MICHAEL O'BRIEN!

I am SOBBING at my desk right now!
Of course it's me! I can't believe
you found my embarrassing old
website—I made that thing in 1997
and completely forgot it existed.
James (my husband) is always making
fun of me for being "uncool mom"
about technology, and apparently
he's right because I barely
remember how to check this old
email account.

You found your David! Please tell
me you found your David from that
night! The beautiful boy who
couldn't take his eyes off you
while you were busy having a panic
attack about the eyeliner?

```
I have SO MUCH to tell you. Married
8 years (James Morrison—he's a
photographer), two kids who think
I'm mortifyingly embarrassing,
living in Portland doing
environmental justice work because
someone has to save the world from
corporate idiots.

CALL ME. Seriously. My number is
503-595-7892. I want to hear
everything immediately.

Still proud of my makeover skills,
Kelly

P.S. - Please tell me you still
organize your books by subject and
publication date. Some things
should never change.
```

Patrick read the email three times before the words fully sank in, then let out a whoop of joy that brought David running from the kitchen.

"She remembered," Patrick said, his voice breaking with emotion. "She remembered everything."

The phone call lasted three hours. David listened from the kitchen as Patrick's voice grew animated in ways he hadn't heard since before the diagnosis, describing their life together, their townhouse, his freelance work. Kelly, for her part, filled Patrick in on eighteen years of adventures—environmental protests, art gallery openings, raising children who inherited her fearlessness and her husband's artistic eye.

When Patrick finally told her about the Alzheimer's, the line went quiet for a long moment.

"Oh, sweetheart," Kelly said finally, her voice thick with tears. "I'm so sorry. How are you doing? How is David doing?"

"We're taking it one day at a time," Patrick said, unconsciously echoing words David had spoken to his own mother years before. "Some days are better than others. But Kelly, I needed to find you because... because I wanted to make sure someone knew. Someone who was there at the beginning."

"Patrick Michael O'Brien," Kelly said, her voice fierce with the same determination that had dragged him to Medusa's decades earlier, "you listen to me. You didn't just find love that night. You found yourself. And no disease, no matter how cruel, can take that away from the people who love you."

They talked for another hour, making plans for Kelly to visit New York in the spring, sharing photos via email, reconnecting across the decades as if no time had passed at all.

After Patrick hung up, he sat quietly for a long moment, then looked up at David with tears in his eyes.

"She said something that I keep thinking about," Patrick said. "She said I didn't just find love that night—I found myself. And that you can't take that away from people."

David moved to sit beside him, pulling Patrick close. "She's right. You became who you were always meant to be. The disease might change things, but it can't change who you are at your core."

"And who am I at my core?"

David smiled, pressing a kiss to Patrick's temple. "You're the bravest person I know. You're the man who got on a plane because he was tired of waiting for someday. You're the person Kelly saw potential in twenty-five years ago, and the person I fell in love with at first sight."

That spring, Kelly and James came to New York for a long weekend. David watched from the kitchen as Kelly embraced Patrick like he was something precious she'd thought she'd lost forever. She was exactly as Patrick had described and exactly as David remembered from that long-ago night at Melrose—fearless and funny and completely unafraid of the changes the disease had brought to Patrick's speech and memory.

"David Chen!" Kelly said, turning to embrace him as well. "Look at you! Still as gorgeous as ever. I told James you had cheek-bones that could cut glass."

David found himself laughing despite the emotional weight of the reunion. "It's so good to see you again, Kelly. Thank you for coming."

"Are you kidding? I've been waiting years to see what you two built together."

She told stories about college that made Patrick laugh until his sides hurt, showed photos of her children that made him cry with joy, and spent an entire afternoon helping him organize his office because "some things never change, and organization is good for the soul."

On their last night, as they sat in the townhouse living room surrounded by the comfortable detritus of a perfect weekend, Kelly looked around at the life Patrick and David had built and smiled with deep satisfaction.

"You know what I love most about this?" she said, gesturing at the bookshelves and photographs and general evidence of a well-lived life. "It's exactly what you would have chosen if you'd been brave enough to choose it at twenty-two."

"I wasn't brave at twenty-two," Patrick said.

"No," Kelly agreed. "But you were willing to let me push you toward brave. And that was enough."

When they said goodbye at JFK, Kelly held Patrick tight and whispered something in his ear that made him smile through his tears. Later, on the drive home, Patrick told David what she'd said:

"She told me that night at Medusa's wasn't the beginning of our love story. It was just the moment I stopped being afraid of it."

David reached across the car to take Patrick's hand, squeezing gently. "Smart woman."

"The smartest," Patrick agreed. "I'm so glad we found each other again."

As they drove through the familiar streets toward home, David reflected on the gift Kelly had given them—not just the reunion, but the reminder that love stories were made up of all the people who helped them happen. Friends who pushed you toward adventure, who saw potential you couldn't see in yourself, who remembered who you were even when you started to forget.

In the rearview mirror, the airport lights faded into the distance, but the warmth Kelly had brought to their lives remained. She would call every few weeks after that, sending photos of her environmental justice work, updates about her children, cheerful reminders that some friendships were strong enough to survive any distance. Kevin, too, had been calling more frequently since learning about Patrick's diagnosis, checking in without being intrusive, offering the steady support of someone who understood that love sometimes required witnessing difficult things.

And when the time came, the following year, Kelly would be one of the first people David called. Kevin would be another. They would both fly out immediately - Kelly not for the funeral but to sit with David in their townhouse and help him remember all the ways Patrick had been loved, and Kevin to handle the practical things David couldn't face: calling Patrick's remaining family, coordinating with the funeral home, making sure David ate something more substantial than coffee and grief.

"He found exactly what he was looking for," she would tell David through her tears. "And so did you."

Some friendships, David would realize, were like the love he shared with Patrick—not dependent on daily contact or constant presence, but rooted in recognition. Kelly had seen who Patrick could become long before Patrick saw it himself, and she'd been brave enough to push him toward becoming that.

In the end, that night at Medusa's had been a gift from Kelly to both of them—the gift of possibility, wrapped in blue-streaked hair and amateur eyeliner and delivered with the fierce love of someone who refused to let her friends hide from their own lives.

# CHAPTER
## Forty~Two

HOPE WAS a cruel thing when it dressed itself up as medical expertise and promised answers that no one actually wanted to hear.

Dr. Sarah Martinez had kind eyes and the sort of gentle competence that made difficult conversations feel bearable, but David found himself studying her diplomas on the wall instead of meeting her gaze as she flipped through Patrick's chart. Neuropsychology, Mount Sinai. Harvard Medical School. Johns Hopkins. All the credentials that should have made him feel confident they were in the right hands, but instead only reinforced how serious this had become.

"The initial screening results are concerning," Dr. Martinez said, her voice carefully neutral in the way medical professionals perfected when delivering news that would reshape lives. "But I want to be clear—we need more comprehensive testing before we can make any definitive determinations."

It had taken David three weeks to convince Patrick to see someone, and another month to get this appointment. Patrick had resisted not out of denial, exactly, but from a kind of protective instinct—as if not naming what was happening might keep it from being real. But after the incident where Patrick had gotten lost coming home from their own neighborhood grocery store, calling David in genuine panic because nothing looked familiar, they'd both known it was time.

The preliminary appointment had been deceptively routine. A young resident asking Patrick to remember three words, draw a clock, subtract seven from one hundred repeatedly. Patrick had performed adequately on most tasks, well enough that David had allowed himself a moment of relief. Maybe it really was just stress. Maybe they were overreacting.

But Dr. Martinez's expression suggested otherwise.

"What kind of more comprehensive testing?" David asked, reaching for Patrick's hand. Patrick's fingers were cold despite the warm September afternoon, and David could feel the slight tremor that had become more noticeable over the past few weeks.

"Neuroimaging—MRI and PET scans—to look at brain structure and activity patterns. More detailed cognitive assessments. Blood work to rule out other possible causes." Dr. Martinez leaned forward slightly, her tone shifting to something more personal. "I know this feels overwhelming, but getting a clear picture of what we're dealing with is the first step in figuring out how to manage it."

Patrick spoke for the first time since they'd sat down, his voice barely above a whisper. "How long do the results take?"

"About two weeks for the full workup. I know that feels like forever when you're waiting, but we want to be thorough."

Two weeks. David felt something hollow open in his chest. Two weeks of pretending everything was normal while knowing that somewhere in a lab, machines and specialists were mapping the geography of Patrick's mind, cataloguing the places where connections were failing, where memories were slipping away like water through cupped hands.

They scheduled the tests for the following week—a series of appointments that would consume three full days. MRI on Monday, cognitive testing on Tuesday, PET scan on Wednesday. David cleared his calendar without explanation, telling his assistant only that he had family obligations that couldn't be rescheduled.

The night before the first test, they lay in bed not sleeping, both staring at the ceiling as if they could find answers written in the shadows cast by streetlight through their bedroom window.

"What if it's what we think it is?" Patrick asked finally, his voice small in the darkness.

David turned on his side to face him, studying Patrick's profile in the dim light. At forty-seven, Patrick still looked young to David —a few more lines around his eyes, silver threading through his red hair, but fundamentally the same person who'd walked into his life at twenty-two and changed everything. The idea that something could be stealing Patrick's mind, his memories, his essential self, felt impossible to accept.

"Then we deal with it," David said, though his voice sounded more confident than he felt. "Whatever it is, we figure out how to live with it."

"But what if I forget you?" Patrick's voice cracked completely. "What if I forget us, everything we've built, everything we've been through? What if I become someone who doesn't know why you matter to me?"

David felt tears sting his eyes. It was the fear that had been living in both their minds for weeks, the possibility too terrible to voice until now. "Then I'll remember for both of us," David said, pulling Patrick closer. "I'll tell you our story every day if I have to. I'll show you the photos, play you the music, take you to all the places that matter to us. I'll love you enough for both of us."

Patrick buried his face against David's chest, his shoulders shaking with silent sobs. David held him tighter, whispering promises he wasn't sure he could keep but knew he had to try.

The testing days passed in a blur of sterile waiting rooms and gentle technicians who spoke in soothing tones while sliding Patrick into machines that hummed and clicked like mechanical prayers. David watched from observation rooms as Patrick followed instructions—identifying objects, reciting word lists, solving puzzles that had become suddenly, cruelly important.

The cognitive testing was the hardest to witness. Dr. Martinez, the neuropsychologist, was patient and encouraging as Patrick struggled with tasks that should have been simple for someone of his intelligence and education. Drawing geometric shapes. Remembering stories read aloud minutes earlier. Following multi-step directions that seemed to dissolve in Patrick's mind before he could complete them.

David wanted to intervene, to help, to somehow transfer his own mental clarity to Patrick through force of will. Instead, he sat in the hallway afterward while Patrick cried quietly in the bathroom, both of them understanding without discussion that something fundamental was being confirmed.

The call came on a Thursday afternoon two weeks later. David was in a client meeting when his assistant knocked on the conference room door, her expression apologetic but urgent. "Dr. Martinez's office called. She'd like to see you and Patrick tomorrow at two o'clock."

David excused himself from the meeting and called Patrick immediately. "They want to see us tomorrow."

"Both of us?" Patrick's voice was tight.

"Both of us."

The silence on the other end of the line spoke volumes. Good news was delivered over the phone. Bad news required a conference room and tissues and the kind of careful explanation that couldn't be rushed or misunderstood.

Friday afternoon, they sat in the same chairs they'd occupied a month earlier, but everything felt different. Heavier. Dr. Martinez's kind eyes held something that might have been sympathy, and the folder in front of her seemed to carry the weight of their entire future.

"The imaging and cognitive assessments confirm what we suspected," she began, her voice gentle but direct. "Patrick, you're showing clear signs of early-onset Alzheimer's disease. The pattern of protein deposits in your brain, combined with the specific areas of cognitive decline we've documented, gives us a definitive diagnosis."

The words hit David like a physical blow. Early-onset Alzheimer's. Forty-seven years old. The man he loved, the brilliant mind that had shaped his world for over two decades, was being systematically dismantled by an enemy they couldn't fight, couldn't reason with, couldn't defeat.

Patrick made a sound that wasn't quite a word, his hand gripping David's so tightly it hurt. David found himself staring at Dr. Martinez's diplomas again, as if academic credentials could somehow change what she'd just told them.

"What does that mean?" David heard himself ask. "In practical terms. What does that mean for us?"

"The progression varies significantly from person to person," Dr. Martinez said carefully. "Some people maintain relatively stable function for years. Others decline more rapidly. We'll monitor Patrick closely and adjust treatment as needed, but I want to be honest with you—this is a progressive condition. It will get worse over time."

"How much time?" Patrick's voice was barely audible.

"There's no way to predict exactly. But given your age and the current stage of the disease, we're likely looking at years, not decades." She paused, letting that sink in. "The most important thing now is making sure you have support systems in place and that you're making the most of the good time you have."

David felt something fundamental shift inside him, like tectonic plates realigning after an earthquake. The future they'd planned, the comfortable routines they'd built, the assumption that they had decades ahead of them—all of it had just been rewritten by proteins folding incorrectly in Patrick's brain.

They left the office in silence, walking through the hospital corridors like sleepwalkers. On the street, surrounded by people hurrying toward their own intact futures, David stopped and pulled Patrick into his arms, not caring who was watching.

"I'm so sorry," Patrick whispered against his shoulder. "I'm so sorry, David."

"No," David said fiercely. "Don't apologize for being sick. Don't you dare apologize for something that isn't your fault."

But even as he held Patrick close, David felt a grief so profound it threatened to consume him. This was the cruelest irony of all— after spending decades fighting geography and timing and every external obstacle that had kept them apart, they'd finally found their way to each other only to face the one enemy that couldn't be negotiated with or overcome through sheer determination.

They'd won everything they'd ever wanted, and now it was all going to slip away, one memory at a time.

# CHAPTER
## Forty-Three

DAVID HAD NEVER UNDERSTOOD the desperation of trying to hold water in your hands until he found himself cataloguing every moment with Patrick as if their love was seeping through.

The weeks following the diagnosis passed in a strange suspension of normalcy. Patrick continued his freelance work, though David noticed he took on fewer projects and spent longer reviewing manuscripts he would have finished quickly before. They still had their morning coffee ritual, still watched the evening news together, still made plans for weekend trips to museums or dinners with friends. Kevin visited that fall, staying for a long weekend, and David watched carefully to see how he handled the changes in Patrick—the occasional pauses in conversation, the way Patrick sometimes struggled to find words that had always come easily.

But Kevin was exactly what they needed. He treated Patrick normally, neither patronizing nor overly careful, including him fully in conversations while being patient when Patrick needed extra time to respond. The three of them went for slow walks through Central Park, had dinner at familiar restaurants, fell into the easy rhythm they'd established over years of friendship.

But everything felt fragile now, temporary, as if they were living in a house made of glass that could shatter at any moment.

"You're watching me," Patrick said one evening in October, looking up from the book he'd been reading—or trying to read. David had noticed him rereading the same page multiple times, his brow furrowed in concentration.

"I'm not watching you," David protested, though they both knew it was a lie. David had become hyperaware of every pause in Patrick's speech, every moment of confusion, every small sign that the disease was progressing. He couldn't help himself.

Patrick set the book aside and moved to sit beside David on their living room sofa. "You are. You've been watching me like I'm going to disappear any minute. And I'm still here, David. I'm still me."

David felt his throat tighten. "For how long?"

"I don't know. Nobody knows." Patrick took David's hand, his grip still strong, still sure. "But right now, in this moment, I'm here. I remember who you are, I remember who I am, I remember that I love you more than I've ever loved anything in my life. Isn't that enough for tonight?"

David wanted to say yes, but the word stuck in his throat. How could it be enough when he knew it was all slipping away? How could he be satisfied with "tonight" when he'd spent most of his adult life dreaming of decades with Patrick?

"I'm scared," David admitted, the words coming out broken and raw. "I'm so fucking scared, Patrick. I don't know how to do this."

Patrick pulled him closer, and David buried his face against Patrick's shoulder, breathing in the familiar scent of his skin, memorizing the feeling of being held by hands that still knew exactly how to comfort him.

"You don't have to know how," Patrick whispered into his hair. "We'll figure it out as we go. That's what we've always done."

But even as Patrick said the words, David could hear something different in his voice—a slight hesitation, as if he was working harder to find the right phrases. It was subtle, probably not noticeable to anyone else, but David knew Patrick's voice better than his own. He knew every inflection, every pause, every breath.

Dr. Martinez had warned them about this—the way the disease would steal Patrick piece by piece, so gradually that some days they might not notice the loss until they looked back and realized something precious had disappeared while they weren't paying attention.

"Tell me about the first time you saw me," Patrick said suddenly.

David pulled back to look at him, confused. "You know that story."

"I know. But tell me anyway. Tell me like it's the first time."

And so David did. He told Patrick about that night at Medusa's, about watching him from the balcony, about the way time had stopped when Patrick turned around on the dance floor. He told him about their first conversation at the upstairs bar, about the slow dance to New Order while everyone else jumped around them, about walking to the diner at 2 AM and feeling like his life was finally beginning.

Patrick listened with the intensity of someone hearing a favorite song, his green eyes never leaving David's face. When David finished, Patrick smiled—the same radiant smile that had undone David completely twenty-five years ago.

"I love that story," Patrick said. "Promise me you'll keep telling it, even when I can't remember it anymore."

David felt tears sting his eyes. "Patrick—"

"Promise me. Promise me you'll tell me about us, about all of it. About the Art Institute and that terrible weekend when we thought I might be sick, about the phone call when you finally came home to me. Promise me you'll help me remember who we were, even when I can't remember who I am."

"I promise," David whispered, the words feeling like both a vow and a surrender.

They developed new routines in the weeks that followed. David began writing things down—not just appointments and deadlines, but memories. Stories about their life together, details about Patrick's family and friends, explanations of inside jokes and shared references. He filled notebook after notebook with their history, creating a map of their love that he could navigate even if Patrick got lost.

Patrick, with characteristic organization, began making his own preparations. He updated their wills, arranged for David to have medical power of attorney, created detailed instructions for managing his freelance business as his ability to work declined. He wrote letters—to his mother, to Sean, to Laura and their other close friends—explaining his diagnosis and asking them to be patient as he changed.

"I want them to remember me as I am now," Patrick said one evening, sealing the last of the letters. "Not as who I might become."

David watched him work with a mixture of admiration and heartbreak. Even facing this impossible situation, Patrick was trying to take care of everyone else, to make things easier for the people who loved him.

"What about me?" David asked. "What am I supposed to remember?"

Patrick looked up from the letters, his expression soft but serious. "Remember that I chose you. Every day, for eight years, I chose you. I chose to leave Chicago, I chose to build a life here, I chose to love you even when it was complicated and scary and uncertain." He paused, searching for words that seemed to be getting harder to find. "Whatever happens, whatever I become, remember that the choice to love you was the best decision I ever made."

That night, they made love with a tenderness that felt like goodbye and hello all at once. David memorized every touch, every sound, every expression that crossed Patrick's face in the lamplight. Patrick was still completely present, still the person David had fallen in love with, but David could feel time pressing against them like a weight, making every moment precious and finite.

The next morning, Kevin found them in the kitchen making breakfast together, Patrick humming Vivaldi while David read sections of the newspaper aloud. There was something achingly normal about the scene, Kevin thought, watching two people who'd learned to treasure ordinary moments because they understood how fragile they were.

"You two look good," Kevin said, accepting the coffee Patrick offered him. "Really good."

And they did. Despite everything—the diagnosis, the uncertain future, the weight of knowing their time was limited—Patrick and David had found a way to be present with each other, to choose gratitude over fear, to love each other through the impossible.

As Patrick slept curled against his side, David lay awake counting heartbeats and wondering how long they had. Kevin had told him before leaving that whatever happened, David wouldn't face it alone—that some friendships were strong enough to carry any burden, and their friendship was one of them.

Weeks? Months? Years? Dr. Martinez had said the progression was unpredictable, that some people maintained function longer than others, but David had seen the statistics. He knew what "early-onset" meant, knew how young Patrick was to be facing this, knew that youth might work against them instead of for them.

But Patrick was right about one thing—tonight, he was still here. Still the man who hummed Vivaldi while making coffee, who got cranky when his books weren't properly organized, who looked at David like he was the most important person in the world.

Tomorrow would bring whatever it brought. For tonight, that was enough.

It had to be enough.

It just had to be.

# CHAPTER
## Forty~Four

DAVID HAD NEVER UNDERSTOOD why people kept photographs until the day he realized they were the only proof that love could transcend time itself.

The townhouse was quiet now in ways it had never been before. Not just the absence of Patrick's voice humming Vivaldi in the kitchen, or the lack of pages turning in his office upstairs, but a deeper quiet—the silence of a life that had been shared for eight years and was now, necessarily, solitary again.

On his nightstand sat two silver-framed photographs, positioned so they caught the morning light that streamed through the tall windows of their bedroom. His bedroom now, though David still found himself making coffee for two, still automatically setting out Patrick's blue mug before remembering.

The first photograph was from those early days at University of Chicago—the one David had kept hidden for so many years, pulled from that photo booth at Old Orchard Mall during their magical two weeks. Two twenty-two-year-old faces grinning at the camera with the kind of unguarded happiness that came from believing the whole world was opening up before them. Patrick's red hair wild from the winter wind, David's arm around his shoulders, both of them looking like they held some wonderful secret.

The second was from their library steps afternoon in New York, taken during Patrick's first visit when everything had seemed possible. The same two faces, older now, marked by a decade of separation and yearning, but lit with that same joy. The photographer at the nearby table had captured them mid-laugh, Patrick's head thrown back, David looking at him with an expression of pure adoration.

Two photographs spanning twenty-five years. A beginning and a middle, with no end in sight.

David picked up the older picture from the mall Photo Booth, running his thumb along the silver frame. He recalled Patrick being so nervous that day, overwhelmed by the idea of David buying him clothes, by the casual intimacy of shopping together like they were something real and permanent. The picture had been Patrick's idea—"Something to remember this by," he'd said, as if he already knew their time was limited.

How prescient he'd been. How heartbreakingly, perfectly right.

The disease had taken Patrick gradually, then all at once. For months after the diagnosis, he'd remained fundamentally himself —still editing manuscripts with precision, still making David laugh with his dry observations about their neighbors, still reaching for David's hand automatically when they walked. But slowly, imperceptibly, pieces began to disappear.

First the recent memories—what they'd had for dinner the night before, whether he'd already called his mother that week. Then the practical skills—how to operate the coffee maker, where he kept his reading glasses, the route to the library he'd walked hundreds of times. David had adapted, becoming Patrick's external memory, his guide through the increasingly unfamiliar landscape of their shared life.

The worst part hadn't been the forgetting itself, but watching Patrick's awareness of what he was losing. The flicker of confusion when he couldn't remember a word that had always come easily. The way he'd started writing everything down, then forgetting where he'd put the notes. The morning he'd woken up and looked at David with polite uncertainty, as if trying to place a face that seemed familiar but couldn't be properly identified.

"I know you're important to me," Patrick had said that morning, his voice careful and confused. "I can feel it. But I can't remember why."

David had shown him the photographs then, told him their story like he'd promised he would. About Medusa's and the Art Institute and all the years of almost connecting before they'd finally found their way to each other. Patrick had listened with the intensity of someone hearing a beautiful myth, tears streaming down his face even as the details slipped away almost as quickly as David spoke them.

But for a moment—one brief, shining moment—recognition had flickered in Patrick's green eyes. "I love you," he'd whispered, as if the words were emerging from some place deeper than memory. "I don't know why, but I love you."

Those had been the last words Patrick spoke to him that David truly believed came from the person he'd fallen in love with twenty-five years ago.

The rest had been inevitable, clinical, heartbreaking in its efficiency. The home health aide who came daily when David couldn't take more time from work. The gradual loss of speech, of mobility, of everything that had made Patrick who he was. The final weeks in the hospice facility, where David sat beside a bed holding the hand of someone who looked like Patrick but no longer carried any trace of the man who'd once stood on library steps in golden afternoon light, laughing at something David had said.

Patrick had died on a Tuesday morning in March, with David holding his hand and snow falling outside the hospice window. Fifty-one years old. Five years since the diagnosis, eight years since they'd finally built a life together, twenty-six years since they'd first fallen in love in a crowded nightclub.

Not nearly enough time. Never enough time.

The call to Kevin had been one of the first David made, his voice breaking as he said the words aloud for the first time: "He's gone." Kevin had been on a plane from Chicago within hours, arriving at David's door with groceries, practical necessities, and the quiet competence of someone who understood that grief required both emotional and logistical support.

Kelly had been the second call, and she'd responded with the same immediate love. "I'm coming," she'd said simply, before David could even ask. "James can handle things here. I'll be on the next flight out."

"I don't know how to do this," David had said, standing in their kitchen while Kevin organized food that neighbors and friends had been dropping off all day.

"You don't have to know how," Kevin had replied, his voice gentle but firm. "That's what friends are for."

Kelly arrived the next evening, appearing at the door with her suitcase and the fierce determination that had once dragged a terrified Patrick to Medusa's. But now that energy was focused entirely on David, on making sure he was cared for while he processed the impossible reality of Patrick's absence.

Kevin stayed for a week, handling the endless details that death demanded—coordinating with the funeral home, helping David write Patrick's obituary, fielding phone calls from Patrick's extended family and publishing colleagues who'd heard the news. He cooked meals David barely touched, made sure David showered and changed clothes, sat with him during the long silences when words felt impossible.

Kelly took a different approach. While Kevin managed the practical aspects of grief, Kelly sat with David in their living room and helped him remember. She told stories about the Patrick she'd known in college—his careful organization, his shy sweetness, the way he'd transformed that night at the club. She helped David understand that Patrick's impact on the world had been real and lasting, that the love they'd shared had changed not just them but everyone who'd witnessed it.

The funeral itself was small but perfect. Sean had insisted on providing the music, playing the guitar and singing "Danny Boy" with a voice that carried all the love and grief the O'Brien family felt for their lost son and uncle. Marcus had designed the program with quiet artistry—a Celtic knot rendered in watercolor, with small shamrocks that seemed to dance around the border, perfectly capturing both Patrick's Irish heritage and his gentle sense of whimsy.

David had been amazed at how many people came. Colleagues from his years at Meridian Press, neighbors from the Chicago house, publishing contacts from New York, runners from the group he'd belonged to years ago. Patrick had touched more lives than either of them had realized, and each person who spoke shared a memory that revealed some new facet of the man David had loved.

A month later, David found himself driving through the familiar streets of Arlington Heights, carrying a manila envelope that felt heavier than its actual weight. Sean and Marcus had invited him to stay with them—his first visit to Chicago since Patrick's death, his first time seeing the house that had been such an important part of Patrick's story.

They met him at the door together, both looking older than he remembered, grief having etched new lines around their eyes but not diminished their warmth. The house was exactly as Patrick had described it but transformed by years of Sean and Marcus's life together—Patrick's careful organization and love of books still evident, but layered with Sean's sheet music scattered on the piano and Marcus's art books stacked on every surface. It was easy to see why Patrick had loved this place, and why he'd wanted Sean and Marcus to make it their own.

"It's good to see you," Sean said, embracing David tightly. "We've been worried about how you're doing."

Over dinner, they talked about Patrick—sharing memories, laughing at stories David had never heard, crying together over the magnitude of their shared loss. It was Sean who finally asked the question David had been dreading and anticipating.

"What happens now? With the house, I mean. We know Patrick left everything to you, and we want you to know we understand if you need to... if you want us to..."

David reached for the manila envelope he'd set beside his chair. "Actually, I have something for you."

He handed it to Marcus, whose artistic hands opened it with careful precision. When Marcus saw what was inside, his face went completely white.

"David," Marcus whispered, staring at the deed transfer documents. "We can't... this is too much..."

"Patrick would have wanted it this way," David said simply. "This house was his gift to you, his way of making sure you had a foundation to build your life on. Making it officially yours just completes what he started."

Sean was crying now, unable to speak, while Marcus clutched the papers like they were the most precious thing he'd ever held.

"You've made this place a home," David continued. "You've filled it with love and laughter and the kind of life Patrick always hoped it would hold. He'd be so proud of what you've built here, and he'd want you to have the security of knowing it's truly yours."

That night, David slept in the guest room, surrounded by remnants of Patrick's life that Sean and Marcus had carefully preserved—a few of his favorite books, a photograph of Patrick and David from their New York life that Sean must have requested, small mementos that kept Patrick's memory alive in the house he'd once called home. David felt peace settle over him for the first time since Patrick's death. The house was in the right hands, Patrick's generosity lived on, and the love they'd shared continued to create ripples of kindness that would last long after both of them were gone.

When David returned to New York a few days later, he found himself drawn back to their bedroom, to the photographs on the nightstand that had become his anchor in the weeks since Patrick's death. The visit to Chicago had given him something he hadn't expected—not closure, exactly, but a sense of continuity, of Patrick's story extending beyond their eight years together.

David set down the first photograph and picked up the second, studying their faces on those library steps. This was how he wanted to remember them—not young and naive like in the first photo, but mature enough to understand how precious what they'd found really was. Old enough to have learned that love wasn't about perfect timing or ideal circumstances, but about choosing each other over and over again, even when it was difficult.

Especially when it was difficult.

The irony wasn't lost on him. They'd spent decades fighting geography—Chicago to New York and back again. They'd battled timing, careers, their own fears and the expectations of others. They'd overcome every external obstacle that had tried to keep them apart, proving that love really could conquer distance and circumstance and the complicated realities of building a life together.

And in the end, none of it had mattered. The enemy that finally separated them hadn't been geography or timing or any of the challenges they'd learned to navigate. It had been something inside Patrick's own mind, something that couldn't be reasoned with or overcome through determination or negotiated away with love and good intentions.

But even that loss, David was beginning to understand, couldn't diminish what they'd shared. Because love—real love, the kind that shaped you and changed you and left permanent marks on your soul—wasn't about duration. It wasn't about how many years you got or whether you achieved the happily ever after that everyone promised was the goal.

It was about recognition. About finding the person who saw you completely and chose to stay. About the way Patrick had looked at him that first night at Medusa's, as if David's face was the answer to a question he'd been asking his whole life. About the way David had felt standing on the library steps, understanding for the first time what it meant to want to build something permanent with another person.

They'd had twenty-six years of that recognition, even when they were apart. Eight years of actually building something together. Five years of learning how to love each other through the impossible. And in those final months, even when Patrick could no longer remember David's name or their history, something deeper had remained—a comfort in David's presence, a peace that settled over Patrick's features when David held his hand.

Love, David realized, wasn't just about memory. It was about something more fundamental than that—a connection that existed in the spaces between conscious thought, in the way two souls recognized each other across time and circumstance and even the devastating loss of everything that made them who they were.

In the photographs, they looked like what they'd always been, what they'd always known themselves to be even when the world tried to convince them otherwise: soulmates. Two people who'd found each other against impossible odds and loved each other through everything that followed.

The disease had taken Patrick's memories, his words, his ability to exist in the world as himself. But it couldn't take away what they'd shared, couldn't erase the impact they'd had on each other's lives, couldn't diminish the profound gift of having been completely known and completely loved by another person.

David placed both photographs back on the nightstand, angling them to catch the afternoon light. Outside, New York continued its relentless pace, but inside their bedroom—his bedroom now—time felt suspended, held in the silver frames that contained twenty-six years of love.

He'd been Patrick's external memory in those final years, helping him remember who he was when his own mind could no longer hold the information. Now David would be the keeper of their story, the guardian of everything they'd built together, the living proof that some connections really were strong enough to survive anything.

Even death. Even forgetting. Even the cruel arithmetic that gave them eight perfect years together after a lifetime of yearning, then asked them to be grateful for the gift.

In the photographs, they were laughing. They were young and then older, naive and then wise, but always, always looking at each other like they couldn't quite believe their luck. Like they'd found exactly what they'd been searching for, even when they hadn't known they were searching.

They'd fought geography and won. They'd fought timing and won. They'd fought fear and convention and their own careful instincts, and they'd won.

In the end, they'd won everything that mattered. The rest was just details.

But first, David wanted to sit here a little longer with the photographs and the afternoon light, remembering what it felt like to be completely loved by Patrick O'Brien. Kevin would call later— he did every evening now, checking in without being intrusive, making sure David was eating, gently encouraging him to get outside, to see people, to slowly rejoin the world. It was exactly the kind of steady, patient friendship that Patrick would have appreciated, David thought. Kevin understood that some losses required time to heal, and some connections were worth maintaining even when they demanded nothing in return.

Remembering the sound of his laugh, the way he hummed while making coffee, the expression on his face when he looked at David like he was the most important person in the world.

Almost always, they'd spent their lives almost connecting, almost being together, almost finding their way to each other.

But in the end, they'd found their always. Brief, imperfect, heartbreaking, and absolutely worth everything they'd endured to get there.

Some love stories don't end with forever. Some end with enough.

Just enough.

# About the Author

Michael Manosca first pursued a career in the arts, studying in Chicago, but storytelling has always been at the heart of his creative expression. His travels across the world have shaped his perspective, infusing his writing with the depth and nuance of the people and cultures he has encountered.

Michael writes in a deeply personal format, inspired by the relationships and experiences that shaped his upbringing. He explores the intricacies of friendship, the search for identity, and the quiet moments that define us. Through vivid characters and emotional depth, he hopes to craft stories that linger in readers' minds long after the final page.

When not writing, he can be found wandering the northern woods, exploring new cities, or enjoying a lively conversation in a tucked-away café. He currently resides along the western coast of the United States and is already working on his next story.

# Also by Michael Manosca

Beyond Ties that Bind

Treffen

Reflections at the Window

Bloodlines

Prism

Flickering

A Language of Water